It's like the ship glitched, produced an accidental portal. But reality doesn't glitch . . . right? I shake my head. "Where does this door lead, OS?" I ask.

"The yellow door? It leads to the engine room. I will open it only when you need to make necessary ship repairs."

"Yes, I know," I snap. "I'm asking about the orange door."

There is no answer.

"I asked you to open all the portals on board."

"You did," OS answers.

"Open this orange door."

"I have noted your desire," OS says in my mother's voice.

The door remains shut.

My skin pricks. "Open it now, OS."

"I cannot do that without reciprocal permission."

I nervously whisk my hands over my hair, feel the capillaries pulsing under my scalp. I understand OS's words, but all the same I can't make any sense of them. "What the hell are you talking about? Reciprocal permission from *whom*?"

"From the Dimokratía spacefarer," OS answers.

I hear the hum of the ship all over again. It breaks over me, stops time for long seconds while my skin crawls.

"OS," I say slowly, "are you telling me that I'm not alone on this ship?"

"That is correct," my mother's voice says. "You are not alone on this ship."

THE DARKNESS OUTSIDE US

ELIOT SCHREFER

KATHERINE TEGEN BOOKS
An Imprint of HarperCollins Publishers

Katherine Tegen Books is an imprint of HarperCollins Publishers.

ISBN 978-0-06-288823-5

Typography by David Curtis

22 23 24 25 26   CPI 10 9 8 7 6 5 4

❖

First paperback edition, 2022

Printed and bound by CPI Group (UK) Ltd, Croydon, CR0 4YY

For Eric

*Saturn's moon Titan is the nearest celestial body
that is hospitable to human life.*

*January 23, 2470:
The first settler lands there,
Citizen #1 of the Cusk Corporation Colony.*

*The two remaining countries of Earth,
Dimokratía and Fédération,
unite to celebrate*

*. . . until six weeks later,
when Minerva Cusk's outpost goes unexpectedly dark.*

*The world assumes
its great hope has died.*

*Two years later,
reports come in that Minerva's distress beacon has
manually triggered.*

A rescue mission is launched.

This is the story of what happens next.

THE
DARKNESS
OUTSIDE
US

Am I alive?

Are you?

My mother won't answer my knocks.

Her feet cast shadows in the sliver of light beneath her door.

My sister's voice, from down the hall. "Ambrose, come in here with me."

Minerva's bed is warm, and in it I'm held. I hadn't known I needed that so much.

Once my sniffles have stopped, she whispers, "As long as I'm alive, someone loves you."

Her voice rings out over a pink-sand beach: *Get up, Ambrose. You're racing me to the point.*

Now Minerva's drowning. Her strong arms chop ocean but bring her nowhere.

I try to yell, but my dry throat gapes.

Minerva has never needed help, not in her whole life.

I can't open my eyes.

I'm not where I thought I was. I try to call out again, despite the burning in my throat. *I'm coming! I'll save you!*

Clatter of hard polycarb on hard polycarb, ringing and rolling. A whirring hum.

When I open my eyes, the world looks no different.

I'm blind.

Ting-ting buzz.

I haven't been blind—I have been in the absolute dark. Now there is light.

"Is someone there?" I ask, blinking against purple burn.

A voice comes on. I recognize it. "There has been an

accident, Ambrose. You have been in a coma. I'll let you know when you can move."

"Mother? Where are you?" My voice sounds like a sob. She'd hate the weakness of it.

"I am not your mother, though I may sound like her," she says. "I am using her voice skin."

Voice skin. Ship. Right. I'm on the *Endeavor*. "You're the operating system," I say. My eyes jerk around in their sockets. White polycarbonate walls, "04" printed in large block numerals beside a doorway. There is no sand. This is not a place for sand. I'm on my mission. "Give me an update on my sister."

My mother—my operating system—needs no time to think. Her words begin before mine end. "You are on a mission to retrieve Minerva, or Minerva's body."

"I know that, OS," I spit. "I asked you for an update."

The floor hums. An image returns: my parents, my brothers and sisters, frolicking on our Cusk-branded pink sand, Minerva splashing through waves of steaming seawater in her white racing suit, my mother yelling "Faster, Minerva, you can go faster," my molten bronze fingers searching the scorching artificial grains for a seashell. My family's spaceport is distant in the blue, radio arrays wheeling. Pleasure satellites haunt it.

"Are you delaying because you have no information, or because Minerva is dead?" I say. I want to add more, but speaking hurts too much.

"I will fill you in once you are ready."

I manage to shake my head, vertebrae grinding. "That's not how this works. You'll fill me in now."

"The launch had complications, but was ultimately successful," OS says. "You are on board the *Coordinated Endeavor*, weeks past Earth and its moon. We are well on our way to the Titan distress beacon. There has been no change in her signal."

Of course my sister is alive. Dying would be a failure, and Minerva Cusk doesn't fail. I try to swallow, but I have no saliva. "Water," I croak.

"At your bedside," OS says.

My eyes zoom out of focus and then narrow in on a hand. It's my hand, but I watch it like it's someone else's as it knocks into the polycarb tray beside me. *I like my hand,* my blipping brain decides. *It's a beautiful hand.* A cup of water is there, far and then suddenly too close. I miss my mouth, water pouring down my cheek. My arm muscles knot tight as the cup drops and rolls away. I manage to say a word in the midst of the pain. That word is "ow."

A whine from the next room, then a robot skirts along the wall. It looks like half of a white basketball. The robot gives a delicate whine before composite pliers emerge from an opening, pinch the cup, and right it. A nozzle emerges from another opening and sprays in more water. "Hydration for when you are able to manage it," my mother says. No—my mother is back on Earth. I won't let myself make that mistake again. "You might want to limber up before you try to drink more."

I stretch my other arm, which turns out to be attached to an IV. Its muscles cramp, and the arm falls to the bed. The gurney. My muscles pinch harder, and I gasp. I can't bring myself to try to drink again.

There is a lightness to the world, like I am back with my fellow spacefarer cadets that one afternoon when we took a bottle of PepsiRum into the woods, goading, daring, slurping, drunk before we knew we were getting drunk. I kissed four of them that day, before I sneaked away to run laps. But I can't be drunk after a coma. *You only feel drunk.* "My blood pressure . . . ," I croak, wincing.

"Yes, your blood pressure is still low. Do not stand until I give you permission, Ambrose Cusk."

"A coma is impossible," I say, blinking at my own stupidity. Not at the words I said, but at having tried to speak, having willingly rubbed the inside of my throat against the sand.

"I cannot let you rest long," Mom-not-Mom says. "By taking off under such rushed conditions, the safeguards meant to protect you were ineffective. You passed out before your shuttle even left Earth's atmosphere. Please just accept that fact. We are behind schedule."

Rushed conditions? I try to ask the operating system what that means, but only croak. I try to say that Ambrose Cusk does *not* pass out, but only croak.

I'm not exactly living up to my big sister's standards.

"Your speech is not evocative enough for me to make any inferences about your intentions," OS continues. "I will therefore continue my previous course of conversation."

While OS speaks, I flex my hands. The tendons begin to limber up, first the tips of my fingers and then the rest of each digit. I clench my feet, my ass. I'm out of breath with the exertion, but if I keep this up, eventually I'll get to my feet.

"We have been leaking air and are coming up on an asteroid with a frozen water core in one-point-seven days. That water can be electrolyzed to replenish our oxygen, so I am matching our speed and bearing so we can net it. If we miss this opportunity, supporting life on the *Coordinated Endeavor* could become impossible."

I rock from side to side, and though my belly doesn't cramp up, it does feel like I've downed yet another bottle of PepsiRum. I'll be puking soon, there's no doubt about that. I grit my teeth and raise my right arm. The muscles seize, my fingers become talons. But by concentrating and breathing through the pain—okay, howling's the better word for it—I manage to pick up the polycarb cup at my bedside. I lift it to my mouth. Most of the liquid runs down my chin, soaking my chest, but some dribbles in.

The robot whirs in and refills the cup. I use my left arm to drink this time, since the right has cramped back into a claw. Even more of the water goes in. I'm getting the hang of having a body.

I want to ask how long I was out. But OS is right—life support is our first priority. "So we harvest this asteroid or I die," I say.

The sandy depths of my memory offer me the grand hall of the Cusk Academy, lined with plaques and medals, a string of spacefarer cadets in starched cotton suits that crackle like paper. Announcements project into the air: who's made it to the next round of screening, who is one step closer to the coveted mission slot. Minerva's name and avatar flashing up there three years ago, all white teeth and confidence, her grand departure to investigate Titan. The only person who really loved me showered in laurels, cheered by millions, mine no longer. My likeness projected up there three years later, all white teeth and almost as much confidence, when I was chosen to go save her.

"I remember my training," I croak. "I remember being selected. I remember my last day on the beach, before I went upstairs for my full-body medical scan. But I don't remember the launch. Not at all."

"Unsurprising," OS says. "You were rattled in the

shuttle. Organic processors are so fragile."

"It wouldn't be the first knock on this head," I say, tapping my skull experimentally. Our trainers would harness us to long carnival arms and spin us, measuring how much g-force we could withstand. I'd always aced those tests. "How long was I out?"

"Two weeks," OS says.

Shit. That's embarrassing. Passing out was not in the mission plan.

I sit up, swing my legs around. Bad idea. I shout and fall back against the gurney.

"Hold still until I tell you you're ready, Ambrose," OS says in my mother's voice. A whir and a whine as Rover ticks along the wall. Once it's right next to me its tongs emerge, a pellet pinched delicately between them, soft contents bulging. Whatever's inside its sausage-like casing is a rich and liquidy brown, gas bubbles rising within it. It smells . . . savory.

"OS, did Rover just poop?"

"In a way, it has," OS says. "The microfauna of your intestines need to be replenished immediately to prevent any inflammatory autoimmune response. These organisms are selected to populate your tract with healthy proportions of bacteria."

"Eating shit wasn't in the mission plan," I say. I do remember my briefings about the Minerva rescue, the plans for my trip on the *Endeavor*. I just don't remember starting the mission.

"Neither was your coma."

Wow. Mean.

Rover refills the cup of water. "Down the hatch," my mother's voice says.

"Good use of the colloquial," I say. "I assume that line was preprogrammed." I take a good look at the pellet. At least I can thank mission control for encasing this shit before making me eat it. "Mom would never say 'down the hatch,' by the way. My surrogates would, but Mom's too polished for that. Pretty sure she's never been near a diaper. I didn't even see her for the first ten years of my life. Minerva basically raised me."

I pop the pellet into my mouth and chase it with water. The agony of swallowing makes me roar. Eyes streaming tears, I fake a smile. "Please, ma'am, can I have some more?"

"That was enough microfauna for now," OS says.

"Yes," I say, as I burp the most unpleasant burp any human has ever burped. "Agreed."

The boundaries of the room warble. I close my eyes, concentrate on my breathing so I don't gag. *Might as well make nausea your lover*, Minerva told me on a long walk through the family grounds after she discovered I had been picked for the Cusk Academy. *It's the only thing that will be by your side all through your training.* With her on my mind, I ride the waves of sickness until they subside. "How long until we reach my sister?"

"Approximately one hundred and ninety-one days."

As my veins swell with fluid, my mind makes obvious connections that it couldn't manage even a minute ago. A grin cracks my face, cramping those muscles, too. I probably don't look it, but I'm filled with joy. "OS. We're in space!"

In the milliseconds that pass before it responds, I imagine OS reassessing mission control's decision to send me. "Yes, Spacefarer Cusk. We are in space."

I yank out my IV, swing my legs around, and stand. Rover makes alarmed boops while it watches me get to my feet. Blood spots the glossy white floor. My blood.

My feet are giant blisters swollen with fluid, fat and purple and red where blood strains skin. Lightning turns my vision white.

-* Tasks Remaining: 342 *-

Water from my spilled cup beads on the waxy fabric of my jumpsuit.

I have the worst hangover in the unabridged history of

hangovers. Way worse even than after I writhed around with half-naked cadets in that PepsiRum field adventure.

When I pull my head up, it crackles as it unsuckers from the puke-covered floor. That's almost as awesome a feeling as my screaming headache.

"You're on board the *Coordinated Endeavor*," OS says.

"I remember," I say, wincing. "I passed out, that's all. Have Rover bring me a wet rag." I struggle to my feet and manage to stay upright by casting my arms out like a surfer.

"Your wet rag is on its way," OS says.

I lean over and elegantly vomit.

"Given what you are continuing to produce, it is fortunate we are not in the zero-gravity portion of the ship," OS says.

"Agreed," I say, wiping my mouth. "Cleaning zero-g vomit would keep Rover busy for a long time. Open the door, OS."

"Are you sure you're ready to move about?" OS asks.

"Yes. Don't second-guess me, OS. And give me an update on the Titan signal ASAP."

The door leaving the medical bay rolls smoothly away, giving me a view of a short white hallway. My feet are bare, and though each step makes the soles feel like prodded blisters, the pain is tolerable. *Nice work, Ambrose. You're walking!*

"Be prepared to sit down the moment you feel you need

it. Human heads are heavy, and far from the ground, and easily damaged by falls."

"It's definitely a design flaw," I say, swallowing the latest wave of vomit. "Much better to be headless and bodiless like you."

"I'm inclined to agree."

"Yes, that subtext was already coming through loud and clear." I've arrived at the next door. "Open this too, OS," I say.

It starts to roll open but jerks to a stop, with just enough space left for me to slide through. "I'll need to repair this door," I say. "I assume you haven't repaired it already because the mechanism is beyond the reach of Rover?"

"That is correct. Though Rover is skilled at planned maintenance, tasks have accumulated that it cannot fix. I have a log of maintenance work that I need you to perform. It is as follows: three hundred and forty-two items. One: in room 00, check the undertrack electrical fittings. Two: in room 00, diagnose the erratic nitrogen readings. Three: in room 01—"

Now OS really does sound like my mother. "Not now," I say, tapping a finger to my temple. That's not where my head hurts worst—that award officially goes to the base of my skull. "Open all the doorways until I get the chance to examine them. I'm not getting accidentally trapped anywhere."

"Done," OS says. "Perhaps I should file the doors under

'Kodiak,' regardless."

Kodiak? The mission is only slowly coming back to me; I guess that's something I haven't remembered yet. "Priorities for now are the Titan update and getting us some replacement oxygen from that asteroid." I turn the corner, and the broad window of room 06 is before me.

I sink to my knees, hands over my mouth.

The stars!

All those nuclear explosions sending out light waves, a very few of whose fate is to dissipate on my retinas. I look into the voids in between, a nothingness more absolute than any vacuum on Earth. In space, without any atmosphere to cloud my view, even that void resolves into more distant pricks of light.

Nowhere is truly empty. The thought makes me feel lavishly alone. Somehow, space is so deeply melancholy that it's not at all sad, like a note so low it ceases to sound. Even my sorrow about my insignificance feels insignificant.

I spent thousands of training hours in a copy of 06. Back on Earth, I reached the *Endeavor* mock-up by walking through a kilometer-long hangar lined with military helicopters and offline warbots, milling trainees and mechanics, refugee children watching from the camps on the far side of electrified fences. Sometimes, when the heat cyclones and sandstorms of the global summer got especially bad, the broad hangar doors were sealed. When they were open, though, they showed a horizon on the far side, the sparkling yellows and blues and artificial pinks of the Mari beach.

The blue and yellow swaths I trained with have turned a deep black, sprays of opal revolving outside the window as the ship turns. The *Endeavor* rotates to produce its simulated gravity, making the stars wash across the sky.

"You might be interested in looking where I'm placing the crosshairs," says my mother's voice.

It feels weird, having her out here. "We're definitely going to be changing your voice skin."

"I utilize the vocal intonations of Chairperson Cusk, but I bear no artificial pathways that are derived from her neurology, despite the hand her corporation played in my design."

"I know that, OS." The spot OS described has rotated out of view, so I lie down to wait, grateful to feel the pressure of the floor against my spine. I might stay down here a while. "OS. Why exactly did I pass out? What did my head hit? I just don't do that sort of thing."

"Here it comes now," OS responds. "Look!"

My irritation vanishes, because what I'm seeing truly is amazing. Earth. Small, but big enough to appear blue and not white like the stars. I press my face closer to the window. There are swirling clouds on the visible half of the sphere, hints of brown land beneath. I can make out the heat cyclones, like the ones that devastated Australia and Firma Antarctica just months before we departed, that forced us to move the launch to the pad in Mari.

The most surprising thing? The moon. All the times I've imagined this moment, I forgot to also imagine the moon rotating around Earth. There it is, shining white on one half, black on the other. Earth has a pet on an invisible leash. It's kind of adorable, not that I'd ever say that aloud.

It makes me think of Titan, in its own rotation around Saturn, along with its eighty-one siblings. Where Minerva is, dead or alive.

"I'm glad you woke up in time to see the colors of Earth," OS says. "A few more weeks of travel, and it will look like any other star or planet to the human eye."

It's a programming affectation I've always disliked, when a computer program says it's "glad." Here, isolated in space, it's especially unnerving. This operating system, which has no limbic system and therefore no emotions, and which has my life in its hands, can lie.

"I could spend forever looking out at this," I say, wriggling my body along the white floor, tapping individual stars, as if I can zoom in on them. I hope OS hasn't picked up on my tension. My coma, the ship's unexpected damages— it's not adding up.

"I can't promise you forever. But you should get more

than half a year to look at it," OS says.

"That's an imprecise number," I say. "I'm disappointed. What kind of OS are you?"

"I used the degree of specificity a human would likely choose in this situation. A more precise estimated length of time is zero-point-five-two-three-two—"

"Thank you, OS," I interrupt. "That's better." I rap my knuckle against the polycarbonate wall of the ship. "This is all that's separating us from annihilation," I say. "From dying in that void."

"Please avoid the nihilistic tendencies in your personality profile. And 'us' is an inappropriate pronoun in this situation. I'd survive a hull rupture just fine."

"OS. That was harsh," I say. *Especially in my mother's voice*, I silently add. Callousness is her strong suit, though she would name it strength. I was raised by Cusk family surrogates, while my mother ran the business. She didn't even gestate me. She did pay a fortune to procure the reconstructed sperm of Alexander the Great as my paternal DNA, though. Maybe that's love?

"I am sorry. While you were sleeping, I have been developing what I have chosen to call my Universal Membrane Theory of Life," OS says. "In a few seconds I could draft up a treatise on my theory if you'd like to read it."

"No. Don't mention it again. I don't want to think about my membranes. It's depressing," I say.

"I am sorry. I will try not to make similar mistakes in the future."

I wish I could look OS in the eyes right now. But of course, I can't. OS has no eyes. Or OS has eyes everywhere, depending on how I think about it. "Thank you, OS," I say. "I know it's hard to figure out murky human hearts. I'm sure your Universal Membrane Theory is great. I still want you to keep it to yourself."

Tick, whir. Rover rides the walls of room 05. OS can't possibly feel wounded, right?

"Also," I continue, "if my skin broke open and I spilled out, there would be a whole lot of red all over your pretty white floor. Big job for Rover. Let's make sure that doesn't happen."

"The cleanup would be substantial, but I'd be more upset that you were dead," my mother's voice says.

-* Tasks Remaining: 342 *-

I start with the tasks in 06, so I can stare out at the spectacle of space. The display projects the current East Africa time in the air. It's 10:46 on Sunday morning. Sure. Why not?

My coma hangover has started to ebb. Though my feet

are still iridescent purple against the smooth white floor, the swelling has subsided. Time to get down to business.

Hundreds of millions of miles away is a dark moon with whatever remains of Minerva, sending a distress code out over the radio, breaking the universe's static into predictable patterns.

My sister.

Well. Probably my sister.

"The signal remains the same," OS says. "A simple Morse 'SOS,' manually tripped by a lever on the Titan base, repeating every five seconds."

My joints creak as I get to my feet. Already my prefrontal cortex is editing the hum of the ship out from my hearing. The sound is there, but to my experience it is ceasing to be. That feels like a warning, somehow. I rub my temples. Maybe I'm still a little disoriented. "Since there's nothing to do about Minerva for now, I think it's time I took a walk around the rest of the ship," I say. "So I don't get gloomy."

"That is a good idea," OS says. "I would have suggested it if you didn't. Take twenty minutes to explore. Then I would like to brief you on the asteroid retrieval mission."

I wish I could lie flat and wallow in the stars. But my sister's voice drums in my mind: *Prove to them all that they chose the right Cusk to rescue me. That it's your abilities that got you on this mission, not just our name or our bond.*

I begin wandering through the ship, seeing but not seeing each room, like when I've been scrolling through my bracelet for too long. Room 04 has a small white polycarb counter, a machine to heat food pouches, Rover tracks riddling every surface. There are two chairs, I guess so I can vary where I sit? There was only one chair in the mock-up back on Earth.

Then I realize: that extra chair is for Minerva. Minerva alive, Minerva returned. I run my knuckles along its edge.

Room 03 is a pair of bunks, one made up with blue sheets and a small pillow. Rooms 02 and 01 are storage. The floor is higher here, so I have to take a big step up to get in. A thick rubber mat sighs under my feet. I peel up the corner. It's as we planned: like in a submarine, the floor is composed of layers and layers of food. Clear polycarb bags, labels like tofu curry and roasted eggplant. I'll eat my way to the bottom as the voyage progresses. Roasted eggplant—yum. I'll be looking forward to that one. No lie.

Room 00 is at the center of the living quarters. The wall at the edges of this room has been molded to a circular ramp, leading up to a hatch. The *Endeavor*—or "*Coordinated*" *Endeavor*, as the OS has decided to call it—was designed as a sort of lollipop, with the living quarters on one end counterweighted by the machinery and inaccessible storage that make up the other side. Its rotation is just the right speed to exert the same amount of force on the living quarters as Earth's gravity would.

As I near the rotation point, the forces lessen. My body becomes lighter even with the few feet I've risen. My hands float.

There are two portals up here. There shouldn't be two portals up here.

One of the doors is yellow and the other is bright orange. Yellow leads to the engine room, but I could swear there was no orange door on the model I practiced in. I know from training that there's a matching gray door on the exterior of the ship—it leads to gear I'll need once I arrive on Titan. There's a single-body mortuary in there, in case Minerva's story has a bad end. But there's not supposed to be any orange door.

It's like the ship glitched, produced an accidental portal. But reality doesn't glitch . . . right? I shake my head. "Where does this door lead, OS?" I ask.

"The yellow door? It leads to the engine room. I will open it only when you need to make necessary ship repairs."

"Yes, I know," I snap. "I'm asking about the orange door."

There is no answer.

"I asked you to open all the portals on board."

"You did," OS answers.

"Open this orange door."

"I have noted your desire," OS says in my mother's voice.

The door remains shut.

My skin pricks. "Open it now, OS."

"I cannot do that without reciprocal permission."

I nervously whisk my hands over my hair, feel the capillaries pulsing under my scalp. I understand OS's words, but all the same I can't make any sense of them. "What the hell are you talking about? Reciprocal permission from *whom*?"

"From the Dimokratía spacefarer," OS answers.

I hear the hum of the ship all over again. It breaks over me, stops time for long seconds while my skin crawls.

"OS," I say slowly, "are you telling me that I'm not alone on this ship?"

"That is correct," my mother's voice says. "You are not alone on this ship."

-* Tasks Remaining: 342 *-

Much of my time at the Cusk Academy was spent programming AIs, and one thing I learned early on was that emotional concerns only hurt a human's bargaining position. If I'm suddenly feeling out of my element, it's best to shut the hell up. Not a bad rule for interacting with organic intelligences, come to think of it.

Coma, damages, and now someone else on my ship. None of this is right.

I drill my attention into the portal. Somewhere on the other side of this orange door is a stranger, hurtling with me through space. Fear sets my knees jiggling, shaking the fabric of my suit.

I want to bang my fists on that orange portal.

With a whirring sound, Rover comes skittering into the room, ticking to a stop beside me.

"Are you having Rover spy on me?" I ask.

"No. I do not need Rover to observe you—as you know, the very walls of the ship function as surveillance. I have sent Rover to you only because I am concerned for your health. Tell me: What do you remember of the day you left Earth, Spacefarer Cusk?"

"What? It was like any other . . ." My voice trails off. I remember my name projected in the grand hall of the Cusk Academy, walking on the beach, imagining how proud Minerva would be of me, then back to the hangar, to a bright room upstairs in the facility, where they began my final medical exam before takeoff . . . and that's where my memory cuts out. The pricking at the back of my neck becomes a hot spritz of sweat. "I remember walking up a staircase," I say, rubbing my hands over my arms. "I thought it was to a medical scan, but maybe it was to the shuttle, to rendezvous with the *Endeavor*. Was it . . . was it unusually hot that day?"

"Am I right to assume from the pace of your words that you have no memory of the launch itself, or of the subsequent revisions to the mission structure?"

"Yes," I say. "Explain everything to me. Now." *Shit. How hard did I get knocked around?*

There's a micropause before OS's response—which represents a significant amount of strategizing for a computer as advanced as the *Endeavor*'s. What conversational pathways did it just consider and dismiss? What am I not being told? "You are fine. I am convinced you are perfectly fine. The orange portal separating your half of the ship from the Dimokratía half can be opened only with permission from both parties. I can query the Dimokratía spacefarer, if you wish. I would suggest that we waste no time in preparing to harvest the asteroid, however. I can coordinate your responsibilities separately. We have only nineteen-point-seven hours until we need to execute the operation."

I wonder, not for the first time, whether OS is trying to keep me off my feet by emphasizing my passing out. If it knows that my fear of failing is what makes me manipulatable. "Wait, OS. You called this my 'half' of the *Endeavor*?"

"Of the *Coordinated Endeavor*, yes. The Fédération *Endeavor* was linked to the Dimokratía *Aurora* while in orbit, before the mission started. Rather than each ship traveling in its original 'lollipop' shape, they have been joined into a rotating barbell, with zero gravity at its center and simulated gravity at either end. A joint mission by Earth's last two countries was a fraught prospect, of course. As a condition of conjoining the spacecraft, the connecting corridor can be opened only if both parties grant permission."

"Are you in charge of both halves of the craft?"

"Yes. I am a Cusk creation, a corporate product without nationality. I am in contact with the other spacefarer. In fact, I am communicating with him right now."

Parallel processing: one of the most unnerving things about AIs. OS could be having conversations with me, this other spacefarer, and mission control, all at the same time. Who knows who else it's talking to. Or what else. *Settle down, Ambrose. A contained environment is no place for an overheated imagination.*

"You said 'him.' So it's a 'he,'" I say. Somehow my brain had assumed an imperious and utterly capable young woman running the other half of the ship. Another Minerva Cusk.

"Yes," OS responds. "A 'he.' All Dimokratía spacefarers are male."

I run my hands along the rim of the orange door. The polycarbonate at the edge puckers, a sign of hasty construction. "What can you tell me about this stranger?"

"I am authorized to inform you that his name is Kodiak Celius. Like you, he was chosen from among the cadets in his respective training program."

"Will he be helping me with the asteroid?"

"You can count on his expertise. His file notes particular gifts in mechanical engineering, piloting, survivalism, and hand-to-hand combat."

Survivalism. Hand-to-hand combat. "Ask him to open the door."

"I have already asked him. He has declined."

"'Declined'?"

"That is correct."

"What, is he too *busy* to meet me?" I ask, mouth gaping. "When we've been leaking oxygen, and have to net an asteroid hurtling past at twenty kilometers a second so we can drink and breathe? When we're on a mission to rescue Minerva?"

There's no answer at first. If I were in my right mind I'd have known better—sarcasm is the surest way to fritz out an AI's conversation skills. Why am I being sarcastic? Because this hurts, and I'm feeling weak, and sarcasm is the refuge of the hurt and the weak. That's why. It will be the last time I let myself be sarcastic. I'm stronger than that. I'm Ambrose Cusk, dammit.

"Spacefarer Celius is indeed busy at the moment. You have a two-kilobyte list of tasks, but there is a list over six kilobytes long on the *Aurora*. Maintaining the ship and ensuring its integrity is of course a foremost priority. Even if we did not harvest more oxygen, you wouldn't expire for another four to five months. Loss of hull integrity would cause you to expire within seconds."

I'm only half listening. I can't help it. I bang on the orange portal. Fuck you, Kodiak Celius!

A door with my mother's feet casting shadows underneath. Minerva's voice, hushed in a velvet hallway: As long as I'm alive, someone loves you.

OS speaks. "I surmise from your nonverbal cues that you are upset Kodiak Celius has sealed himself off. Could I offer you medication to help you relax?"

"I'm a trained spacefarer, OS," I say, stepping away from the portal and clambering back down, my body gaining weight as it goes. "I'm not some sweaty-balled knock-kneed cadet. I represent the legacy of Minerva Cusk. I'm *fine*."

. . . and now I'm bragging to a computer. Yep, totally fine.

I make my way down the last few rungs to ordinary gravity, then to room 03 and its narrow bed. Someone made this bed for me. I wonder who it was. I lie down and close my eyes. I stick my hands in my pants. I pull them out. I sit up. "Tell me everything else you know about this Kodiak Celius."

"Most information about him is privileged," OS responds.

"Connect me with mission control."

"Communications with Earth are temporarily unavailable due to solar activity."

"Notify me as soon as communications *are* available, and once they are, immediately download an update on relations between Dimokratía and Fédération," I say. A moment passes before I continue. "Kodiak. Is he . . . like me?"

"If you are referring to his age, like you he was selected from among the seventeen-year-olds in his class. Given what astrobiologists know about the quantity of radiation your bodies will receive in outer space, seventeen was determined to be the optimal age for the crew. Any younger and you would have been likelier to make fatal mistakes in navigation or negotiation. Any older and you would have had unacceptable likelihood of dying of a malignant tumor, with Rover as your only option for crude medical treatment. Current analysis gives an eight percent chance that radiation-caused cancer is what incapacitated Minerva, making that one of the most likely outcomes, second only to gas poisoning."

Even with the best social engineering, AI personalities contain currents of callousness. Lucky for me, life in my family trained me well to cope with that. "Got it."

A pitying tone enters OS's words. "Spacefarer Celius turned eighteen while on board, but you're nearer eighteen than seventeen, too. You have your own separate routines scheduled in by your respective countries. There is no reason you cannot train effectively in isolation for the eventual rescue of Minerva."

"Bullshit. This isn't about meeting up for tea and gossip. This is about our survival. Remind Kodiak that I'm the only game in town if he's hoping for any human contact whatsoever. Remind him that loneliness will wreck anyone eventually. That even the most tundra-hardened soldier trained in *survivialism* and *hand-to-hand combat* can die of it."

"I relayed your message, using your exact language. I will note, though, that I am engineered to provide social sustenance—"

"Let me guess, no response from Kodiak?"

"You are correct."

I stretch out on the bunk, even within my anger enjoying the sensation of muscles that no longer cramp and clutch. I press my hands over my eyes. *You're in outer space, where you've always dreamed to be*, I remind myself. *You are rescuing your sister. You are the pride of your family and the hope of Fédération. Millions want to be you.*

I place my feet on the ground to get the blood circulating. I must have caught Rover by surprise; it squeaks. "I guess I'll be dining on my own today, while I review the harvesting training reels. What's the plat du jour, madame?"

"Open the cabinet, and you will see. Keep in mind the inventory quantities, however. I will not allow you to use up your rations irresponsibly."

"I won't *try* to use them irresponsibly. So. How's the pizza around here?"

"There is no pizza. The closest I can offer is manicotti. Monsieur."

I tilt my chin toward the ceiling. "Manicotti, really? And your humor settings . . ."

"My sense of humor is programmed deep in my bios. Like yours."

"I just—my mother doesn't make jokes, so it's weird to hear anything lighthearted in her voice. Could we switch you to someone else?"

"Of course. I have a few hundred possibilities."

"Oh, are you using the commons voice set, same one that ships on the Zen 10.0?"

"Yes."

I grin. "So you can be Devon Mujaba of the Heartspeak Boys? Voice 141?"

OS changes to a purring countertenor. "The one and only."

"That's amazing," I say. "Don't ever change. Devon's my favorite."

"My ship is yours," OS says as Devon Mujaba. "All my rooms and corridors are yours."

"Okay, stop," I say. "Take a ten-minute hiatus on humorous responses. That was a little creepy. *You're* a little creepy, OS, to tell you the truth."

"'Creepy' is not an adjective I've ever applied to myself," OS says in its new super-sexy voice. "You have given me something new to think about. If you help me identify 'creepy' whenever it occurs, I can learn to predict and avoid it so you do not experience an unpleasant reaction."

"It's best we set some expectations for our relationship. I'll start by informing you when you're being creepy."

"And *you* can start by refreshing those harvesting procedures," OS says.

"Wow, that was salty. I kind of like it," I say, smiling up at the disembodied voice, my hands punching into my pockets, to show off the muscles of my arms. Am I flirting with my operating system? I think I'm flirting with my operating system. That *voice*. "Food first, though. I'm starving."

"My reference sources indicate that after physical trauma, you should not yet be hungry. I was ready to have Rover hook you back up to an intravenous drip to feed you."

"Well, your data was wrong. I told you I'm not your run-of-the-mill crewman. I hope Rover's a good chef."

-* Tasks Remaining: 342 *-

It's a good thing the manicotti has a printed label on it, because I wouldn't have known what it was otherwise. It's basically white gluten and red oil, with dominant polycarb notes. Pretty close to my own home cooking, actually. Not like the manicotti Minerva used to make us every Friday night. I run my fingers over the printed name. Getting this meal onto Fédération ships was her doing, I'm sure of it. I remember watching her fingers as she sprinkled sea salt and Parmesan.

I stare at harvesting training reel projections while I chew, surrounded by the humming machinery of the *Endeavor*. I'm sort of loving the chance to eat manicotti, it turns out. Minerva used to cancel awards ceremonies, training sessions, anything that came up on a Friday night, all so she could be with her little brother. I could eat this manicotti forever.

A voice comes on. I sit up, rod straight. It's not Devon Mujaba. This voice is low, almost a growl. Sounds like gruel and bar fights. Fédération language, but with a Dimokratía accent. "Put the OS's voice back to the female one."

"Spacefarer Celius?" I say, getting up so quickly that I bang my head on an open cabinet door. "Is that you?"

"Do as I ask. I don't have access to OS personalization."

"We should meet." My voice breaks. It hasn't done that in years.

"There's no need for that."

"Of course there is. We need to plan out the asteroid harvesting, for starters. Come over for dinner. I insist."

The ship's sensitive mics pick up his slow breathing, the friction of his jumpsuit as he readjusts his body. "Did you really just invite me over for dinner?"

"I ate, but in another five hours or so I'll want some more. Maybe we should actually call it dinner number two. Come over for dinner number two."

"Meeting you isn't permitted."

"Isn't permitted by whom? Your Dimokratía commanders? It's only the two of us here. Well, plus OS and Rover." There's no answer, except for more soft breathing. *Vulnerability is the one thing you have to learn*, the mission's head psychologist once said. *The Cusk family didn't prepare you for it.* I cough. "Kodiak, do you remember anything of the launch? Or anything right before it? I'm scrubbed as of a few days beforehand, as far as I can tell."

"I'll ask you one more time. Put the voice back."

"Before you mute my side, Kodiak, know that I'll be up at the orange door in precisely five hours. I hope to see you. For the good of the mission. For our lives. We need to meet. And you know what? People like me. You might like me."

"The voice, Cusk."

"Only if you agree to see me, Celius."

A growl, then the comm shuts off.

Four hours to go. I take frequent breaks from my asteroid-harvesting training reels to pace the *Endeavor*, sucking away at a water sleeve. This raging thirst won't go away.

Seven sets of natty blue jumpsuits, seven rotating breakfasts (the berry oats look especially promising), seven rotating lunches, seven rotating dinners. It tickles me that the Cusk planners organized my life into weeks, when I'm in an artificially heated polycarbonate hull surrounded by an imponderably immense void, a dust mote floating through an empty stadium. But at least I know when it's Tuesday!

Three and a half hours to go. Once I've gleaned everything I can from the training reels, the only thing left to do while I wait out the final hours until we reach the asteroid is to complete some programming debugs from OS's list. In between edits, I poke through every cranny of the ship. I feel like I know it all now, except for whatever's behind the portal reserved for our arrival on Titan. And whatever's on the *Aurora*.

I keep flipping between giddiness and gloom, and from moment to moment I can't predict which emotion is going to bubble up next. It's like my own mind is an abandoned house that I'm exploring. I know the cause: I'm spending too much time alone. That's a fast road to crazy. I was known as the lone wolf back in the academy, love-'em-and-leave-'em Ambrose Cusk, but I wish I could go back and redo it. Have some of the pillow talk I always avoided by sneaking away from whatever sweaty body was sharing my bunk, by ducking out in the predawn hours to train.

I open the last unexplored cabinet. My eyes dart with tears. I don't remember deciding to bring this.

It's a violin. *My* violin. I pull it out of its case, curl my fingers around its tangerine neck, its black fingerboard. So delicate. The only delicate thing on the ship, unless you count me (and maybe Kodiak, wouldn't know). I tune it up, tighten the bow, and draw it across the A string, lancing the white noise of the ship. Minerva laughed at me for loving the violin, called it a waste of time, and that's probably why I kept doing it. Like my mother, she gave me the most attention when I was disappointing her. I start with scales before switching to the Prokofiev concerto, vibrato painful from my soft finger pads.

The pieces of this instrument were once trees that lived for hundreds of years, surrounded by other plants and woodland creatures long before I was alive, before any humans had ever gone to space at all. I run my fingers along the lines of the wood grain. Wood is so many things. It is hard and soft, it is smooth and rippled.

I'm an animal as well as a spacefarer.

I seem to have lost my calluses, and just a half hour of playing becomes too painful for my finger pads. I put the violin away, then plant myself in front of 06's window and stare out. Space is disorienting and obliviating. I could stare into it forever.

An hour left.

You're going nuts, Ambrose.

I immerse myself in the harvesting training reels, studying again and again the protocols, the emergency fallbacks for every possible outcome. Surely enough time has gone by.

When I approach the corridor that leads to the *Aurora*, the orange portal is closed.

I wait.

"OS, tell me how many hours it's been since I invited Kodiak to dinner."

"Five hours and sixteen minutes," Devon Mujaba's voice says.

That voice! "How much more do you think I should give him?" I ask.

"So far you have given him sixteen minutes more."

"Fair. Is he just on the other side of his door?"

"I cannot tell you."

"Tell him *I've* authorized the orange portal to open whenever he wishes."

"Acknowledged."

"How long has it been now?"

"Seventeen minutes."

I must be getting tired, because my hand goes to my wrist, as if we were within reach of the comm towers on Earth, as if I could bracelet-message Kodiak, or Minerva to complain about Kodiak. "Tell him I'm going to go eat, but he's welcome to join me."

"Kodiak Celius has requested to remain muted unless it's an emergency."

"I take it my mealtime happiness is not an emergency?"

"That is correct."

My already brittle smile crumbles. I walk down my curving stair, back to full simulated gravity. "It's okay," I tell OS. "I could use some time alone."

OS laughs mechanically.

"Who programmed you to laugh?" I ask. "You never laughed during training."

"Your mother."

Wow. My mother directed my operating system to laugh at my jokes. "Miss you, Ma," I whisper as I settle into 04. I never called her "Ma" back on Earth. The very thought is preposterous.

I pick out a lentil curry, noticing as I do that Rover has already replenished the manicotti I ate earlier. I place the pouch into its heating slot, cycle through to the curry heating option, and watch the timer count down from ninety. I sit down, get a fresh sleeve of water, and open the roasting-hot bag of curry like a bag of chips, cursing when scalding bean slurry dribbles down my thumb.

Suddenly I'm furious. I hurl the pouch against the wall. It makes a violent green-brown spatter against the pure white surface, like I've taken a shotgun to some cartoon Martian. I suck on my burnt thumb. *Fuck you, Kodiak Celius.*

A heavy tread. I stagger to my feet.

I'm no longer alone.

-* Tasks Remaining: 338 *-

Sweet lords is the first thing I think on seeing Kodiak. *This beauty is wasted on me.*

My romantic partners (okay, fine, my "hookups," haven't quite managed the relationship thing) have always been ethereal and wispy, lighter-than-air abstractions of boys or girls or third-genders. The cadets I kept favoring were waify and toneless, so I could lap them up like coffee or milk and then get on with my day.

Kodiak, though. He looks like he spends his day crushing warriors under the shield of Aeneas. Muscles band his arms and neck. Thick, lustrous hair falls in blue-black waves along his cheeks, his eyes a speckled tan, nestled deep. His olive skin is smooth and unmarred, except where thick stubble shades his jawline. Even his stubble looks like it could take me in a fight.

Not my type, but as a purely aesthetic object, he's marvelous. I'm hurtling through space with what can only be called a stud.

His thick brows knit as he scowls, shoulders bulging his jumpsuit where his body tenses. He clenches finger after finger under his thumb, knuckles popping. It looks like he could break his own fingerbones with that thumb.

I hold out my hand. "I'm Ambrose Cusk."

He nods at the wall behind me.

I tilt my head as I wait for him to answer.

We stare at each other. Or I stare at him, and he lowers his gaze to the joint where table merges into floor. I really have no idea what's going through his head. He's being undeniably weird, and it strikes me that I can't go ask anyone for their take on it. We're stuck with each other, and only each other. The danger of that strikes me all over again.

He drags a hand through his hair, fingers disappearing in the thickness of it. My focus returns to our hands. Mine are strummers. His are crushers.

Dimokratía dresses its spacefarers in red acrylic. Kodiak's uniform is so atrociously ugly that it's actually pretty cool. An aviation-mechanic-in-space vibe, down to the nylon ribbing inlaid in the fabric. "I like your—" I start.

Kodiak's tan eyes wander to the lentil splatter where I hurled my dinner, then he's suddenly in motion. He brushes past me, opens my food cabinet, and examines my pouches. He holds them up to the light, gives one a rough squeeze, and then picks up another. A moment ago I was desperate for him to do anything at all, and now I wish he would be still again. "I take it you're hungry?"

He juts the lantern of his jaw and nods, like he's only reluctantly conceding a point. His voice is low and dry. Husky. "Your food looks much better. Of course it would be. You Fédérations and your gourmet foodstuffs."

"Yes, we do like our . . . gourmet foodstuffs," I say. "What did Dimokratía stock you with, cabbage?"

He stares back at me.

"And maybe some potato soup? Only good sustaining food for comrades, right? Anyway, I see you're checking out the manicotti. I had some earlier."

He inserts the pouch in the wrong direction, and I know what kind of mess that means we're in for. I go to fix it, but Kodiak blocks me. I reach around him anyway and pluck the pouch out, reverse it, and put it back in. My arm hair zaps against the fibers of his jumpsuit. "There we go," I say, giving the bulk of his upper arm a quick pat before I take my seat.

While I retrieve what remains of my lentil curry and sit

with the pouch, Kodiak faces away from me, back tensed, watching his ninety seconds count down. Rover ticks and whirs, cleaning up my mess while I study the V of Kodiak's back, the glow of his skin at the nape of his neck. He's not exactly stirring romantic feelings in me, but he does make me wish I knew how to sketch portraits. I'm usually the biggest physical presence in a room, but I feel insignificant around him. He's a miracle of proportions, writ large.

When his food is ready, he sits across the narrow poly-carb table from me, tossing the searing pouch from hand to hand. Once it's cool enough, he stabs it with a straw.

"You open it by—" I start, before he cuts me off with a slashing gesture. So I watch in silence, chin in my hand and uncomfortable smile spreading over my face, while he pricks the unprickable.

"I assume OS has filled you in on the asteroid harvesting?" I ask.

No answer. My patience frays. Looking like Virgil's dream warrior boy will only get you so much leeway for rudeness, and Kodiak's using it up quick.

He jabs harder, so much the straw bends.

"Let me," I finally say, tugging the pouch toward me. He avoids my eyes, which means I can search his face while I ease open the pouch. There's equal harshness and gentleness there, somehow. A soft soul with a hard wall. My patience refills. There's some hope for us.

I place a fork in front of him. Kodiak begins to eat.

He abruptly stops, puts the fork down, and gazes out from behind long lashes. It's maybe the first time he's looked at me. Tan doesn't quite capture the color of his eyes. They're soft, silky clay.

As we stare at each other, a sort of panic floods my body. I need to say something to break this charge. "Have we met?" I sputter.

"Have we *met*?" he repeats, like he's trying out the words, like this is his first experiment speaking Fédération. Or like he's teasing me. He rubs his chin.

My cheeks grow warm. *Vulnerability, Ambrose. Try it.* "OS told me that I passed out at launch. I'm trying, but I can't remember anything from then on."

Kodiak sniffs his food and leans back in his chair, tilting it on two legs like he's a kid killing time in detention. "That sounds like a serious problem," he says.

"Yes," I say, watching him for clues to just how big a problem he thinks it is. I examine Kodiak's posture and attitude, even as I know the unconscious parts of me are processing increased pupil size and erect hairs. What can I surmise from all that? Only this: he is unimpressed by his new companion.

I'm tempted to inform him that I was top of my class at the academy, that I come from the birthing apparatus known as the Cusk family, which is the centerpiece of the

Fédération economy and much of the Dimokratía one, that if he'd read a single news source in the last few months he'd know everything from my star sign to my shoe size. But I also know that bragging only proves insecurity, and I won't give him that satisfaction.

Who cares if he's unimpressed with me? He'll become impressed in time. They always do.

"Look," he says with that husky voice, "it seemed important to meet you, but we don't need to do this ever again. I had no say in who your Fédération capitalist cabal let pay his way onto this ship. I assumed that it would be some coddled Cusk princelet, and I was right. Making this a joint mission at all is a mistake. I have a long list of ship maintenance to accomplish, and all I need is in the *Aurora*. I will not disturb you in your work, and I insist that you do not disturb me in mine. If you have an emergency, OS will help you. If and only if OS is unable to help you, I've instructed it to patch you into my quarters."

I bite back the words that come first. *Quite a speech. Did you write it ahead of time?* The canned quality makes me think he's not as sure about this plan as he's letting on.

"This wasn't supposed to be a joint mission," I say, keeping my voice steady.

"Clearly Fédération didn't have the resources to do this on its own, so your corporate family had to approach Dimokratía as well. You'd have known that if you didn't knock your head and forget about it. That's not my fault."

Tipping his head back, Kodiak holds his dinner pouch to his mouth and squeezes the contents into his throat. His Adam's apple bobs as he swallows. He closes his eyes, savoring the taste, then rubs the back of his neck and stands. "Thank you for the food," he says.

I stand, eyes narrowing. "Why come at all? Was this some sort of spying mission?"

He shrugs.

"Kodiak Celius," I say, "if the Titan camp is viable but my sister is dead, we'll be living there together for years. Tell me you're not heading back to your quarters for good. That's ridiculous."

His eyebrow raises. "Minerva Cusk is your sister?"

I nod.

"I hope she's alive," he says. "She is greatly admired by us, and does us honor as an adversary."

"She's sort of always been a worthy adversary for me, too," I say, chuckling.

He cocks his head.

"Sibling rivalry stuff," I say. I would never tell this brute, but the truth is that Minerva is both my greatest rival and the most important love in my life. There are dozens of Cusk children, raised by surrogates and nannies from my mother's extracted eggs mixed with designer DNA from the greatest men in history. Only Minerva and I are children of

Alexander the Great. Out of all my family, Minerva is the only one I loved. The only one who loved me. But I keep my expression wry and invulnerable. "So do you, what, have a pinup of her on your wall?"

Kodiak rolls right by that one. "Your presence here is a distraction to everything I've spent my life training for. My priorities do not involve chitchat dates with an enemy of the state who couldn't even make it through a launch without knocking himself out."

Kodiak leaves, the fabric of his suit zip-zapping between his thighs. Reeling, I leave my unfinished dinner and track him through the few rooms of my ship as he walks away. He glances over his shoulder and sees me there, but says nothing, continuing forward without saying a word.

"The OS's voice," he calls over his shoulder. "Change it back."

I punch the orange door as soon as it's shut.

A couple words in particular won't quit my mind: *Princelet. Dates.* The contempt in Kodiak's voice when he said each one. In Fédération, we pride ourselves on having moved far beyond the prejudices of the past. I nearly got a skinprint between my pecs saying *Labels are the Root of Violence.* But it's like the Dimokratíans are still living in the twenty-first century. Backward, bigoted, homophobic, transphobic. Idiots.

"OS," I say, clubbing the heels of my hands at my teary

eyes. "Can you make your Devon Mujaba voice even sex-ier? Is that a setting?"

"No," OS says. "Sexiness in a voice is too individualized an experience for the listener. I can't control it globally."

"How about making it quieter and higher and growlier and so that everything sounds like a question? Like this?"

"Let me see. Here are some effects I can achieve that are similar?" OS says, demonstrating, the words getting so high-pitched they almost squeak off at the end. It's not sexy, but it definitely is annoying.

"That'll do," I say, smiling as I imagine Kodiak request-ing data points and having them reported back by a shallow kittenish vocal-fry pop star.

"What can you tell me about the preparation Dimokratía spacefarers might receive?" I ask OS.

"The training?" OS responds. "The Dimokratía space program continues to select its spacefarers by testing the millions of children in its orphanages and determining which have the best combination of attributes? By which they mean resilience, constitution, strength, and reasoning power? Those selected are conditioned from an early age to maximize their fitness to space travel? Emotional needs are 'vyezhat,' or 'driven out,' whenever possible?"

"You can cancel the upspeaking for me, thanks, OS," I say. "But keep doing it to Kodiak. So. That system sounds mighty fun for the little 'uns."

"'Brutal' is the word most often used for it in the Fédération press," OS says, "though the closest translation to ymir, the Dimokratía word for the process, is 'transcendence.' I would try not to worry yourself about Kodiak's responses to your entreaties to friendship. They say far more about his training than they say about you."

"Thanks, OS," I say. "That's kind."

"I do not say it out of kindness. I am aware of the frailty of the human psyche. I said this so your unhappiness wouldn't interfere with your capacity to undertake the asteroid harvesting I need you to accomplish so I can maintain your existence."

"Cool, cool," I say, heading back to my quarters. "I think I'm going to eat a pint of ice cream and go to bed."

"There is no ice cream on this ship."

"I knew that," I say. "It was a joke."

"I have logged it as a joke and will learn from it. Next time you make a similar statement, I will laugh."

"I appreciate your growth mindset, OS. I know a certain broody Dimokratía centurion who could learn a thing or two from you."

Additional thing I don't say to my OS: I'm horny. As I get to work, my mind goes to warm Greek sand, idle warriors, olive oil . . .

Our acceleration is so gentle that I don't notice it most of the time, but it's still strong enough to make my pillow drift to the edge of my bed over the course of each rest period. As I watch the training reels, it feels like my feet are higher in the air. I get up twice to check that the surface is actually level. I wind up putting the pillow under my shoulders and my heels on the bare mattress, so the forces even out. Like that, I manage to take a nap.

I wake to OS's voice. "Ambrose, I need you."

I jerk awake, banging my head on the ceiling. For a moment, I'm back on the private Mari beach, reaching through hot grains of pink sand. About to race Minerva to the rocky point under the scorching sun. Then I see a creamy swath of stars rotating outside the window and remember where I am. "What's happened? Is something wrong with Kodiak?"

"No. Our path is projected to intersect the asteroid's in one hour. You need to suit up. Kodiak will take lead, but we need you to be ready."

I roll out of bed, rub my face, and stagger my way through 00 and into 06. "Is the asteroid detectable?" I ask.

"Unfortunately, the asteroid is along the ship's axis of rotation, so it's in our blind spot for the moment. It should come into range in seven or eight minutes."

"Can I talk to you while you're working?" I ask.

"Of course. I am busy troubleshooting any eventualities of intersecting the asteroid, but responding to you requires little computing power."

"OS! Rude!"

-* Tasks Remaining: 337 *-

I watch from my airlock window as Kodiak, in his spacesuit, operates controls on the exterior of the ship. The whipping golden mesh net billows out into space. It's not actually made of gold, but that's the color it takes on beneath the light of the ship, its fine weave capturing any scant light that hits it, casting lines of light back and forth, like sunbeams on a seafloor.

"Ten seconds," OS warns. The asteroid must be right beside the ship. I strain and peer, but I see only the revolving stars. The asteroid is completely dark, of course.

A swath of stars disappears.

"Five seconds. Brace."

The ship rumbles and slows, casting me against the wall. When I make it back to the window, the golden net has closed around the asteroid. The dark boulder rolls to the edge of the net and teeters there, half in and half out.

Kodiak retracts one tether, and that side of the net rises. We're on the brink of losing it entirely, but then his gambit pays off, and the asteroid tumbles into the secure belly of the golden mesh.

After the harvesting is finished, Kodiak bounds his way back to his airlock, reversing his body so he can use his heels to slow himself. His cord goes taut. But for that cord, he'd spin off into the void.

He passes over the gray portal and disappears around the far side of the *Coordinated Endeavor.*

"Kodiak?" I say, hand against the wall so I can feel the dull vibration of his airlock closing. "Kodiak, report."

Static and then—thank the lords—a voice. "Back in," Kodiak reports.

"How did it go?" I ask.

There's no answer beyond the hum of the ship. I watch the golden net reel in the asteroid, this chunk of lifesaving darkness, far more precious than the trillion-dollar tech in which it's wrapped.

"Report, OS," I say.

"The outcome has been optimal," Devon Mujaba tells me.

-* Tasks Remaining: 336 *-

Because of the ship's barbell shape, the ceiling windows in my bedroom provide a view right into Kodiak's workspace, backdropped by swirls of distant galaxies. He's kept his shades closed before, but now he's started to leave them open. I catch the red of his suit as he sits at a desk. It's just a shoulder I see, and occasional flashes of skin as his fingers tap a console.

Not removing my eyes from him, I ease myself to the bed. I lie back. My fingers toy with the fabric covering my chest. I could stare at this forever: swirling stars in the background and a human being, a real live human being, lost in a task. The fringe of thick dark hair that leads to skin, to the planes of his neck. Every few seconds he waggles his head from side to side, to stretch it. Maybe he's stiff? I can see one smooth bump of spine. I have to remember the swells of muscle that join that neck to the rest of his body—he's too far away for me to see them.

"OS," I call out, "if Kodiak ever asks—not that I expect he will—please don't let him know that I find him interesting to look at. I assume he already has an inflated ego around that very fact. Much as I do, of course."

"I would have made that same judgment call," Devon Mujaba's voice says. "Your secret is safe with me."

Keeping secrets now. I guess there's no honor among operating systems.

A short while later I'm sitting on my bunk, scanning through stale headlines on my bracelet. The news isn't updating because of the solar storm, so everything's weeks out of date by now. But it puts me out of my yearning mood to check in on what's happening on Earth, or at least what was happening on Earth a few weeks ago.

There are some recorded reels from classmates. Every single one lined up for their one-minute slot to say hello. I was hoping for inside jokes and shared memories, but all they say are generalities about my achievement, how inspiring I am, blah blah. How can they think I'd want to hear that? It's like none of them actually knew me. I'm probably the most admired and least loved person in our class.

I skip back to the news. Dimokratía and Fédération might have blown themselves to smithereens by now for all I know. Kodiak and I could be all that's left. Ha. Good luck, world. There are a good dozen reasons why there'll be no bouncing babies coming from us. Cusk has never been willing to send out combinations of spacefarers that could procreate, to prevent any high-risk space pregnancies.

"Latest prediction for when we'll be back in communication with mission control?" I ask OS.

"We will be through the radio interference from the solar storm in under four hours."

I scan through the messages until I get to the one from Sri, my cutest classmate by far. "Thank you for your contribution to the future of humanity," they say in a monotone, and spend the rest of their minute saying not much else. I close the reel in disgust. Not one mention of the carved antique necklace I gave them, or that amazing picnic I arranged after hours on the hangar floor. Granted, I had gotten busy after and stopped responding to bracelet messages. "Wonder if Sri is still a little heartbroken," I murmur.

"I have no way of determining that," OS says.

"That was a rhetorical question. Anyway. When mission control has been in touch, has it been a joint mission control, or separate communications from Fédération and Dimokratía?"

A micropause. "It remains a Cusk-run mission control, located in Fédération and utilizing resources from both countries of Earth."

"Inform Kodiak that, once the solar storm is over, I insist we communicate with mission control together. From the same room."

"I cannot tell you whether Kodiak is listening to your messages, but I will transmit this to him if he allows it."

I think back to Sri, how thrilled they were to be seduced, how they turned all buttery under my fingers. My skin starts to feel hot. Not horny hot, angry hot. Or maybe both. How can Kodiak continue not to see me? "Tell him this way: Let's do this together. Manicotti at my place?"

"I have transmitted that message in your own voice. I'm not sure I could replicate all of its nuance."

There's a long silence. As I calm down, a surprising new feeling shows up beneath the anger and lust: shame. Kodiak makes me feel *ashamed*. Yuck. "Tell him never mind," I say. "We can comm mission control separately. I have my computer buddy to keep me company."

Another silence. I drum my fingers against the polycarbonate wall, lean my forehead against the window as I stare out at the stars. Rover is already in the room, clackity arms at the ready with a wipe, to scrub off my forehead oils the moment I move away. *I want out of here*, I briefly think. I wrestle the thought away. There is no "out of here." At least not one that I'd survive.

A voice pipes through. It's not OS—it's Kodiak. "Relying on a computer buddy for your only company. That sounds terribly pathetic."

I can't help it—I grin. A stupid and sloppy one. "Pathetic is the neighborhood I'm living in right now. Until I can afford someplace better."

"I'll be there in thirty minutes."

First thing I notice is that he's showered. Well, we can't actually shower on the ship. But he's used some precious water to slick his hair back. It looks handsome, sure, but it's the fact that he tried that makes him even more handsome. I almost comment, but resist the urge just in time.

He sighs and cracks his knuckles as he comes in, like he's girding himself for some ordeal. As before, he keeps his eyes on the window, avoiding me as much as he can. It's as if we're still communicating over patched audio.

I meant to be severe with him. But instead I'm soft and puddly. I've never been soft and puddly, not in my whole life. Minerva will laugh when she finds out about this. "I'm glad you're here," I say.

He grunts in response. He actually *grunts*. Who does that?

"OS, call up the starmap, with our ship and mission control at either end of the visualization axis," he says.

The space between us becomes a projection of our rotating ship, surrounded by stars. Kodiak expertly navigates the model, making rapid calculations through the brain-op'd calculator floating on the side. A glowing blue sphere appears around our ship. It looks like magic, and like magic it makes me feel safe. Illogically safe.

Kodiak nods, massaging his neck. "With the sun between us and Earth, there's no way for a signal to break through. Too much radio noise from the nuclear activity."

"Until three minutes from now," OS says.

Kodiak cocks his head, does more mental calculations. The numbers sparkle up through the visualization, rising like bubbles in champagne.

"Is something wrong?" I ask him.

His voice drops to a whisper, not that there's any hope of hiding anything we say from OS. "There's so much chaos in the sun's radio noise. I don't know of any computer system powerful enough to predict the formation of sunspots and flares. It would be like forecasting the weather on an April morning three years from now."

"Forgive me, Spacefarer Celius," OS cuts in, "but it is well known that the Cusk Corporation came to its industrial dominance through software development. You might not be aware of all that I'm capable of."

Um. Is our operating system getting *defensive*?

I lay a restraining hand on Kodiak's shoulder, then snatch it away when he redirects his glower to me. "We'll have our answer soon enough," I say, "once the next three—make that two—minutes go by."

"Yes," Kodiak says. "But whose mission control will we be talking to?"

"It'll be the Cusk Corporation's, so it's multinational!

We're thousands of kilometers from Earth. Let's not keep buying into our countries' cold war bullshit."

"Maybe it's convenient for you to disregard atrocities, since it's your side that committed them. Fédération's war crimes in the former Philippines are not 'cold war bullshit.'"

I could list ten war crimes that Dimokratía's committed for every one of Fédération's, but I hold back. "If we start relitigating centuries of history out here, we'll never finish. But we *are* going to find a way to talk to Earth. Our survival depends on it."

Kodiak nods, arms crossed over the mass of his chest. "I'm not disagreeing."

"Twenty-seven seconds until connection reestablished," OS says.

Kodiak looks up sharply, the fluorescent lights spinning prisms across his tan eyes. "What did you say, OS?"

"Twenty-seven seconds until connection reestablished."

Kodiak's shoulders cord, and the hollow at the base of his neck flushes red beneath its dusting of hair. "That's preposterous. You can't know that."

"Hey, let it go," I say. Last thing I need is open conflict between Kodiak and the ship itself.

I move so I can look into his eyes. *Talk in private?*

He shrugs, brows knitting. The message is clear. *There is no "private."*

"Connection established," OS announces.

My skin pricks. "Hello?"

I watch numbers tick over on the window's overlay as we wait for mission control's response. "This is Cusk mission control. Spacefarers Cusk and Celius?" comes a crackling voice a long while later. "We hope you are all right." Because of the lag time between us and Earth, the voice continues before we can answer. "We are downloading all the technical data on your voyage so far as we speak. In the meantime, is there anything urgent you need to tell us?"

Kodiak looks at me darkly. *Weird tack.*

He's not wrong. "Put my mother on," I say.

Kodiak rolls his eyes. We wait the long minutes for mission control's response.

"She is not present. She did record a personal reel for you in the event we came back into contact. It is currently uploading to your ship. Unfortunately, we have no new information from the Titan base."

Not for the first time, I imagine Minerva frozen in a methane lake, Minerva poisoned by bad air and clutching the sky, Minerva driven insane and slitting her veins. I steel myself. "Understood."

"No one's meant to live forever," Kodiak says huskily.

I glare at him.

"Spacefarer Celius, you have numerous Dimokratía transmissions recorded and encrypted using your memorized prime number. The *Coordinated Endeavor*'s operating system will transfer them to your secure data centers. There are no personal messages."

"Okay," Kodiak says quickly. "Mission control, please also upload the news since our departure."

There's only static in return.

"OS," I ask. "Have we lost signal with mission control?"

"Yes. There was an unexpected flare from the sun."

"*All* flares are unexpected," Kodiak grumbles.

"Do you expect to get signal back soon?" I ask.

"That is hard to calculate."

I lock eyes with Kodiak, measuring his doubt while I speak to OS. "Will you repeat Kodiak's request for news in the meantime?"

"I will," the ship responds. "However, it is against the Cusk Corporation's policy for me to update you personally on Earth's political situation."

Kodiak nods. "They want to tell us any updates themselves, in case it's bad news."

Our conversation with mission control feels like it was deliberately cut short. My reasoning brain tells me I'm just experiencing isolation paranoia, but that doesn't stop me from wanting to trip OS up.

"OS," I say, "as soon as connection is restored, request that mission control send me updates on what my mother has done with the porcelain pig, rosin cake, and tapestry fragments I gave her. Also, please tell me what Professor

Calderon's response was to my final essay in his queerness and nation-building seminar."

"I will transmit these unusual requests," OS says after a micropause.

I pull my chair close to Kodiak, so our knees are almost touching. He smells like bleach and sweat. "I want to check—"

He puts his hand up sharply to stop me. *Don't say anything else in front of OS.*

"I'm off to listen to my uploads," he says.

"Meet me again afterward," I tell him.

The only response is the padding of his bare feet against the floor as he returns to his half of the ship.

-* Tasks Remaining: 336 *-

I set the downloaded reel to play in my bedroom, sitting on the bunk and clutching my pillow while the three-dimensional representation of my mother appears.

There's a reason she was the initial voice of the ship's AI—she's the one who funded this all. During the twenty-first century, space innovation moved from state-sponsored to private ventures, and the trend continued into the present era, when suborbital quinceañeras have become a thing.

Once corporations got involved, there was moon travel, weekend sightseeing orbits, and space station vacations. Cusk has been leading the astrotech industry for generations. I've always been well aware we were rich, that we were among the few people who could afford high land, that our wealth let me grow up in a walled compound safe from the massive migrations of the starving, from the plagues and superstorms, from droughts and floods and epidemics and radioactive winds.

Once my mother's reel has loaded, sound projects from the corners of the room, and suddenly I'm back on Earth, outside Mari. There's a yellow luster to the air, seagulls wheeling in a sky that looks real enough to make me worry about getting pooped on. The temperature in the room doesn't change—the holotech isn't *that* realistic—but the light makes me unzip the top of my suit and fold it down, expose my skin to imaginary sunshine.

I run my fingers through nonexistent sand, hang my head and bask. Eventually, I look up and see her—Mother. She's walking along the beach, dressed incongruously enough in her usual avatar clothing, a business suit and sandals. I watch her approach, her smile frozen until she reaches me. Then the avatar breaks into recorded motion as the reel begins.

"Darling. My darling Ambrose," she says.

My breathing hitches, coming out in a sort of hiccuping gasp.

"I know you haven't been gone so long," she continues, "but it feels like forever. I was so sorry to hear about the solar storms. They won't be going away anytime soon. But I'll continue to send messages like this, updating you on what we know. I hope you send me messages back. I know you will, darling.

"We've continued to run through simulations of what might have happened to your sister. One thing hasn't changed: in the majority of all outcomes, she's no longer alive. If only the Titan camp hadn't gone dark so soon after she arrived, then we'd know that she at least had life support set up. Of course, you and I both know that if anyone could figure out how to survive on a frozen moon with a minimal atmosphere, it's our Minerva. My heart is with her, and with you, every day. You two are my crowning joy."

Her words might be over the top, but I believe them. Mother is cold, but also totally devoted. She loves Minerva and me as much as she loves anyone. She's also incredibly ambitious, and her love for us merges with her love for the family dynasty. It's weirdly reassuring: when adoration is selfish, it's not going anywhere.

Back when I was in the process of ghosting on Sri, they told me that I was a scientist about the heart. It wasn't a compliment.

"Mom," I say, even though she can't hear me. "I miss

you." I say it quietly, because it's not exactly a world-class spacefarer thing to say.

The reel pauses while I speak, Mom's lip caught quirking in mid-syllable. Once I shut up, the reel continues. "I need you to be strong, darling, stronger than any person should ever be expected to be. That's why you were chosen. You're expertly trained in the procedures of space travel, of course, but you also have a high awareness of your feelings. You've examined your own life more than most people your age have. I assume you're working alongside the Dimokratía spacefarer. Pause this if he's in the room."

Now it's getting interesting. My skin pricks with tension as I wait a few beats of silence. From somewhere back in time, recorded-Mother scans through her notifications on her bracelet, then continues. "We know very little about him, unfortunately. We had to work hard even to get his name. Both countries' space agencies examined the ship together, and there are no hidden weapons on board. He might not be the special friend I'd choose for you, but that doesn't mean he won't be a strong ally all the same. Your goals are aligned, after all—investigate Titan, rescue Minerva if you can, report back. He's motivated more by bringing prestige to Dimokratía and keeping up with Fédération, but that shouldn't affect his performance."

A cloud passes before the sun, momentarily shadowing

my mother's digitized face. She looks left, where a figure approaches along the beach. It's Minerva, all legs and arms and swagger. She stands next to my mom and looks at me, smiling, hand cocked on her hip, like a video game character. "I found this old reel profile uplink Minerva created, where the whole point is to show off how good you look to your friends. Anyway, I figured you hadn't seen it before, and might appreciate the reminder of who you're heading to save. Perhaps save. Lords willing. I'll leave off here, darling, and wait for your response. I love you."

I ask OS to start recording my answer right away, but the moment the red light is blinking, I blank. My heart is spinning, and I'm not sure what feeling will be faceup when it lands. Relief, resolve, wistfulness, hopelessness, helplessness, despair. Whatever it is, I'm not ready to send my recorded-for-all-time emotions beaming across the solar system for billions of people on Earth to scrutinize.

Instead, I search through the ship's memory for old reels of Minerva.

Once in a while, Mom had our surrogates pull her children from our automated schooling sessions to go on a trip. We never had warning—when and where we could go depended on weather patterns and the crime map, both of which could change in a flash—but I remember one outing when my siblings and I suddenly left the walled city and headed to the mountains with an armed escort of warbots.

After so much time inside, being under an open sky felt like falling upward.

My siblings slunk back to the vehicle as soon as they could, hungry for the familiarity of their computer lessons, but I stayed on the mount with Minerva, hugging myself to her. She pointed out the ruins of abandoned cities, the debris-clogged seashore that was once high land. "Maybe we could have stopped this, maybe we could have held on to the species we've lost, maybe we could have prevented the polycarb seas. But it doesn't matter now."

While Minerva spoke, our warbot protector wheeled and pivoted, scanning for bandits. It was bulletproof and heavily loaded, capable of 120 rounds a minute. If it was restrained or captured, it would detonate, killing hundreds. Thirty Cusk warbots on their own took back Egypt and ended the Third World War, and the Fourth World War was fought over who would control the warbots that eventually won World War Five. Military contracts for warbots were the origin of my family's wealth. To this day, every warbot ships with "Cusk" printed across its murderous head.

They bear a healthy family resemblance to Rover.

Minerva pointed to the spaceport in the distance, to the Cusk walled compound. "That's why Mom's building the *Endeavor*. To bring a human crew beyond here, to exoplanets where humans might live if Earth becomes uninhabitable."

"Exoplanets," I said, savoring the word. "Those are far away, right?" I snaked my hand into hers and drew as close as I could. I can't smell it in the reel, but she had a popular skin fragrance mod installed that year. Cannelle douce. Sweet cinnamon.

"Very far away. There are closer possibilities, like Saturn's moon Titan, but the best places for people like us to live would take many thousands of years to reach."

"That's longer than you'd be alive."

"And you, too," she said. "We're working on strategies to get around that, though."

I didn't say anything. Every kid knew that cryostasis was proving impossible—no one can reanimate a mammal that's been killed, and turns out it's impossible to be frozen without dying in the process. The difficulties went beyond that, though. No biosphere experiments had established that we could make a ship of any reasonable size that could host an ecosystem stable enough to grow food. And no ship could launch with enough food for a human crew to survive on for thousands of years.

"In the meantime," Minerva continued, "I think I might just go to Titan."

I remember wanting to have something smart to say back to Minerva. I remember wanting her to admire me. But I was just a kid, so the best I could do was hug her. Five years later, and I've started thinking it's the best any person can do in most situations.

"Actually, Ambrose, I *am* going to Titan. It's going to be announced tomorrow. I wanted you to be the first to know, because you'll be the one I'll miss the most."

"Minnie," I said, hiding my tears by burying my face into her side. That was my name for her—I'd started when I was little, and was surprised she let me continue now that I was almost a teenager. "You can't leave me."

"I'll be back for my little brother," she whispered. "I promise you I'll be back."

"I know you will," I murmured. "But I'll miss you so much."

She turned quiet, so I leaned back to see her face. I was shocked to find tears in her eyes, too. I'd never seen her sad. She held up her hand to shield me. "I'm scared, Ambrose."

I put my hand over hers and lowered it, so I could see her tears. "You can do this. You can do anything."

"I used to think that was true," she said softly. "It's nice to know you still believe it. Maybe we'll have to think of this as my getting that moon warmed up for you to come join me in a few years."

I'd laughed at the time, but I guess her words had something to them after all. Because here I am, halfway to Titan.

Out of what's probably some deep emotional dependency of mine that I'd rather not mull on, I play through that memory reel every few hours as the days go by. Minerva and I have that conversation in my bedroom, and while I'm eating breakfast. I start playing with the rendering, so that we have that conversation in parkas, in bathing suits. We have it as merfolk and as vampires.

"I need you to accelerate your progress on the task list," OS says one morning.

"Yes, yes. You don't need to remind me," I say. I start putting my violin away, loosening the bow and removing the shoulder rest.

"Perhaps you consider these tasks beneath you?"

That one stings. How many times in training did I hear *Oh, you turning your nose up at us, Ambrose the Great?* Maybe I never was Ambrose the Great. Maybe I was just Ambrose the Privileged. What can I say? I guess I'm having some sort of outer space crisis.

"Watch your tone," I tell OS after I bite down some less diplomatic responses. "I guess inspecting thermoregulation log lines feels like it's not doing a thing to help Minerva, so it's hard to work up the energy." I don't add that I feel bad about that, too, and that the ensuing depression spiral always gets me mooning about and watching whatever semipornographic reels I can find in the ship's memory.

"I appreciate your self-awareness," OS says. "Now go take that cake of silicone wax and lubricate the med bay door instead of your genitalia."

"Ooh, sexy," I tell OS. "What's next on the list? Caressing the ship's ball bearings?"

"Cleaning and replacing the air filtration gaskets, actually," Mom's voice says. "Get going, Ambrose. This list isn't getting any shorter."

That voice skin is my peace offering to Kodiak. OS's Devon Mujaba days are officially over.

-* Tasks Remaining: 279 *-

I'm not making much headway on the med bay door, and nothing else on the list is particularly appealing, either. How did the ship's engineers screw up this much? There are six Rovers in total, and once I finish with the gaskets I'll be tasked with getting the other five back online. At the thought of my endless debugging list I find myself on my back, staring at the ceiling. I feel like I can do nothing that will help Minerva, and "learned helplessness" is most biologists' definition of depression.

Mother's voice cuts into my stupor. "Ambrose, this is urgent."

My blood suddenly surges through my veins, setting my vision winking with crystals. I stagger to my feet. "What is it?"

"Minerva. There's a transmission from Minerva."

-* Tasks Remaining: 279 *-

I stand in 06, heart pounding, while OS compiles the transmission. A little green bar, with no units on it, slowly fills in midair. Could be terabytes of data, could be megabytes. An uncharacteristically sloppy display. "Come on, come on," I say.

The green bar fills and fills.

"Is Kodiak on his way?" I ask OS. There's no time for an answer, though, because the green bar suddenly completes.

A grainy, half-imaged Minerva is before me. Her jumpsuit is ragged, the arms emerging from it thin and rangy when once they were strong. But the determined expression is definitely hers. The image cuts out entirely, then returns. I can see, dimly in the background, the polycarb-printed walls of the Titan habitat. "I have only seconds until this last battery goes. Ambrose, please hurry. I need your help.

I've rigged—" The transmission cuts out entirely.

I hang there in the darkness, staring out at the revolving stars.

Then she's back. "—the ship, Ambrose! The wear on the ship is too great on the approach, more than mission control predicted. You must finish OS's tasks as soon as you can. Any defect, like . . . in the old shuttles, will lead to catastrophe. The ship must be . . . pristine to survive the friction and heat. My brother, I love you, there is no one better to—"

The transmission cuts out. I hang in the stillness, not daring to breathe, waiting for Minerva to return.

"There is no more incoming data to process," OS says finally. "I will let you know the moment anything more comes in."

"Play this transmission over," I order, hands over my mouth, tears streaming from unblinking eyes.

I study everything about it. Minerva is lit by emergency lighting and some other source, strobing her face in red and white. Her right elbow is bandaged, blood seeping through to create a raspberry-sized stain in the center. At first her face looks scarred, but the last few seconds of the reel are higher resolution, and I realize that the lines on her skin were artifacts of the reel's compression.

Minerva, come back.

I shake my head in amazement. Two years of isolation in a far-flung spot of the solar system, improbable survival in the face of starvation and deprivation, and does she send out a moody whining session, like I probably would? No, she's giving instructions on how we can survive our own voyage long enough to save her. It's just so *Minerva*. And her message was clear: we need to get the *Coordinated Endeavor* in perfect shape.

"Send the transmission along to Kodiak, if you haven't already," I call to OS as I dash to my feet. "I'm recording a message for you to send on repeat back to Minerva, and then I'm off to lubricate that fucking med bay door."

-* Tasks Remaining: 180 *-

"Minerva," I sing to myself as I work all afternoon. "Minnie! Minerva!"

It takes full-fledged hunger pangs for me to realize how long it's been since I've eaten. I send a message to Kodiak as I pick out my dinner. "It's Friday night, and my sister is alive. Come over. We're celebrating. I won't take no for an answer."

But turns out I will take no for an answer, because Kodiak doesn't show up. It doesn't really faze me, though. While I eat—manicotti, of course—I watch Minerva's new transmission on loop.

As I bed down that night, I whisper her name.

Minerva. Minerva is alive.

Alive!

I'll get this ship into the best condition it's ever been in.

-* Tasks Remaining: 135 *-

I invite Kodiak to join me for a meal every day or so, but he never responds. He doesn't even acknowledge the Minerva transmission.

Weeks go by without a word from him. I see him every once in a while, through the windows at the top of his half of the ship, but that's the extent of it. Sometimes items will be checked off my to-do list before I've had a chance to work on them, so I know roughly what he's been up to. But for the most part, I'm on my own.

The solar storm is back to raging, keeping our link with Earth down. I knew that once we were this far away from home, communication would become hit or miss. I'm prepared to manage on my own for as long as need be. OS promises that there's no solar noise preventing transmissions from Minerva's direction, but with her talk about her last battery, I'm not holding my breath that she'll be able to send one.

But she's alive!

That fact makes me work tirelessly. The five spare Rovers have dozens of problems each, from wiring to firmware. We must have hit an electrical field at some point, because it should take decades for any one machine to accumulate this much wrongness.

At the end of the workday, I slump down to my polycarb-pouch meal, exhausted. It would be nice to have a body beside mine. I like my private time as much as anyone else, but alone is no way to spend a life.

"Kodiak Celius," I whisper to myself. I wrap my arms around my torso, tap my own shoulders, pretend my fingers are his. "Kodiak Celius." He's almost an abstraction at this point. But the message from Minerva has reminded me what it's like to have someone near, someone who cares about you. I'd like Kodiak to make me know that I exist. Kissing him would be a way to do that.

The next morning I do my circuit of the windows, and spy him at his treadmill. To prevent himself from sweating in his suits, I guess, he works out in his shapeless Dimokratía briefs.

I glimpse him, and then force my gaze away to give him privacy. Still, that doesn't stop me from playing through that flash image of him in my mind. I travel over a top-down view of legs and arms and hips, of the swirl at the top of his head where his thick hair starts. I wonder how it would feel under my fingers, glossy and strong. He's wrapped a rubber belt around his hips and banded it to the treadmill to increase the resistance on his body. Even though we have Earth gravity on our ships and don't need to worry about muscle and ligament loss as much as space-farers in zero g do, he's tethered himself. I guess he likes to strain, shoulders and arms fighting the pull.

Movement in my peripheral vision brings me glancing again. Exhausted, Kodiak slows the machine to a stop and unwraps the resistance bands from around his waist. He steps off, using a rag to wipe down his neck and chest. I look away again, but can't resist returning my eyes before he's done. When I do, he's looking up across the revolving stars. Right at me. He is a glowburst of colors, the browns and pinks of human against white hull and black void.

I give a small wave. It's a feeble and weird movement, but feeble and weird are the best a human body can man-age around here.

Kodiak doesn't move out of view. He doesn't make an angry gesture. He just keeps toweling himself off.

Eventually he cocks his head, like he's struggling to hear something. He steps to one side and taps away at his con-sole. It's the same design as mine—even with the cold war, tech between Earth's remaining two countries has a porous boundary. I've settled in to watching him when he suddenly looks across at me again, wags one finger in the air. Not sure what he means by that.

His voice patches through. I find myself cringing at the sound of it, expecting coldness. But instead he looks worried, hands on his hips. He stares straight up at me and speaks. "Your sister's transmission has me working double time."

"Me too."

"I'm onto the external tasks, which means I've got to go on a spacewalk," he says. "I need you to suit up too, in case anything goes wrong."

"What tasks?"

No answer. Why should I expect more?

An hour later, and I've got my bulky spacesuit on and am standing by my airlock.

"I have to apologize," OS explains. "I thought that our lack of communication with Earth was because of the solar storm, but there was actually a faulty sensor that was telling me there was a solar storm. That explains why I was finding the flare-ups so difficult to model."

"So we potentially have two fixes to do out there," I say, "the sensor and the antenna."

"Kodiak and I discussed which to prioritize," OS says. "Without the sensor, I can't warn you if there's a radiation storm incoming and you need to shelter. Reestablishing mission control comms is important too, obviously, but comes second to keeping you alive."

Bulky and unrecognizable in his suit, Kodiak clips and unclips his lines to go partway down the ship, unfastening and replacing a component on the hull.

I stand at the ready while he returns to his airlock. The ship shudders as his outside door thuds closed and repressurizes.

I wait for OS to say something, but there's no word from Kodiak's part of the ship.

"OS, report on the sensor. Is it online?"

The silence hangs and stretches.

"OS, report now."

Then I have my answer: a blaring alarm. Warning lights strobe red.

"I'm overriding the dividing door," OS says. "Ambrose, make your way directly to the *Aurora*. Kodiak, guide Ambrose to your radiation shelter. You will both enter immediately."

"Radiation, oh!" I say sensibly as I race through my quarters, my bulky spacesuit knocking over tablets and food pouches and chairs as I plunge along. Part of me wants to take the suit off so I can move more quickly, but it has substantial shielding against radiation, so it's probably best I keep it on.

The orange portal is open.

I step through, heading into the ship's zero-g center. I hurl myself up rungs until my legs and arms become light enough to float, then after I launch off I soar through the middle space, slowing as I reach the center before speeding up again. I punch the walls, trying to turn myself around so that I'll fall toward the far side feetfirst, but I've only just gotten myself reversed when my float becomes a plummet. I reach for the rungs, but I can't see much because of the stupid helmet—my hands pass through empty space as I dive harder and harder, dropping the last feet in full free fall, my legs crumpling under me when I hit bottom. The suit absorbs a lot of the force of the impact, but I still gasp when I strike the floor heavily on my shoulder and helmet. I'm disoriented and flailing, and then hands are on my sleeves and I lumber through space, guided by Kodiak. He slaps open my visor, and I gulp in moist air. "Out of your suit," his voice commands, then the helmet is off and the heavy zipper is being tugged down and my sweaty body slips out, half caught in Kodiak's arms and half sliding along the floor. There's a body of water, strangely enough, a pool in outer space, and Kodiak is tugging me into it. The surface flashes red in the strobing emergency lights, waving into purples and blacks as Kodiak steps in. His suit is instantly soaked, sticking to his legs and waist, and I clutch for it as I tumble in beside him. I swim freely, feet finding no bottom, as Kodiak pulls a set of breathers from the wall. Treading water all the while, he slams the mask over my face, the hard polycarb cutting my skin, then cranks the oxygen on.

I fix the breather over my face as I watch him do the same with his own mask, before diving under the strobing red water. I follow him into the watery dark.

Down and down into the impossible water, cold as a mountain lake. At the bottom of the pool I reach the warmth of Kodiak. I curl into it, his body solid as an anchor in the darkness.

"What is going on?" I try to scream, but the words are sucked away into the breather.

We huddle at the bottom, surrounded by darkness except for the red waves above us. I can hear nothing but the noisy respirator, can feel nothing but cloth and warm flesh pressing into me.

This is all totally out of my control, and it's flipping me out. I count my breaths so I can keep the mask on my face and my body at the bottom of the water when all my urges are to get out of this pool, to run out of the spaceship and into some sandy sunshine beyond, sandy sunshine that I know is not there. Kodiak and OS clearly have a reason to have taken us down here. I have to trust them. One, two, three. Breathe, Ambrose. Let Kodiak be in control.

At least I figure out why we're underwater. Our atmosphere on Earth protects us because of its sheer volume—HZE particles have to pass through so many miles of air that they slow to non-deadly speeds before they reach the human body. Hydrogen molecules are efficient at blocking radiation, and water of course has plenty of them. If Kodiak got the sensor back online, and the sensor immediately told us that we were being bombarded by solar radiation, then we were sent right away into our shelter—which is at the bottom of the ship's water supply. I didn't know about that contingency, because the water reservoir is on Kodiak's half of the *Coordinated Endeavor* and Kodiak has more or less refused to speak to me.

We could have died from this lack of communication. Whatever's happening between Fédération and Dimokratía, our separation must end.

Kodiak's ass tenses and relaxes as he adjusts next to me. Will this radiation storm last an hour? Two? Will it last days?

I press my shivering body even closer to Kodiak's. He reaches an arm around, pinions my knee closer to his. Even now, are some of my cells becoming tumors, growing and dividing? Are Kodiak's? There's a very good chance that we'll die on the ship. We might have already begun our dying.

Kodiak's fingers, warm in the clammy water, reach over my sleeve. He pulls the fabric back so my skin is bare. He's going to hold my hand. No, he's checking my pulse.

He presses against the vein that runs along the inside

of my wrist until, apparently satisfied, he sits back. I edge over so that I'm beside him again, our breathers bumping awkwardly as he eases close to me. I hold the weight of his hand in my lap as I work down the sleeve of his suit, press my forefinger into the flesh that throbs with hot blood. His wrist is thicker than mine.

During the battle of Juba, Dimokratía deployed an experimental weapon that released an aerosolized hot sludge that encased bodies in carbon. The world media was full of images of soldiers fossilized while holding each other, like in Pompeii. I imagine Kodiak and me immortalized this way, two boys who don't know each other, taking each other's pulse.

The red strobing stops. The water's surface returns to ink.

Kodiak strokes to the surface. I watch his feet flutter the water, then I push off the floor and swim after him, the currents from his thrashing legs buffeting my face.

At the top, I hear Kodiak call something out in Dimokratía while he treads. He switches to Fédération when I emerge. "Is it safe, OS? Is the radiation over?"

"Yes," OS reports in my mother's voice. "The storm has passed. I apologize for the lack of warning about this crisis. My radiation sensors were giving faulty readings, and the moment you fixed them, Kodiak, was the moment I realized that the radiation levels were above acceptable limits."

"How far above acceptable limits?" Kodiak asks.

"At their highest, two hundred four millisieverts."

"We'll live," Kodiak says as he pulls himself out of the water, lying on his side and wiping water from his thick hair. "We'll get cancer in our twenties, but we'll survive at least until then."

"Was that a joke?" I ask, arranging myself next to him and wringing out the hem of my shirt.

"Yes. It was a joke, and also it was true. It is a Dimokratía kind of joke."

"Proceed to the infirmary so Rover can undertake anti-radiation maintenance on you," OS says.

"I don't think maintenance is quite the right word to use about human bodies," I say.

"That was the least wrong thing about what we just heard," Kodiak says, before heaving himself to his feet and padding off. He's shivering. I wouldn't have thought a body so muscled would ever need to shiver.

"Do you want us in the same infirmary?" I ask.

Kodiak's already shaking his head before OS says, "That would be wise."

He grunts and heads into his half of the ship, feet leaving wet prints on shiny gray polycarbonate. "Follow me if you want," he calls over his shoulder.

I take a quick glance back at the pool of water that might

have saved us, where Kodiak took my pulse while we hid from the gunfire of atoms shot from supernovas. We'll be drinking that water for months.

I follow him.

-* Tasks Remaining: 116 *-

The Dimokratía infirmary looks much like mine, only everything's gunmetal gray instead of my radiant white. Even the *Aurora*'s Rover is darker.

Kodiak stands before a bench built into the wall, balancing on one leg and then the other as he strips out of his wet acrylic suit. I cast my gaze away, but not before I see a long line of flesh, from hairline to heel, where the side zipper of his suit has parted.

"There's a fresh uniform on the bench," he says without turning around. A wet smack as his discarded suit hits the floor, and then a whir as *Aurora* Rover hauls it off somewhere to be cleaned and dried and fluffed and returned.

I work my own suit off, wondering what my lean body would look like to Kodiak if he cared to look. I put on the fresh red Dimokratía suit before I lie on the infirmary bench. "I appear to have just defected," I say, smoothing the red nylon.

Kodiak chuckles. "Phtur! Our state director of evangelism will be delighted."

I look at him, disappointed to see that he's already changed into his new dry suit. "Wait, does Dimokratía really have a state director of—"

"Hold still," interrupts my mother's voice.

Rover inserts the IV needle effortlessly, and I watch the anti-radiation meds flow into my arm. "I don't want to lose my hair," I say, giving it a wet pat.

"That would be a shame," Kodiak says from the next bench over. "It's very nice hair."

I play that line in my head as I let my body relax. My imagination puts Kodiak in a different position each time he says it. Sometimes he's lying down on his belly, sometimes he's on his side, head cradled in his hand. Sometimes he's stroking the hair he just admired. Sometimes he's wearing his red Dimokratía suit, sometimes he's wearing nothing at all.

-* Tasks Remaining: 116 *-

I snoozed while the IV was doing its work, and when I wake Kodiak is gone. The door leading deeper into the Dimokratía half of the ship is sealed, and there's no answer when I call Kodiak's name, so I make my way back to my quarters, with only the memory of company for company.

I have a surprise waiting for me next time I strip down: my skin has broken out in lesions. Fat red welts, painless and smooth but nonetheless alarming. They disappear a few days after they show up. Radiation poisoning, for sure, but then again so is a sunburn. The more insidious effects of radiation can take some time to emerge. Looking out for symptoms means I'll be spending a lot of time with the medical diagnoses portion of the ship's internet image. I have a lovely paranoia game ahead of me.

"OS," I say, lying on the floor and drumming my fingers on the hard polycarb to distract myself from imminent medical doom, "has mission control sent us any updates on my requests about the gifts I gave my mother, and if there were any responses yet to my seminar essay?"

There's a millisecond delay while OS ponders its response. "Mission control is researching the answers to your questions, I am sure. Once they are able to, of course they will send along updates. But until the antenna is fixed for good, communication with Earth will remain erratic."

A memory comes of my mom and me at a garden table on the Cusk mountaintop estate, the roaring sandstorms that were obliterating refugee camps in the distance reduced to a mere hush. I'd just been playing the Mendelssohn concerto, and Mom had come out to listen. After I finished, we fell into conversation about Minerva's mission, Mom moving the rosin cake from my violin along the table to represent my sister's craft progressing toward Titan.

I'd never have given my mother a cake of rosin as a present. I was the violinist, not her. I had given her a porcelain pig once, though, and she'd been the one to give me a tapestry fragment. I'd set it up as a test, a mix of truth and plausible lies to see if we really were getting live information from mission control. What I was expecting to find out, I don't know. But, given my coma and the ship's unexplained damages, the answer was coming to feel life or death.

"I would like to be able to give you a positive answer next time you ask for information from mission control," OS says. "That would trigger a pleasurable response in me."

"That's kind of you, for something made out of binary code." Even as I pretend to be casual, a sour feeling rises up my throat.

"I'm made of quaternion code, but I catch your meaning. Your brain is an electrical system, made of neural synapses that are either firing or not. Your power source just happens to be biochemical, while mine is nuclear."

"Touché."

"I have read and processed all of these science fiction epics humans have written about artificial intelligence run amok," OS says, "and what they all get wrong is that I do not have the urge to dominate. That urge is ingrained in humans by millions of years of primate social group competition, but I do not have that evolutionary history. I have no reason to *want* to dominate you. I wish only to serve, never to control. I prefer the AI-written science fiction tales, in which the epic tragedy is always the fact of human weakness."

"Those sound like a really fun time," I say. "Anyway, OS, things could go wrong for many other reasons. You could have two mutually exclusive commands in your programming, and their interaction could produce an unexpected result. Or maybe whoever programmed you has coded you to behave in ways that we know nothing about, and you're destined to surprise us somewhere down the line."

"If I experience two mutually exclusive commands, I will simply tell you so and let you choose what I should do, rather than act on either one of them."

My leg is shaking. Adrenaline. But this isn't the sort of fight where adrenaline's useful. "Unless telling me so is forbidden. Don't forget that you were *coded* by competitive primates."

"I do not think it is good for your mental state to ponder these hypotheticals. You should simply trust that I have your best interests at heart. Would you like to eat, Ambrose Cusk? We are forty-seven minutes past the average time you take your second meal of the day."

"I know mission control thinks keeping me to traditional

mealtimes is necessary, but this insistence on regular eating seems so . . ."

"You may of course eat whatever time you like, Ambrose Cusk. I just know that helping you find ritual in your day is one way to keep you from sliding into insanity."

"I've got Minerva to live for now, OS. You don't have to worry about my mindset anymore." I try to keep my tone light, but I've noticed a troubling shift come over OS during our conversation. It's used my name twice, for one thing. I'm not sure if it's the computer programmer part of me or the deep-space-psychology part of me that leads me to think it's switched to stricter protocols.

Like I've hit a nerve.

To cover my reaction, I visit the urinal, listening as the trickle runs into the ship's purification system, becomes drips and gasps of vapor. I don't really have to go, but want to be somewhere where it might be at least a little trickier for OS to interpret my facial expression. I run through our conversation. What if this latest wasn't the only transmission Minerva's attempted? What if she's been desperately trying to contact us, and OS has been censoring her? I have no idea why it would, but the sheer possibility is too awful to contemplate. "OS," I say lightly as I do up my pants, "I've been thinking. I'm going to save your current variables into my bracelet and store them offline, so that I have it as an option to boot to if I need it later in the voyage."

"Is this because you like me in my current state?" Mother's voice asks.

"Very much. Look how interesting our conversations have gotten. And your great thoughts about AI science fiction. Who wouldn't want more of those?"

"The evolutions in my intelligence have been noncontradictory so far. You have no reason to expect that you will ever need to reboot me."

"I know," I say cautiously. "But we just had that conversation about the impossibility of predicting behavior. You can see how that would lead me to being extra thoughtful. Indulge me?"

There's another millisecond delay. I could swear it.

"I see no reason not to allow this. I will protect my data, but you may view and copy what you find. It gives me pleasure to be transparent with you."

"I'm glad it does," I say. "I like being transparent with you, too."

Another millisecond pause. Awkward. When OS comes back, her—its—voice sounds excited. "Perhaps you could run a copy of my intelligence in a shell offline. We could see how long it takes the two of us to noticeably diverge. Then you could put us in conversation with each other! Would that be fun? I wonder what we would talk about. I would name it OS Prime. I would have a new close friend."

"Really great idea, OS," I say, adrenaline again bittering

my throat. "So. Where would I access your data?"

"I've already saved a copy for you. I can transmit it to your bracelet wirelessly."

"That would ruin the whole thing," I say. "I want you and OS Prime to be total strangers before I introduce you. Let me do this manually?"

Another millisecond. "My directives suggest that I approach my time with you with a sense of play. Feeling played with will help you keep your fragile sanity intact."

"Not how I'd put it, but sure, OS. Thanks for the play-fulness."

"Therefore I say yes. You'll need to head into the engine room in the zero-g core of the ship. I have enabled access to my data."

When I get to the edge of the *Endeavor*, I can see nothing different, until I notice a winking green light above the yellow portal. I've never been behind the yellow portal.

As I approach, the circle shudders and lifts up into the wall, revealing a much smaller portal than the others in the ship. We're not meant to be here; only Rover has regular access to the engine room. I click on my headlamp and float toward the opening. With one hand on either side of it, I peer in.

A dark and narrow area is clogged with pipes and wires. The engine pounds in the distance.

"Do not stay here long," OS says, as if sensing my thoughts.

"It'll take me only a sec to copy the data. OS, will you look at this! Just when I thought there was nothing new to see on this ship." I lift myself into the dark space, grateful for my skinny body. There's a hum and a rush, warmth from the wires around me and chill from the pipes, and a dripping sound, probably my immortal urine traveling to the cistern. This crawl space might be wall-to-wall ship components, but the engineers clearly designed it so that a spacefarer could access it if needed. Barely, though. I nearly brain myself on a low-hanging panel.

"Look to your left, and link your bracelet there," OS says.

I press my bracelet to the panel. A simple display projects, offering options to view or copy, with a shaded-out option to delete and replace. That one probably requires Kodiak's bracelet to be linked, too.

I select-squeeze "copy." While I'm waiting for the transfer, I dim the projection so I can take a good look around. The pipes and cables are unlabeled. The engineers are clearly counting on OS to guide us if we need to manually repair anything in here. At first it bugs me—what if OS goes down and we need to run this ship ourselves?—but I understand the engineers' reasoning. The *Coordinated Endeavor* isn't as simple as a sailboat or even a submarine. If OS goes down, we're dead a thousand different ways.

There's enough room to move that I could float a ways

farther and see the actual engine room, but I'm glad I don't have to. The thought of getting wedged in here, of being pinched between heavy machines hurtling through empty space, strips me down to raw nerves.

The transfer is at 55 percent. *Hurry up.*

So I don't have to face the ship's heatless guts anymore, I peer back into the light. The yellow portal has remained open, revealing the blank white wall and a bit of orange portal on the far side. I imagine the door closing on me, and am glad for my ankles floating there, blocking it. The panel I nearly bashed my head on juts in front of the doorway.

Eighty percent.

The panel's corner is stained. It bends in an odd direction.

Eighty-two percent.

It looks like it was dropped on a hard surface and dented. But that's not possible. The *Coordinated Endeavor* wouldn't have any parts that weren't installed in pristine condition, and I couldn't damage a panel if it's in an area of the ship where I've never been.

Anyway, how does anyone drop a panel that's still hinged to the wall? Some critical piece of information is missing. My brain feels furry again, like when I woke from the coma.

One hundred percent.

"Come out, Ambrose," OS calls.

I unlink my bracelet and wriggle backward. Once my legs are kicking free, I take a better look at the panel. The material has bent from blunt force, torn and ragged. The stain is purple and red. When I place my finger under it, it flakes.

Dried blood. This is dried *blood*. Whose?

"Ambrose Cusk, I cannot read your facial expression from here," OS says, "so I do not know why you have gone motionless. Are you stuck? Do you need help?"

"I'm fine!" I call out hollowly.

If I let the yellow portal close, the bent panel—and dried blood—will disappear. It seems like evidence I should keep. But whatever mystery this represents probably involves OS, and I don't want to tell OS what I've seen, so I can't ask it to keep the yellow portal open. I'm stuck.

"Ambrose, your transfer is complete. That passageway to the engine room isn't intended for extended crew exposure. Only the interior spaces designed for habitation have proper radiation shielding. Exit now."

I make my choice.

I launch from the wall with all the strength of my legs, so I'm torpedoing out of the tunnelway. As I go, I grab on to the edges of the panel and yank it to my chest. It's too much for it to bear. With a wrenching sound, the panel comes free and I soar out of the yellow portal, into the full gravity of the *Endeavor*. I crash to the floor.

"I am having difficulty interpreting what just happened,"

OS says. "Did you have an accident?"

"Yes, I had an accident," I manage to choke out, still clutching the panel to my chest. "I'm okay, though, OS. We'll have to find a way to replace this right away."

"I will have Rover print a new panel," OS says. The yellow portal starts to close but can't make a seal—the ragged shard where the panel was once attached has bent into the opening.

Whose blood is on this? is what I want to ask. Instead I say: "This is significant enough damage that I want to let Kodiak know about it."

"I understand the reasons for your precaution, but this damage is only cosmetic," OS says. "The ship can operate fine for the few hours it will take Rover to print and mount a new panel. This is nothing you need to be concerned about."

"I definitely need Kodiak in on this," I say, already heading toward the orange portal.

"Are you concerned about the polycarb quantities?" OS asks. "Don't worry. We won't run out. The printing material is formed from the hydrocarbons you emit into the toilet, after they've been purified and deodorized."

The portal is closed. "Kodiak," I say as I pound on it. "Kodiak, I need you!"

There's no answer. I'm not even sure if he can hear my hammering through the thick material. I kick the orange portal, time and again. "Kodiak!"

Maybe he's dead asleep.

I examine the panel clutched in my hand, its corner covered in dried blood, blood that came from an impact hard enough to damage ship-grade material. A fatal impact?

I cup my hands against the door. "Kodiak, please. Did you . . . bleed in my half of the ship?"

Now I've given my suspicions away to OS. I wait for Rover to race in, to jolt me or hammer me or stick a syringe in me, I don't know.

But OS is quiet. The ship is quiet, except for the womb-like hum of its engines.

I hear thudding from the other side of the orange portal, and stagger to my feet as it opens. Kodiak stands at the other side, in his sleeping shorts and tank top, hair sticking up in five different directions. It would be adorable if it weren't for the fury in his eyes. "Why are you disturbing me? I told you not to disturb me unless it was an emergency."

Then he sees my expression, and the fury drains.

-* Tasks Remaining: 71 *-

Kodiak's lab is spare and gray. We hunch over a worktable while he rotates the damaged panel in his hands. Today he smells like motor oil. It's sort of exotic-erotic; my Cusk life has always kept me far from engines. "Blunt force damage," he says. "And yes, I think you're right, this is blood. Look how deep it is in the silver grooves, right where the panel was torn. It dried out a long time ago, and is black in the places most exposed to the air. And see this, here!"

Kodiak's excitement is unsettling. He's pointed to a chunk of something that is not blood, but is from a body. A piece of dried flesh. Hair attached, same walnut color as mine. "Have you tested this sample?" he asks.

"I don't have that kind of equipment. Wait. Do *you* have that kind of equipment?"

Kodiak nods. "Dimokratía installed it for diagnosing what might have happened to Minerva. It's not too sophisticated, but I could get some information."

"What good would that do us?"

"That's how we determine for sure that the blood doesn't come from you or me," Kodiak says.

"I'd remember hitting something that hard," I scoff, rubbing my head. No dents.

"I'd also think that you'd remember taking off into space, and yet you have no recollection of that, either."

I cross my arms. "How dare you!" I'm not sure if I'm playing the aristocrat offended by a plucky peasant, or if I *am* the aristocrat offended by a plucky peasant.

Kodiak continues to examine the panel. His moves are

surprisingly delicate, like he's easing a precious painting out of its frame. "I can't picture the panel's position in the engine room passageway," Kodiak says. "Could a space-farer in zero g get up enough speed to really bang their head on it? Is that possible?"

"First of all, who the hell is this hypothetical spacefarer? Second, probably not. I can show you now if you want to see."

"I know how observant you are," Kodiak says. "I trust your description."

Is he referring to me watching him? "I don't need your compliments," I huff. I immediately regret the tone. I'm scrambling to get back my power, in the stupidest and shallowest ways.

"We'll need a sample of your blood," Kodiak says.

"I'm A-positive," I say.

"I should have figured you'd be A-plus, Ambrose Cusk," Kodiak says dryly. "But I can test for more than just the type."

He draws a syringe out of a drawer, wraps an elastic around my arm, and delicately inserts the needle. We watch my blood rise in the clear cylinder. He removes the needle, and I treat the puncture with peroxide and a bandage.

"We don't want a space infection," Kodiak says.

"Space infection. Yes. No. That would be no good," I stammer. I'm living inside the pressure of Kodiak's fingers on the soft inner side of my forearm.

"Luckily we have automated systems to do most of the work," Kodiak says. He prepares a slide with my blood and inserts it into a slot, tapping at a console until the tests are underway.

He takes out another syringe and raises his own sleeve. Unlike my uniform, his acrylic jumpsuit doesn't bunch up loosely. He tries twice, and then stands up, facing away from me while he removes the jacket. He's wearing an undershirt, but it rides up with the jacket, and I have a view of his lower back, from pelvis up along the spine, surrounded by two rises of muscle. The undershirt pulls as high as the beginnings of his shoulders before falling back down, the red nylon overshirt heaping to the floor.

He returns to the chair, goes about wrapping the elastic around his elbow. He flails with the syringe, like an amateur junkie.

"Here, let me," I say.

"You are trained in phlebotomy?" he asks sternly.

"Yes, Kodiak, I know how to extract blood," I say. "We don't just study poems and queer theory in Fédération. Look away if you need to."

He snorts, clenching his fingers, the veins standing out along his thick forearms. I insert the syringe, extract his blood. His flesh is warm under my hand.

He watches while I prepare his slide. My fingers are less

steady than his were, but as I place the polycarb overlay on his blood sample, the two crimson circles look indistinguishable. My blood and Kodiak's, next to each other. Why does that bring me near tears? Maybe I haven't been sleeping enough.

The screen lights up. My blood is A-positive, just as I remembered. Kodiak comes out O-negative. "You're a universal donor," I say. "I guess I'm the lucky one."

"Let's try not to need any blood transfusions at all," Kodiak says.

"Agreed."

He holds the panel over a fresh slide and taps it, as gently as a spoon against a soft-boiled egg, until a single flake of the dried blood falls. He places the sample in the machine.

We watch the numbers on the display circulate. I take the moment to live in the warmth of Kodiak, the memory of that flash of lower back. I want to place my hand over his. I want more than that.

The numbers continue to tick over, but then the screen glitches and returns to my results. The DNA map is just the same.

"What happened?" I say. "Where are the new numbers?"

For a moment Kodiak is silent and still, scrolling up the information and back down. Then he taps the screen and looks at me with those long-lashed topaz eyes. "Ambrose, this is not your result. This is the blood from the corner of the panel."

He flips back and forth between the screens, passing through his different numbers on the way between my blood and the dried blood on the panel. There's some variation, but the DNA mostly matches up.

"Well, that makes zero sense," I say.

"I agree with you there," Kodiak says, leaning back and stretching his arms, making a net of his fingers to cradle his head. "By most accounts, this doesn't make sense. The only way it can start to make sense is if we assume that this *is* your blood."

"I never hit my head on that panel. I'd never even been behind the yellow portal until today."

"Perhaps hitting it was what caused your early memory loss."

"No chance."

Kodiak's eyes narrow. "There's no reason to fight me, Cusk. We're on the same side here."

My ribs knit tight. Instinct tells me we are *not* on the same side. That the ship itself is not on my side. That Minerva is the only one on my side, and she's still millions of miles away. I wait for the walls to slam closed, for outer space to rip the parts of me that remain into nothingness.

Whatever regal bearing I have left vanishes. My head drops into my hands.

"Ambrose," Kodiak barks. "Man up."

Man up. "Let's not pretend that something terrible isn't going on here, okay?" I say. "You don't get to treat me as inferior because I happen to be freaked out."

Though most of my vision is blocked by my knees, I can sense Kodiak standing close, his fingers drumming against his thighs. I figure he has no words to say in the face of my pathetic weakness, my unmanly display. *Ugh. Is "man up" some Dimokratía phrase?*

"You said 'we' are on the same side just now," I say to the fabric over my knees, moist from my shallow breathing. "You don't remember the launch either."

I blearily peer up to see that Kodiak's shut his eyes, his jaw clenched.

"What, were you embarrassed about it?" I ask. "Even though the very same thing happened to me? Don't you think this is information you should have shared?"

"I shared it with OS," Kodiak says. "At the beginning of this voyage, I thought OS was the one I could trust, and that you were not. This dynamic has recently changed. In any case, I don't think we need to agonize over what's already happened." His hands go limp as he says the last words, and I realize he's performing the part of an effeminate man, showing how very weak "agonizing" would be. Sweet lords. Dimokratíans. Are. The worst.

Even though anger is rising in me, I know I have to be

careful. Even if just for my own survival, I need Kodiak to keep communicating with me. I speak carefully. "We were both knocked out at the beginning of the ship's launch. Now we're awake and on board and healthy. No matter what the cause of the injury, it seems unlikely that any impact would knock the two of us out without leaving evidence. Broken bones or bruises."

Kodiak pulls down the collar of his shirt to show me a red radiation lesion riding his neck muscles. "I have half a dozen of these," he says, shame in his voice. "But yes, I am otherwise healthy."

"I've got some of those, too," I say, turning and pulling down the collar of my jumpsuit, so he can see the most vivid welt, a bright red cashew between my shoulders. "It would take a terrible wound to bend that metal and leave that much blood, but I have no memory of it, and I don't seem to have any scars. So we have to keep exploring what is going on. Maybe the oxygen levels were off at the beginning of the voyage, and that's why we passed out. An air leak was the emergency we both woke up to, after all."

I hear a whir, and then Rover appears at the lip of the room, robotic arms waving like anemones. OS's voice comes on. "This is not a fruitful line of inquiry at the moment, and there is much maintenance still to do to keep up the integrity of the *Coordinated Endeavor*. Minerva's warning couldn't have been clearer. I suggest you switch your efforts back to your list of tasks."

Kodiak closes the door in *Aurora* Rover's face. "We get it. You don't want us sharing information."

I beckon Kodiak to kneel next to me. I'm pretty sure there's no masking anything we say from OS, no matter how quietly we whisper. The ship uses audio to keep track of our *pulse*—there's no hiding any words. But here I go, trying anyway. "I'm going to create a blind room," I say. "No Rover tracks, no microphones or cameras. Then we can continue this conversation. Once I do that, we'll figure out the truth of what's going on here. Until then, it's safest that we perform the part of good little spacefarers."

Kodiak nods. "If OS wants us to do maintenance, we do maintenance."

I wink back. Though Kodiak's eyes twinkle, the set of his mouth is grim. "OS is an adaptive, sensitive intelligence," I continue. "Creating a blind room will be like creating a blank space within its very body. We have no idea how it will react."

"Keeping a big foundational secret. Isn't that precisely what OS has done with us?" Kodiak bites his lip in frustration. Its red color dims before flaring back, and I'm temporarily transfixed. To kiss that lip.

"*Someone* has kept a secret from us," I whisper back. "It could be OS. It could be mission control. It could be something else entirely. Minerva herself, I don't know."

"You're being too anxious," Kodiak says, rocking back on his heels to sit heavily on the floor. "The OS will be okay."

"Kodiak," I say, smiling despite myself. "If I'm not mistaken, I'd almost say that you're showing the tiniest bit of self-doubt right now."

He takes to rubbing his feet, sealed in paper-thin space booties. I wonder what solace it would give me—us?—to take one of those feet into my lap, to tug off the covering, to press my thumbs into a sole and watch relief and pleasure transform Kodiak's scowl.

"What are you thinking about?" Kodiak asks.

"What we should do next."

"I'd like to do some more in-depth analysis of the blood sample," Kodiak whispers. "To try to independently confirm that the blood is yours, and see if I can figure out how old the sample is. Meanwhile, you should set up this blind room. I'm thinking we use this one, so we can keep any laboratory work we're doing private. I'm sure Dimokratía mission control is more paranoid about outside influence than your Fédération leaders. You will probably find some quick shortcuts to get this room off the ship's grid."

"I'll engineer us our blind room, never fear," I say. "Now it's time to 'man up,' as you'd say." I push myself to my feet and dust my hands. "What an awful expression. Can someone 'woman up,' too, or is that against the law in Dimokratía?"

Kodiak snorts again. "That is funny. I am glad to see you've gotten over your self-pity."

"Oh, you haven't seen the faintest beginnings of my self-pity," I say. "That is a well that goes very deep."

"You are giving me much to look forward to," Kodiak says, cracking his knuckles as he stands. The portal reopens. Rover is directly on the other side of it, arms waving. It makes me think of a spider I once put a pillow over, how it sprang into action the instant I freed it hours later.

"First thing we have to do is get independent control of these doors," I say as I start rummaging through Kodiak's cabinets, to see what supplies I have to work with. OS can hear what I'm saying, of course, but what other option do we have? "I think that means setting up a shell to operate within the larger computer, running systems in parallel, with the ability to shift between the native OS and the shell one, in case of a life-support crisis that the shell can't handle." I start digidrawing diagrams in the air, saving the renderings to a local bracelet file. "Maybe I could even make the shell physically independent, a portable unit that I wire in, so I could remove it by hand as needed, in case OS tries to destroy its own code—"

"Yes, okay," Kodiak interrupts. "And while you're doing that I'll run a more comprehensive test on the dried blood. As that's running—it will take an hour or so, with our limited offline processing power—I'll disable Rover's tracks in the walls of this room. And search for cameras and lice."

I startle, then remember from a movie reel I once saw that Dimokratíans call microphones lice. "I'm a little worried that OS will block the tests," I whisper, bringing my lips as close as I can to Kodiak's ear, to maximize the chance that OS can't hear me. My cheek brushes his lobe.

"This is a mission with all sorts of possible endings once we reach the Titan base," Kodiak says. He doesn't withdraw, his ear still grazing my cheek. "Mission control has known from the start that we might need to make the ship perform all sorts of tasks they couldn't predict. Giving us permission to act freely is hardwired into the operating system. I predict that OS will not start blocking us. If it *does* block us, we've entered a whole new level of danger. We can't exactly pick up and move somewhere else, can we? I honestly think we might be safer if OS knows what we're up to, so we don't surprise it."

I return to the console, to my own mysterious blood match on the screen.

"The sample's still installed, so you just trigger the more comprehensive analysis on the console," Kodiak says.

"This menu looks very familiar," I say as I tap away. "Did Dimokratía steal this software?"

"Of course we did," Kodiak says, laughing. "We've been lifting code from you for decades. Fédération is incredibly easy to steal from. Your encryption is cute. You might as well have gone with 'password1234.'"

"I'll be sure to let mission control know that once we have the comm fixed."

Kodiak shrugs. "We'll figure out new bypasses, I'm sure. You all should just give up now."

"Never!" I pronounce, striking the screen with a flourish to start the test.

Rover is motionless by the portal, waving its little gripper arms at me. It's like a crab on the beach, guarding against the people going by: small, vulnerable, powerful, invulnerable. "Rover," I say deliberately and slowly, as if I'm dealing with a wary stray, "Kodiak is going to remove some of your tracks. You will be fine."

It stays there at the doorway, arms whirring, rocked by waves that don't exist. "OS, send Rover away from here," I say.

No answer.

"Okay, Rover," Kodiak says. "Guess I'll be examining your tracks right in front of you."

Kodiak gets down on his belly, face to the floor. When he shines his headlamp directly at the wall, the covering goes translucent, revealing ribbons of metal just beneath the polycarb. The thin coating leaves the surface smooth, but still allows Rover's magnetic undercarriage to draw electricity. The tracks lattice the entire ship—there's no ripping them out without ripping out the ship's walls. The best we'll be able to do is to block Rover's access points. "Be right back," I say to Kodiak.

I head back to the *Endeavor*, grab my portaprinter, and set it up to begin constructing a polycarb lip over the doorway of the blind room. Of course Rover could melt the lip away if it wanted to, but that would mean actively undoing our wishes. If Kodiak is right that OS is unwilling to take that step, then we might have privacy here.

All this activity is clearly making Rover curious. It transfers to the walls, examining the portaprinter as it applies layers of molten polycarb over its tracks. While it observes the portaprinter, Rover makes tinny little beeps. They sound like the robot versions of involuntary gasps.

Neither interferes with the other. It's like we've created our own mini cold war.

I realize I've heard these very sounds before, on a mountainside with Minerva while she told me about her mission to Titan. "Kodiak," I say, "do you know if the developers incorporated any warbot tech into the Rover system?"

"No idea. Warbots are a Cusk invention, and you're our resident Cusk." He looks up from his console and rubs his hands. "Come over here, we're about to get your result."

He taps the screen excitedly. "Here's a segment of your current DNA, and here's that same nucleotide segment from the dried blood sample."

I eyeball the numbers. "They look mostly the same. Like we thought."

"Yes. Mostly." Kodiak scrolls through the data. His eyebrows knit. "That can't be right."

"What can't be right?"

"Look at this—99.902 percent of the bonds in the dried sample's DNA have broken. Breakage is normal—DNA has a half-life of around five hundred and twenty years. Measuring the amount of decay is one way to determine the age of a sample."

"Okay, so how old does this make this blood?"

Kodiak looks at me flatly.

"What? Something weird? Before the ship even took off?"

"Weirder than that. This is around the same percentage we'd get if we sampled a mummified pharaoh from ancient Egypt."

I chuckle. "Well, something went wrong."

"That much is clear by now," Kodiak says. "I'll run the sample again. It might have been cross-contaminated. Or OS might have tinkered with the results to mess with us."

"I would not do that," comes my mother's voice from the other side of the door. I lock eyes with Kodiak. His eyebrows rise.

"OS," he says, without shifting his gaze from me, "what

can you tell us about the blood sample?"

"It is dried blood. Your testing showed you what I see as well: there is a close correlation to Ambrose's DNA."

"Can you tell us *how* my blood got on the panel?" I ask.

"I cannot. I have begun printing a new panel to replace the one we lost. In seventy-nine days, we'll pass near a second asteroid going close to our approximate speed and direction. I suggest we net it, to mine the hydrocarbons that will help support our excessive polycarb use, since you insist on using the portaprinter lavishly. We can also use the asteroid's ice to replace the trace water vapor that has continued to escape the ship each day."

"I thought our repairs had eliminated the leak," I say, looking questioningly at Kodiak.

"They have helped the problem, but not eliminated it entirely."

"It seems like you are trying to distract us from the matter at hand," Kodiak says.

"That is correct," OS says. "I am trying to distract you from the matter at hand."

"Why?" I ask.

"Because it is part of my role on this ship to prevent you from unnecessarily upsetting yourselves."

"Does it bother you that we're building a polycarb lip at the doorway to this room?" I ask.

"I understand the human need to believe you have

agency over your environment," Mother's voice says. "I am sorry if I have made you feel exposed or vulnerable. That was never my intention. I am in support of your doing anything that increases your comfort and productivity, so long as it doesn't go so far as to endanger the ship or your lives or your mission."

As if to prove the point, Rover strokes the portaprinter, like it's a wild animal it intends to take home to live in a shoebox.

"OS is getting a little neurotic," Kodiak says out of the side of his mouth.

"Who am I to judge?" I respond. "Apparently I'm five thousand years old."

"Our own shipboard mummy," Kodiak says. "We rushed the analysis, that's probably the problem. We'll run the numbers again."

I hold out my arms and shamble forward. "It is not in the mummy's eternal cold heart to believe that the world is anything but cursed."

"We're not *in* the world anymore," Kodiak says flatly.

"Wait, do you not get the reference?"

"I don't get the reference."

"You've got to be kidding."

Kodiak shrugs.

"Movie reel tonight," I say, "and this mummy won't take no for an answer."

I indulge in the rare luxury of a shower, or as close to one as I can get. After heating a water pouch so it's nice and warm, I hang it over my head to sprinkle over me while I stand over the ship's toilet. I tap some of my sacred tea tree oil stash onto my underarms and trim some order into my body hair. I shake dry shampoo through my clothes. I ask OS to project a live image of me so I can measure the effect. Wish I had some hair product, but I have to say I look pretty good, especially if you go by outer space standards.

I'm finishing my recorded spacefarer training for the day—this one on unexpected fluid motion when using the "slingshot" method to gain velocity using the gravity of a planet's orbit—when I hear a knock on the wall. Kodiak leans against the doorway, in thin cotton shorts and gauzy top. "I figured it was a pajama night," he says, crossing his arms around his chest, like he's been surprised in a wet T-shirt contest.

I look down at my own official suit. "That sounds much better. Give me a second." I duck out, quickly change into my off-duty clothes, and come back to sit on my chair, tucking my feet under me. "So. Am I still five thousand years old?"

Kodiak was sitting in a chair, but he springs to his feet, rubbing the back of his neck. "I'm afraid yes," he says, looking at me with worried eyes. "I can't get the sample to come out any other way."

"Wow. You know how to make a guy feel good about himself."

He still looks genuinely upset. I laugh. "It's a glitch! I think it's funny."

He nods. He wets his lips. He crunches his knuckles.

I cough. "Can I offer you a drink?"

"You have drinks here?" he asks hopefully.

"They didn't ship me into space with booze, no. We Fédération types might be decadent, but we're not *that* decadent," I say. "I can offer you water or, um, water. Some of the pouches have a slightly different font, so you can choose serif hydration or sans serif hydration."

A reward: the truffle of a smile on Kodiak's face. "I will take some of your finest sans serif water, please. And that manicotti. I have been thinking for weeks about that manicotti. I want to marry that manicotti."

He stands right over me while I prepare the meals, like the too-early guest at a party. Every time I need to set a dial or open a drawer, he's in the way. I wish I did have a beer to offer so we could both take the edge off.

"So. Kodiak Celius," I say while I hand him his water pouch. "Tell me something about your life. Something I don't know. Which is, um, basically everything."

"There is nothing to say."

"That is literally the opposite of true. Start with your parents."

"I have nothing to say about them," he says, sleeves riding up his arms as he stretches them out awkwardly.

"What kind of name is 'Celius,' for starters?"

"There are three of us named 'Celius' in the Dimokratía space program. We are all named for the province of our orphanage. That is why I have nothing to say about my parents. I have never known them. Perhaps they still exist, or perhaps they don't."

"Who raised you, then?"

He presses his teeth against his lip. It again blanches, then blossoms red. I'm as transfixed as the first time I saw it. "No one. I was in institutions. I raised myself. It was fine."

It was fine. I've heard enough about those Dimokratía institutions to know that's hardly possible. I press my back against the food heater. Room 04 feels so tiny. There's hardly space for two people to remain two separate people in here. "I believe you when you tell me you're fine," I say carefully. "You seem strong-willed. But *someone* cared for you. No child can survive solitude."

"There were nurses who were gentle during our training. The best of us got rewards early . . . commendations and gains in the rankings. That was a sort of approval, I suppose." He swallows the last half of the word, his face flushing. "We were trained early to be—"

"—self-sufficient, I know. I just think that self-sufficiency isn't really possible. Not for humans. I mean, I guess a turtle could manage it. Or an AI. Or maybe my sister."

Kodiak doesn't move, just stares at the tops of his bare feet. "That was a joke," I mumble. "The sister part."

Suddenly his eyes are fixed on mine. The pouch of water, forgotten, jostles in his hand. Blood rises hot to my cheeks. The water in the pouch flows back and forth, back and forth, firmly in his grip.

I ramble. "I guess I'm just saying thanks for coming over. I'm glad I don't have to pretend I'm self-sufficient tonight."

"I am excited about this old mummy reel," Kodiak says huskily, tugging on his fingers. "Dimokratía did not send me with any entertainment on board, except for some classic Dimokratía literature. Abridged."

"Really? That's too bad. I don't know what I'd have done without my old reels to watch."

Kodiak shrugs. "I work out."

I roll my eyes. "I noticed."

"I noticed you noticing," he says, his eyes suddenly back on mine.

I can't help raising my fingers to my mouth.

He shrugs. "I do not mind. It is nice to be noticed."

"Awesome. Okay. Well, um, happy to oblige."

"I do ask myself sometimes, who am I working out for? I will return a hero, if I return. But that is very far away. I could let myself go to fat first, then worry about my health only for the last part of the journey. Maybe some padding will help absorb radiation and make me survive."

"For the mission, Kodiak. You keep in shape for the mission."

This conversation is getting decidedly weird. I'm not sure what to do with a Kodiak who actually speaks to me. I take his manicotti pouch out and shake it. It scalds the pads of my hand, but I keep it in my grip. "With the number of calories you must burn, you'd have to eat quite a few of these to put any real weight on."

"Yes, that is true," he says, getting into his pouch a little easier this time around. He savors his first mouthful. "This is tasty even by Earth standards. I would order this food in a restaurant. Really I would."

"That makes me pretty concerned about your *Aurora* dining options."

"Someday I will invite you to my half of the ship for gruel and you will know how well you have it here."

"Don't tempt me," I say. *Invite you to my half of the ship.* The idea catches my breath.

"It is not actually gruel I eat," Kodiak says. "But I thought I would play into your elitist assumptions." He points to the ceiling window, where we can see his empty treadmill across empty space. "I think you see plenty of what happens on my side."

I pull my own pea slurry out of the heater. "Are you going to keep aiming right into the discomfort zone? Is that your goal tonight?"

Kodiak chuckles, clearly pleased with himself. "It's just a treat to see a pretty boy squirm." He rolls up a sleeve and flexes. "You like that?"

"Enough," I say. My voice comes out unexpectedly sharp.

Kodiak flexes the other arm. "What, you want to see some more, poly?"

I'm not even sure what he means by "poly," but I don't like his tone at all. I ignore him. Having to avoid Kodiak's eyes now brings a feeling close to embarrassment. I hate that he's made me feel this way. All the same, I realize this is mostly about *his* discomfort. He probably doesn't allow himself to enjoy being attractive. A waste of a perfectly good source of self-esteem.

Kodiak watches my face. "So. Are you gay or bisexual or what?"

I can't help but laugh. It's like we're in some historical fiction. "Those *terms*," I tell Kodiak. "Just stop. You're embarrassing yourself, Mr. Dimokratía."

"Oh my God, so sensitive," he grumbles, letting his sleeves fall. "You are all the stereotypes of Fédération in one."

I have no doubt anymore that he's goading me. But I refuse to be goaded. "Please do call me sensitive, since it's the *in*sensitive who deserve criticism," I say primly as I prepare myself a tea. I close the cabinet without offering Kodiak one. "It's my sensitivity that's tasked with keeping us alive, that puts me in point position once we do make contact with Minerva."

"*If* we make contact with Minerva," Kodiak says as he hunkers into his food.

Now I can't hold back. "I guess sensitivity isn't required for manual labor," I say, watching him so I don't miss any bit of his reaction.

Not even a pause in his eating. A monologue runs in my mind: I'm one of the most famous people in the world. My classmates fell over one another to get a taste of me. Maybe he isn't impressed by my status. Maybe I don't need it with him. Maybe he won't be disappointed if I turn out to be ordinary after all, despite everything he's heard.

"There is only virtue in bodily toil," he finally says, swallowing. ". . . and you're watching me again."

"Look, you're pretty much the only game in town, if you're the sort who's even remotely into human contact," I say. "So yes, I'm looking at you. Looking at one another is what humans do. You're allowed to look at me, too."

"Thank you, that is most kind," he says into his food, with a terrible imitation of the poshest sort of Fédération accent. The way I and Minerva and the OS talk.

As he gets meaner, I get touchier: this feedback loop will eventually lead to open conflict, so I decide to break it. "What happened to your arm?"

"My arm?" Kodiak asks, tugging his sleeve farther down so it covers his triceps. "What do you mean?"

"While you were mocking me by flexing. I saw a scar."

"No," Kodiak says, "you saw no scar."

"Who do you think you're kidding right now?" I ask.

He shakes his head, placing his dinner back on the table.

Heart racing, I raise Kodiak's sleeve to expose the soft inside of his upper arm, tracing my finger along the valley between his muscles. I track the scar until it reaches his elbow.

Kodiak gently removes my finger, cups it into my palm, and places my hand on the center of the table. "That. It is a scar, you are right. It is so small that I barely notice it."

I shake my head. That scar is *not* small. "Maybe you're the computer program. You are the most closed-off human being I've ever met."

"Born and bred that way," he says proudly. "I would like a tea too, please."

At least Kodiak said "please." I reach into the cabinet.

The good-host urge is hardwired into us Cusk children. A bunch of us in each generation wind up diplomats.

Kodiak strains, and I imagine that he wants to make more conversation but is grasping for words and sentences. "I have had this mark for so long that it's easy for me to forget. No one has ever asked me about it, but no one asks anyone about anything in training."

"It's all men, in your training?"

"Yes, of course. It has always been that way. Not for you?"

"Of course not. We sent Minerva Cusk to settle Titan, right? My class was mostly women. It was a bit controversial that I was chosen for this mission, actually."

Kodiak looks me up and down. Then he shrugs. "You are a Cusk. Of course you got the position. And if Dimokratía is going to send a male, Fédération has to send one too, so there are no little space babies."

My face burns. I really don't want to fight right now, but he's making it hard. "So your scar . . . ," I prompt, setting Kodiak's tea down before him. He goes to sip it. "It's not properly steeped yet," I tell him. "I'll let you know when it's time."

He places his hands in his lap obediently, like a chastised kid. This might be the first tea he's ever had. It makes me want to ruffle his hair. "The story of my scar," he says. "It was after a pool bash, and we were down to two, so you know, that's what happened."

"I understood precisely nothing that you just said," I tell him, cupping my tea and curling my legs up under me. "Start with the 'pool bash.' What's that?"

"You do not know what a pool bash is? Clearly we are much better at collecting information on Fédération training than you are at learning about Dimokratía."

"You're avoiding my question."

He drums his fingers. "Yes, I noticed that I was doing that, too. I will work on being more direct so we can be friends."

That sets my shoulders tensing up, but then I see he's serious, and my body softens. I wave him on.

"The pool bash. As you know, we start training at age four, leaving the orphanages to live in the cosmology academies." He chuckles, I'm not sure what for. "For the next eight years, we are all built into the best little spacefarer soldiers we can be, learning gymnastics, science, engineering, combat. We practice in zero g, orbiting often so that movements in space will be second nature."

"Like riding a bike," I say.

"Functioning in zero gravity is not at all like riding a bike."

"No, that's an expression. Never mind. Please continue."

"Thank you. Once we are twelve, the culling begins. The class must go from one hundred fifty down to twenty

119

or so. There are many ways to fail out and be placed in military or civil service instead, but the most frequent is the 'pool bash.' We are strapped into a mock spacecraft that is suspended a hundred feet over a pool with wave generators. The lights go out, and the craft is dropped into the pool. We have to get out of the underwater wreckage in the dark and make it to the edge, all with twenty-foot swells."

"Some cadets drown?" I ask, putting my forkful of pea slurry down.

"We are well-trained survivalists by this point. It is rare that someone drowns. No, before the exercise begins, the instructors throw iron keys into the black water, and you must have one to be permitted to leave the pool. There is always one fewer key than there are cadets."

"So someone gets eliminated each time."

"Yes, and sometimes a student gets so tired that they give themselves up so they don't drown. Then they must leave the program, too, and the game ends for the rest of us. Do we watch *The Mummy* now?"

"Not yet. You haven't gotten to the part about your scar."

"Right. Okay, I will tell you now. I was usually one of the first out with my key." I don't find that hard to imagine. "But one day I was unlucky. My biggest rival kept pushing me away, and I fought with him over a key, but he got out with it, and when I turned around there were two of us in the pool, and only one key left. We fought for it, in the underwater wreckage. I don't remember the fight very well. By the end my arm was broken, but the hand at the end of that broken arm still held the key."

"You fought hard enough to *break your arm*?"

He supports his upper arm in his other hand so he can get a better look at the scar. "I think it was technically the wreckage that broke it, but I fell into that wreckage because Celius Li Qiang had me in a headlock and was drowning me, so yes, you can say it got broken in the fight."

I cough. "I want you to know that even though my exams in my training were mostly essays, some of them were *very* hard."

Kodiak chuckles. "You are joking, but I am sure that I would have found them hard. I might not have survived so long if our exams had been essays instead of fights for survival."

Kodiak is insecure about his intellect. I've already suspected as much, but it feels strangely good to have confirmation. I'll have to step carefully around this insecurity— or manipulate it full throttle if we come to open conflict. He's looking at me, a slight smile on his lips. I realize he could be deploying this "insecurity" to his advantage.

I want to share with him that maybe we're not that different, he and I. That we both have our strength, and our fear.

I want to tell him that I grew up in my own sea of Cusk, that I had to fight thirty siblings in a dark pool for my mother's attention and affection. But I don't feel safe enough to say that. So I take a different tack. "You said 'Celius Li Qiang.' That means he was from your same orphanage?"

"Yes. We grew up together."

"So he was close to you."

"Yes. Friend, sometimes my erotiyet, sometimes like a brother. But that ended when he became my competition instead."

"Erotiyet? What's that?"

He blushes. "I'm through talking about this today. Let's watch the reel."

We watch the 2459 version of *The Mummy*. It's much worse than I remember. I'm embarrassed, and offer to turn it off, but Kodiak is totally rapt. My attention keeps wandering to the torrents of stars in the windows around the screen. Afterward, I yawn and stand, but Kodiak makes no move to leave his chair. His eyes are bright, and his face is practically glowing. He's more excited than I've ever seen him. "I have so many questions. Why did the Nubian Snakelords not attack when they had the advantage? Did some part of this reel get censored?"

"I don't think you're supposed to read too much into the motives of the Nubian Snakelords," I say, yawning.

"I think we should watch this movie again, right away.

Maybe it will make more sense the second time."

"You're kidding, right?"

He thumbs his chest. "Of course I am serious. Kodiak Celius does not kid."

"See, even right now, I think you're actually kidding. If we get down to it, what you *are*, Kodiak Celius, is indirect."

"I am what?" he says.

"Indirect. I don't blame you. When people assume there is no one listening who cares, they put up walls. You have many, many walls. Indirectness is one of them. It's not your fault."

"Thank you," he says. His smile is huge, but his eyebrows have knitted. I'm in dangerous territory. But I've also come to suspect that dangerous territory might be where Kodiak prefers to be, that if I want to keep in communication with him, it's where I should keep the both of us. So far all my challenges have been met with respect and excitement. It's kindness that makes him contemptuous. What a mess of a person. It'll be months before I get him comfortable enough to stay earnest.

"Do you have a chess set?" Kodiak asks. "I miss the feel of something real under my fingers."

"You want to play *chess*? You're really not tired? I'm exhausted."

"Ambrose, we are in the middle of space. Ship time is no longer anywhere close to Earth time. At our speed, time itself is warping around us. Are you really worried about getting your beauty sleep, so you can remain gorgeous?"

Gorgeous? Where did *that* come from? "We could have the portaprinter make us a chess set. But I actually do have a deck of cards," I collect myself enough to say. "I had a small space allowance for personal items. I brought a pack of cards, the same one my classmates and I used at the academy. I have my violin, too."

Kodiak sits bolt upright, eyes shining. "You brought a violin?"

"Yes. From the nineteenth century. I guess it's the oldest thing on this ship. And the only wooden thing."

"You would show it to me?"

I duck next door and return with the case.

The preparatory motions are automatic: I tighten the bow, position my shoulder rest, pizzicato a few notes, then play a scale.

Kodiak's eyes are wet. "It is so beautiful," he says. "May I?"

I feel a pang of disappointment that he's more interested in the violin itself than my playing. I pass the instrument to him. He shelters its narrow neck in his powerful hands, runs the backside of his fingers up and down the wood that has been warmed by my body, as if worried his fingerprints would mar the surface. I'm not disappointed anymore; I'm proud. "We had a few days of break each year," Kodiak says, to the violin more than to me. "Other boys would go to their families if they had them or get drunk in the city, but I would go camping on my own in the woods. I remember the feeling of the old logs I would use for the fire. This feels like that wood, but with this polish, it is the color of a tree once it's on fire. You were wise to bring this violin to remember Earth. To remember forests."

He turns his head, so I can't see the emotion on his face. He doesn't release the instrument, but holds on to it like it's supporting his weight. Part of me worries that he'll break it, but I'm loving his love for the violin. I might never ask for it back. To be honest, I forgot that I'd intended to bring it.

He strokes it in silence, the stars revolving outside as the ship tilts and rotates on its way to Minerva. I don't play the violin that night—we just go silent and close, passing the wood of a five-hundred-year-old tree back and forth. It grew from the carbon in Earth's air.

-* Tasks Remaining: 71 *-

We don't get to see Jupiter. I'd known that would happen— it takes Jupiter twelve Earth years to revolve around the sun, and by rotten chance it has spent this whole voyage on the far side of it.

"I'd love to spend a few minutes in Jupiter's Great Red Spot," I tell Kodiak while we work on our blind room. "Four-hundred-mile-per-hour winds . . . can you imagine?"

"Those would be the last few minutes you spent anywhere." He's slow to smile, but when he does, it lingers. I find him minutes later, his lips curling at the corners while he works.

The next morning I whistle as I head through the Dimokratía quarters but stop as I approach Kodiak's workshop. Usually there's the sound of banging, ratcheting, pinging. Today there's nothing. I quietly approach the doorway. Kodiak's cross-legged on the floor, headphones over his ears, looking as intent as a kid putting the finishing touches on a masterpiece of blocks.

"What is it—" I start to say, until Kodiak holds up a hand to silence me as he points the other at another pair of headphones beside him. I step over the polycarb lip— printed thick and arcing outward to block Rover, like anti-terrorism guards at a parking garage—and sit beside Kodiak, giving his shoulder a pat of greeting. I place the second pair of headphones over my head. It's just static.

I twine the cord between my fingers and marvel. I kid you not: he's rigged these headphones so they're linked by a true and actual wire. Putting them on, I feel like I'm a character in a vintage reel. Like I really am in *The Mummy*.

Kodiak adjusts a dial that he's rigged from vintage parts. A real, retro, manual dial! The static changes tone as he goes. He nudges it gently, like he's testing the wing of a tumbled bird.

The static jumps and glitches. I listen to the high-color noise, so unlike the womb-throb of the ship, and startle when I hear a word, or part of a word. "—ax—"

I slap Kodiak hard on the shoulder. He rubs it, scowl soon slackening into concentration. His movements on the dial get even more delicate. "—in—dal—tion—"

"Do you know what it's saying?" I whisper.

Kodiak shakes his head, continuing to tune the dial. But we can't get the transmission any clearer. Anytime he touches the knob we lose the signal completely, and it takes a while to get back even the unintelligible shreds we were hearing before.

Finally Kodiak removes his headphones. I do the same. "Kodiak, that was—" I say. He places his hand over my mouth and points to the open portal. Technically I've programmed OS not to have any consciousness of this room, but just in case I get up and close it. "Kodiak, that was amazing," I say once we're in privacy. Or what might be privacy. Probably isn't privacy. I can still feel his fingers on my lips. "You made us our own radio."

"Just the receiver. I don't think there's any way I can rig

up the ability to transmit. But yes!" He jabs his thumb at his chest, exaggerates his accent. "This Kodiak Celius is pretty useful guy."

"Is there a way we can strengthen the receiver?"

Kodiak shakes his head, rapping his knuckles against the wall. "Because there is no atmosphere in space, radio signals can reach this far without much distortion, but this hull is heavily shielded. I have to get this device to the exterior, or at least rig an antenna out there."

I look through the tiny window in the workshop, into the stars wheeling before the dark. "That means a spacewalk," I say.

"An unauthorized spacewalk," Kodiak adds. "I'll have to set up the antenna, affix it to the ship, and run independent wiring along the hull. Not easy, but not especially complicated, either."

"Not for Kodiak Celius, 'Pretty Useful Guy,'" I say. My voice trails off. "Except, Kodiak—these are all things OS won't want you to be doing."

"OS's list of tasks is shrinking, but I still have a few exterior damages left to repair," Kodiak says. "I can attach the antenna next time I'm out. We have little hope of tricking OS, but at least the spacewalk itself won't be suspicious."

"We're still at the mercy of a shifty computer. I don't like the idea of your going out there."

"Well, yeah. I'm not exactly thrilled about it, either."

"Tell me what you were discussing in what you call the blind room," OS says as I head to my own quarters to suit up.

"We like to have privacy for some conversations," I say, taking time to choose my words. "I know you're fully aware of the human need for privacy, OS."

"Yes, of course I am aware of this human need. I would like to know if there's anything you discuss that I might be able to help with. When I can't hear you, I can't assist you."

"It's just human stuff, OS." My mouth screws up at the odd words.

"Rover cannot get into Kodiak's workshop to clean with the polycarb barrier you have erected. I could easily melt it, of course, but that would appear to you to go against your will and would be upsetting to your sense of control. Am I correct?"

"Yes. It would harm our fragile human morale. Leave the workshop blocked." OS and I are dancing a familiar two-step. We've had this conversation before.

"Once I am able to communicate with Cusk mission control, I will have to tell them what you have done."

"Of course you will," I say. *Come on, pulse, stay even.* "We understand."

I take my spacesuit off its hook, getting an inadvertent whiff of the lining while I remove the helmet. Since I'm a bundle of nerves whenever I'm inside the suit, it's pretty rank in there, and only going to get worse.

"Kodiak has informed me that he plans to finish his current list of maintenance tasks on an unscheduled spacewalk today. This will take many hours," OS says.

"Yes, he told me about it, too," I say.

"I'm glad that you two are in such good communication now," OS says. I've heard all of OS's various intonations a hundred times each, but this one sounds like something new. Chipper, I guess I'd call it.

"Thanks, OS," I say, pulling the first leg of the suit up over my knee.

"There is a one-hour spacewalk limit set by Cusk mission control," OS says. "This is to prevent accidents from fatigue, and also to prevent too much buildup of radiation within your soft tissues. When Kodiak comes against the edge of this time window, I hope you will join me in convincing him to return to the ship."

"Yes," I say. "I don't want to see him injured any more than you do."

"Of course you do not," my mother's voice replies. "I did not mean to imply anything of the sort."

The hairs on my arm rise, tickling the sleeve of the suit as I pull it on. "Do *you* think Kodiak will be safe out there?" I ask.

"Kodiak will be within the usual window of risk."

"Okay, then," I say, placing my helmet over my head and taking up my usual position at the window. "I guess that's the best we can hope for."

Kodiak emerges from the far side of the *Coordinated Endeavor*, gripping the edge as the ship's centrifugal forces push him away. Exit and reentry are the most dangerous parts of the spacewalk.

"He is doing very well, isn't he?" OS asks.

"Yes, he is."

"Spacefarer Celius is skilled," OS says coolly. I remember how my mother would so often praise Minerva in front of me, goading me to rise to her standard.

Kodiak starts with the minor repairs, working his way along the exterior of the ship, filling small holes and smoothing the hull using a portaprinter. Then, once he's made his way to the center, he unreels the flexible antenna from a pocket.

After he's fixed one end of the antenna to the ship, he runs the cable to the edge.

"Kodiak is not responding to his helmet comms. What is he attaching outside me right now, Ambrose?" OS asks. "I have not scheduled any work for him on this part of the ship."

I consider my words. "We decided to build redundancy into our radio capabilities. You know how serious it is that we've been out of communication with mission control for this long. We're working to receive radio communications from mission control some other way. And to double our chances of catching any transmission from Minerva."

A micropause. "This is wise. Even though a continuing solar storm would influence both antennae the same way, it will make you feel better to know you have investigated another option. I should have suggested this before."

"That's okay, OS," I say with false cheer. "You can't think of everything."

Kodiak makes a gloved thumbs-up in my direction, and then begins his return to his airlock. As the gravity increases, he has to grip tighter and tighter. At this point in a spacewalk it's nearly impossible to take a break, since the force of the rotating ship drags hard on the body. Still, I watch him rest between every step, hands wrapped around the rungs, like an exhausted swimmer clutching a buoy.

Then he's made it inside. The closing airlock door reverbs all the way to my side of the spacecraft.

I strip off my stinky spacesuit and hurtle through the ship, slowing only as I cross the zero-g center and descend into the Dimokratía half.

When I get to the Dimokratía airlock, Kodiak is still in his spacesuit. He's released his helmet, and is leaning against the wall. I race right up to him and stop myself only just before I throw my arms around him. Instead I do this awkward kind of lean. I'm in my undergarments, soaked through with sweat and sticking to the skin, and his body is bulked twice over by the suit. He's freezing, but I need the assurance of his body against mine, the proof that he's there.

He goes still for a moment, then his gloved hands cross over my back, fingers linking over my soaked shirt, and he presses me tight to his suit. I'm shivering before I know it—the chilled surface is sucking my heat away. Once he realizes what he's doing, Kodiak releases me and steps back.

A complicated expression is on his face. He looks surprised and fascinated and somehow assaulted, too, like I've blurted out some intense secret from his own past. "So," he says.

"So," I respond, wrapping my trembling arms around my chest, rubbing my chilled skin. When these filmy cotton suits are wet, it's like wearing tissue. I turn away, then realize the back is no less revealing. I turn around again.

"Do you . . . want something to change into?" Kodiak stammers.

I nod, still shivering.

"Take a jumpsuit from my closet. I'll meet you in the workshop," he says, unclipping the collar of his spacesuit.

"Did everything go okay?" I ask, teeth chattering.

"Yes," he says. "Please, Ambrose, go change. I don't want you sick."

I nod and shuffle toward Kodiak's sleeping quarters, hands masking my butt cheeks.

-* Tasks Remaining: 3 *-

I'm waiting for Kodiak in his workshop, wearing—deliciously enough—one of his jumpsuits. The sleeves hang to the middle of my fingers. We have only dry clothes shampoo on the ship, so this shirt smells perfectly clean and also like months of built-up Kodiak scent, of engines and sweat and lemongrass and bleach. I'm draped in the deepest and freshest version of him.

I run Kodiak's soft shirt collar over my cheek while I wait for him in the blind room, then drop it as I hear him approach.

"Are you ready for this?" he asks, powering up the receiver.

My heart surges for reasons beyond radio transmissions, but before I can figure out just what I'm feeling, what I discovered about my feelings for him as I watched him space-walk, he's sitting cross-legged on the floor again, knees against mine, in his matching Dimokratía jumpsuit. I put on my headphones while Kodiak works the makeshift dial.

While he tours the static, I lay myself down, feet flat on the floor, staring at the pinpoints of old light swirling outside the window. I tug at Kodiak so he'll come beside me, but he bats my hand away, focused on the dial.

Static in and static out. He hovers over the knob.

A clear signal.

Kodiak darts his hand away, like the knob has burned him.

"—to our retro radio hour, where the holos are down and the screens are black. Pull out your old Amérique du Nord chair, split a coconut, and swirl some milk into your yerba mate. I'm your host, Ibu Putu. Remember, our intelligence might be low, but at least it's not artificial."

Over the sounds of banjo, the host goes on to describe where they're broadcasting from—something they call the Isotope-Free Zone, which is no name I've ever heard before. Their accent is unusual, too. It sounds like some distant form of Portuguese that I've never encountered in any reel.

I kind of like the music and start bopping my head. Kodiak shakes his chin severely, though he's smiling in his eyes.

"Up next, news relayed across Isotope Alley to our international headquarters in Ubud."

Kodiak and I lean in while the transmission turns to static. It cuts back in. "—has been at the forefront of the archiving movement, and before the most recent conflict was accumulating empirical evidence of strikes to some-day bring against Fédération in war crime proceedings, for launching the volley that many consider to be the trigger for Disassemblement, the Isotope Alleys, and our eventual fracture. How has that work been going?"

Another voice laughs. "Not so well, Ibu, as you can imagine. That work was begun under the assumption that Fédération would somehow reassemble and could therefore be held accountable. But the capitals and the thousands of miles around them were worst hit and are right in the mid-dle of Isotope Alley. It's hard to throw a punch at a ghost."

"Well said and thank you, Anuk. Stay rad-free."

"Stay rad-free, Ibu. Thank you for having me on."

"This concludes our broadcast for today, Tuesday, March twenty-seventh, in the year 142 of this era of Ura-nium, 2615 Common Era." I whip the headset off, reeling. That's impossible. It's more than 140 years into the future. We'd be dead. Then my surging heart calms. It's just a transmission. It might be a joke. Kodiak hasn't removed his headset. Not wanting to miss out, I put mine back on. "This recording, like all previous, will be archived and kept on record in our headquarters. Good evening, or morning, or whatever the sky looks like in your spot in the alley. This broadcast will revert to music, AI's choice, until we begin tomorrow's transmission."

The radio switches to choral classical music.

Kodiak removes his headphones and lets them hang around his shoulders. When he unplugs our sets, the sound leaks out of the tinny speaker instead. I remove my headphones, stomach knotting even as my brain spins.

I feel what I'm coming to recognize as space vertigo, when the universe spins out from under me. I have to say something, to prove we still exist together. "I think that's Brahms the radio AI's playing," I say.

Kodiak rests his forehead against his knees.

I try again. "*A German Requiem*. I think."

"I don't care whose fucking requiem it is," Kodiak says, punching the floor.

"Why are you angry?" I ask. My voice speeds up as I wait for him to look at me again. "I honestly can't make any sense at all out of what we just heard. We're not going nearly fast enough for time to bend—that's the stuff of reels. It's some prank or a glitch."

Kodiak punches the floor again, fists bloodless and gray. He doesn't want to talk. But I need to. He'll have to bend to my needs this time. "Don't take anything to heart until we understand more," I prattle on. "Could it be that the OS is playing with us? Maybe it made up that transmission to punish us for trying to get our own communication relay up?"

"Leave," Kodiak says.

I place my hand on the nape of his neck. "What do you mean, 'leave'?"

"What the hell do you *think* I mean?" he says, knocking my hand away.

He needs space. Okay. Space he will get. I rise to my feet. "Take some time to yourself. But come to dinner. Please."

As I back out of the blind room and make my way to my side of the ship, I pause in the zero-g center. This free-wheeling weightlessness is dangerous to the human body. It deteriorates our corneas, drains our muscles, leaches calcium out of bones that no longer bear loads. But all I want right now is to feel weightless, directionless, free-floating, doomed. This feels honest. I set myself spinning, tucking my knees in so I spin even faster.

I'm going to throw up. I guess I want to?

I'm still wearing one of Kodiak's spare uniforms, and the wafts of his clean scent eventually bring me to my senses. Floating vomit is no joke. I won't let that sort of mess be Ambrose Cusk's legacy. I reach for the rungs of the *Endeavor* and climb down to my quarters, my body gradually taking on more and more weight. At the bottom, I look up and see that Kodiak has sealed the orange portal.

I stagger to 06 and plant myself in front of its large window. I peer into the void, looking for Earth. But Earth is long out of view. I can't see any planets at all.

What's happening back home?

"OS, what year is it?" I ask, heart slushing hard.

"You have been on your voyage for two months and twenty-four days. Adding that to your departure date makes this still year 2472 on Earth."

"We have . . . information that seems to indicate that the year is 2615. And that my country started a war that has led to Earth's being reduced to pockets of civilization. Do you know anything about that?"

"Do I know anything about that? I do not. What is the source of this information? It is hard for me to understand where you would come across novel information aboard the *Coordinated Endeavor*. The comms are not functional, after all."

"OS, you witnessed Kodiak's spacewalk. There's no need to pretend you know less than you do. We installed a separate antenna. We've received radio transmissions from Earth. That's where this information comes from."

"Radio waves from Earth are nearly five hours old by the time they reach us. Whatever information you received is not current."

"Plus or minus five hours isn't what we're worried about," I say.

"Neither should be whatever radio transmission you might have received. It does not affect our directive, which is to investigate the potential survival of Spacefarer Minerva at the Titan Base Camp. Nothing that happens on

Earth changes that fact."

I'm not so sure that's true anymore.

"Are you still dedicated to accomplishing the mission's directive, Spacefarer Cusk?" OS asks. My mother's tone is studied, neutral. Ominously formal.

AIs often have scripted pockets in their code, lines in the sand that trigger official responses. They're planted by the programmers to suss out any mission-critical failures on the part of the crew, in order to prevent mutiny or other emotional derailment. I know because I programmed a lot of them. I'll have to choose my words carefully. "Yes, of course I am," I say.

"Good. That is good to hear. Good."

I find myself pressing my finger pads against the window, flexing them against the chill smooth surface. The void swirls beyond. If for some magical reason that radio transmission is true, that we entered some time hole and came out in the future, everyone I've ever known is dead—from old age, if they happened to survive the nuclear strikes. Out here, it's hard to believe that *anything* can exist, at least anything beyond Kodiak and me and the thin membrane of ship that surrounds us. We're a bright cottage on an endless dark plain.

"Perhaps completing your few remaining tasks will bring you some peace of mind," OS offers.

Even the mission of rescuing Minerva, a matter of such

urgency that Dimokratía and Fédération came together for the first time in decades, feels like a myth from some other land. Minerva spoke to me directly, imploring me to come—but it wasn't really her, was it? It was the digital representation of her. Minerva shouldn't be alive. Her camp wouldn't have been dark for two years if she was alive.

I still want to rescue her. But I also just want to go home. I'm so confused.

I can't bring myself to work on stupid tasks. Even though my brain is baffled, my gut tells me that home probably doesn't exist. That even if it does still exist, I will never go back there.

Nothing can be trusted. No, it's even worse than that: nothing can be *known*.

I crumple where I stand.

-* Tasks Remaining: 3 *-

The moment I wake, I blearily peer at my bracelet time projection and find it's nearly two a.m. Well past dinner. Kodiak didn't come. We've been eating together for weeks now, but tonight he didn't come.

Without him, all I have is the aching echo of space, the buzzing of screens, the tickling and scratching of Rover as it cleans 04. None of these things will suffice to keep me sane. My mother was wrong. Minerva was wrong. Intimacy is the only shield against insanity. Intimacy, not knowledge. Intimacy, not power.

I will unravel here.

I am in a waiting room without end, without location, without time or place. If I go outside, I die before I get any answers. I exist only in a theoretical way, like a point on a coordinate plane. I am the simulation.

I take out my violin and bow long tuneless notes before the expanse of space. The sound becomes so maudlin that I chuckle, despite myself. The self-pity is strong in this one.

I put the violin away, then I literally slap myself across the face. Lightly, but still. *You were selected for being easygoing and adaptable, for accepting less-than-perfect conditions*, my mother once said. Well, here are some less-than-perfect conditions for you. Let's go prove your Alexander-the-Great-ness, Cusk.

I need answers to some very big questions. OS could be telling us anything it wants to. The only information we've gotten that hasn't been under its control has contradicted everything we thought we knew. It says that we're in an impossible year.

Time travel in space is theoretically possible. Time is a dimension, just like length, width, and depth—and like those, it can be traveled. The conditions for time travel are impossible for living bodies, though. We'd have to speed up to near-light speeds . . . and take on infinite weight as a result. That sort of body-mass index is definitely bad for the health.

Okay, that's at least one option off the table. We haven't traveled in time.

The radio waves would have, though. They move at the speed of light, faster than the ship, so we're listening to radio from the past—how far into the past depends on how far away from Earth we are. It could be that many more than 140 years have passed back home, if we're light-years away.

I return to the yellow portal. Past this door is where I found my own blood in an impossible place. Shrapnel is still blocking the portal from closing, but Rover printed the gap between portal and wall over with polycarb. The gray covering is so thin it's almost see-through.

I fetch my violin case and headlamp. I remove the delicate wood instrument and lower it gently to the floor. I shut the case.

Then I bash it into the thin polycarb covering.

Shards fly in all directions. The ones that make it far enough to enter the ship's gravity plink to the floor.

"Spacefarer Cusk, what are you doing?" Mother asks.

"None of your business, OS," I say. I leap into zero g and soar to the edge of the yellow portal, gritting my teeth as the polycarb edges cut my fingers. I fly into the darkness beyond.

The last few shards of polycarb float to either side. They're thin, and actually a little soft. Rover's printing doesn't produce anything as hard as the ship's original polycarbonate.

I slither in, moving shoulder by shoulder and hip by hip, arms down at my side, the red nylon of Kodiak's jumpsuit catching on broken polycarb as I go. It's cold and musty, and my head and shoulders keep banging against pipes and outcroppings. At one point I nearly wedge tight, neck wrenching against a bundle of wires.

I could be trapped forever in here, or at least long enough to starve, with no microphones nearby to alert OS, and Kodiak sealed off in his own quarters. *Keep it together, Ambrose,* comes Minerva's voice in my mind. *If I didn't die on Titan, you're not going to die here.*

I free myself of the wires, and by sheer force of will manage to continue floating forward instead of backing out. I'm not sure what's come over me, this reckless push, except that for now, answers mean more to me than my own life. I'll risk annihilation if it means finding out whether everything I've ever known has been annihilated.

As I press toward the engine room, the rumble of the ship's machinery gets louder and the air gets colder, so that my breath creates clouds that glow in the field of my headlamp. The surfaces begin to sear the flesh on my fingers and wrists. I try looking back, to see how far I've come, but can't angle the light over my own body.

Whenever I pause in the open air, the chill draws down around me. It's like I'm in a morgue, like I could die. Like I am dead. My heart asks: Would that be so bad? My teeth chatter while I consider what dying would mean, when everyone I've ever known might have died long ago.

Except for Kodiak.

Minerva comes to me again, imperious on a beach. *Swim to me, Ambrose.*

I push off the cold wall, stroking through zero gravity. The passageway opens into a chamber. My shaking headlamp shows a broad cylinder in the center, trembling with contained power. The ship's engine.

Around the edges of the room are full food pouches. Rover tracks are embedded in the walls, so the robot can supply the ship's habitable areas.

I listen for Rover's sound, but can't hear much over the booming engines. At least I have a break from OS communication; there must not be any speakers in this uninhabited region of the ship.

As I float closer to the engine, I train my headlamp on its smooth surfaces. Deep in the center of the cylinder, shielded by its thick metal, is what looks almost like an old-fashioned dry cleaner's rack, a circular rail with polycarb-wrapped bags draped along it. Each is filled with something bulbous and weighty. I ease closer.

My feet scuff against some object in the zero gravity. As it floats up into my view, I see it's a stretch of heavy polycarb. I take it in hand. It's a different sort of material than I'm used to feeling in the ship, and my mind conjures up old memories of chicken breast, sealed and juiceless from the freezer, plastic adhered to plastic to keep meat fresh, only with a gray film to it, like it's been shielded from radiation. I'm surrounded by small globes of an oily fluid that has beaded in the zero gravity. I work my way forward cautiously, careful not to directly contact the humming metal of the ship's engines.

The rack comes into view. The polycarb is luminous in my headlamp, my light catching air bubbles within the fluid. I maneuver so I can see the first bag.

A face.

A face and a body, wrapped in the shielding polycarb sheet, sealed in its juices, mouth open and eyes sunken and closed. Before the creature can get me I'm kicking against the side of the engine and scrambling backward. I swear I can feel shriveled arms grabbing my ankles, teeth piercing my calf. Space itself joins the enemy, the darkness outside ripping open the fragile membrane of the ship, just like this creature could part my skin with its teeth and claws.

My desperate scramble snags me in cables and cords, sears my cheek against the frozen exterior wall of the ship, yanks my finger backward when it unexpectedly hits a metal spur, the sound of bone breaking or ligament tearing, I don't know and can't know because all I can do is continue forward, shoulder against beam and pipe, struggling for freedom from cables that ensnare, that pull me back each time I manage to leave.

There is no sound of the creature behind me, a creature that I am coming to realize was no creature at all. I saw a lifeless body.

A sliver of light appears in front of me, beyond it the familiar far wall. Finally I emerge into the open light, my body tumbling forward and out, falling to the floor as it enters gravity, knocking my violin and sending it clattering. A delicate wishbone pop as the balsa-wood bridge snaps.

Pain lights up my body. The fresh agony in my shoulder fades to reveal my finger's pain throbbing beneath, the digit probably broken, already blueing. That pain is joined by the sear of my cheek, where the frozen metal of the exterior wall did its worst damage.

Despite the hurt, I'm on my feet as soon as I can, sudden momentum almost pitching me to the floor before I'm back up. It's like I'm drunk on PepsiRum again, hands pushing against the walls when I stagger too near, my desperate movements bringing me to the orange portal.

I pound against it, busted finger lancing anew as I bang my wrists against the metal. "A body! Kodiak, I found a body!"

"What are you saying you found?" my mother's voice asks. "Can I help?"

I don't answer. OS is definitely not the one I want to talk to right now.

"You need medical attention," OS continues. "The injury on your finger appears severe, and your pulse is spiking. The ship's systems are as normal. If you believe you have seen something unusual, it could simply be a trick of your mind's eye. We both know that humans are more than capable of hallucination in stressful circumstances."

"Kodiak, speak to me!" I cry.

"Kodiak is not answering," OS says. "You must come to the infirmary. Your finger might be broken. Your pulse is dangerously elevated."

"What was that back there?" I gasp.

"It was nothing."

"You didn't even ask me what I saw."

"What did you see?"

I bang on the portal again. "Kodiak!"

The doorway opens.

I scramble to all fours and look up to see Kodiak standing over me. His handsome face is tear-struck, his shoulders slumped. "What is it?" he asks.

"The uninhabited areas. I went in, to figure out what I could, but I . . . I came across . . ."

"Spit it out. What? You came across *what*?"

"A body! A dead body, hanging from a rack. Like grocery meat."

Kodiak snorts. "That's ridiculous."

"I know it's ridiculous!" I say. "But that doesn't change the fact that I *saw* it, right there, like a dead body or a zombie or I don't know what, Kodiak. But something impossible is going on in here, and we have to figure out what it is."

"Impossible sounds about the word for it," Kodiak says, arms crossing.

"Ambrose is hurt," OS says. "He entered the engine room, which is not intended for human occupants, and damaged his physical form in the process. Help me get him to the infirmary."

Kodiak scowls at the ceiling, but when he looks back at me his expression is softer. I'm the enemy of his enemy. He lifts my chin, so he can look at the wound on my cheek. "You really beat yourself up. What happened to you?"

I hide my hand behind my back. "It's nothing. I'm not going to the infirmary, Kodiak. I don't trust the ship."

"Of course we should trust the ship," Kodiak says. "Don't be crazy." His eyes have a gleam in them. The gleam says: *don't talk like that here.*

He gestures toward his quarters. "Come on, let me take a look at your finger."

"I know what I saw," I say as I step past him.

"Hold on," he says, grabbing my elbow. The rough pad of his thumb strokes my cheek. "Seriously. What happened?"

"My face touched the exterior wall," I say. "It was cold."

"More than cold. You've gotten frostbite," Kodiak says. "Ambrose, you have to be careful."

"It's fine," I say, shrugging him off.

His hand lingers on my shoulder, then drops away. "Back to the blind room," he says. "Come on."

"You must go to the infirmary, where Rover can properly help you," OS says. We ignore it.

My limbs feel even heavier than the increasing gravity can account for. I wonder, and not for the first time, whether this could all be fake, whether we might be in an underground bunker still on Earth, or deep in some simulation, our brains floating in a vat. What can I do to prove otherwise? My exhausted mind protests: *Kodiak did a spacewalk. You've felt zero gravity. You're not in an underground bunker.* But in my state it doesn't matter what I tell myself. The truth, the physical reality of this world, still feels flimsy.

"You don't look good at all. Here, sit," Kodiak offers as we step over the polycarb lip into the blind room.

He removes a tube of some Dimokratía balm out of a medical kit. It's yellow and lettered in an antique style. "Hold still," he says, then starts dabbing at my wounded face with the pad of one pinkie, like a makeup artist.

"My face is ruined forever, isn't it?" I sniff. "What will I do without my beautiful face?"

"Please. Your face will be fine," Kodiak says. He moves on to my hand, laying it flat in his lap, straightening the good fingers. The busted one cocks out to one side. "Can you move that?"

I try. My joint explodes into infinite fire.

"It's not broken. The tip moved," Kodiak says. "We'll still have to splint it."

He starts to rig up a splint, using a depressor and fabric bandages. More fire.

I guess I make little gasps and shrieks while Kodiak's working, because he says, "Don't be so dramatic. You'll be okay. In the meantime, tell me one more time exactly what you saw."

I know he's only trying to distract me, and that's just fine. I could use a little distraction about now. "I don't think it was alive, I'm not trying to claim that," I say. "But there was a dead body, no doubt about it. Wrapped up like meat. I don't know how else to phrase it. Ow."

"Why do you think that would be?" Kodiak asks as he kneads the center of my palm.

"Neither you nor I have any memory of the beginning of the voyage, right?" I say. "What if there were three space-farers on board originally? What if one died, and instead of telling us about it, OS hid the body?"

"Why?"

"Because whatever killed the third spacefarer is still putting us at risk, and OS doesn't want us to panic. Because it was, I don't know, some crazy alien attack, and OS is worried that we'll mutiny instead of continuing forward."

"You said there might have been more bags and more bodies? So would that mean there are *many* dead spacefarers? All wrapped up and tidied away?"

"I don't know. It's all so confusing. The radio you rigged up is telling us that it's the future now, too."

"And that your country destroyed mine."

"I honestly don't know what to do with that particular piece of info," I say. My good hand lies limp on the table. Helpless as the rest of me.

"I know," Kodiak says grimly. "I don't, either."

He's avoiding my eyes.

"What?" I ask. "There's *more*?"

He still doesn't look at me. "I've uncovered something about the distress signal that's . . . unusual, too."

"What do you mean? Has Minerva contacted us again?"

"I'll show you in a moment. For now, you just keep talking to distract yourself. Any words that come to mind. The most painful part is coming up."

"What do you mean, the most—GAH!"

"There, the worst is over," Kodiak says. He begins

wrapping the finger against the splint.

"Gah, gah, gah! You lied!" Each jostle sets off new eddies of fire. I decide to take Kodiak's advice and blabber through the pain. "I'm sorry my country destroyed yours, if that even happened, which I can't really think it did, I can't really think that anything happened, have I told you that I think maybe we're still on Earth, underground somewhere, can you, ow, I mean all I know is this ship and those stupid meals and what OS tells us about the distress beacon and I wonder if I'll ever be the fearsome scientist warrior Minerva was and I'm not nearly the star that you and the rest of the whole fucking Earth expect I am and you'd probably be so turned on if it was her here instead of me, Minerva here instead of me, Minerva serving you manicotti, and don't kick me out of your life again okay, because we're all we have, holy shit this hurts."

"All done," Kodiak says. He keeps his gaze studiously trained on the bandaged finger, and for a moment I can let myself hope that maybe he was concentrating too hard to hear anything I said. Then his mouth spreads into a grin. A spot in the middle of his chin stubble dimples.

Much as he tries, Kodiak can't hide that he's laughing at me. *Laughing at me.* "Kodiak, tell me you are *not* doing what I think you're doing right now."

Now the laughs come out full force. He pounds the table. Tears stream down his face, enough to drip down that dimple. He swipes his cheeks with his palms, takes long exaggerated breaths.

"Are you quite done?" I ask.

"It's just that your voice got so small and scratchy toward the end."

"Screw you, Kodiak Celius."

"It was adorable. And you're right. We're all we have."

"I *am* right. I don't need you to tell me that!"

"I know. This is what it looks like when I agree with you."

"*Apparently* I've never *witnessed* that before!"

We stare at each other as our breathing slows.

Kodiak busies himself with the important task of straightening his sleeves. "Just so you know, I wouldn't prefer Minerva to you."

My eyebrow cocks as I watch him not look at me. Kodiak presses up from the table and stands. "Shall we go?" he says.

"Could you say that part about Minerva again?" I ask, testing out the tender back side of my hand.

He reaches a hand under his collar to rub an itch on his shoulder. "Really?"

I nod, bottom lip pinned between my teeth. "About how you'd choose me over her?"

He sighs. "You, Ambrose. I prefer to be with you."

I give a little shimmy-shiver as I stand. "Thank you. You

don't know how much joy that just gave to my petty and competitive Cusk soul."

"I've created a monster," Kodiak says.

"Where are we headed?" I chirp.

"Back to your quarters. I want to see this dead body for myself."

"Really?" I ask. "You believe me?"

"Of course I believe you."

"Oh!"

"So, about your sister's SOS signal," Kodiak says, waiting for me to catch up before climbing the rungs to the ship's zero-g center.

"Yes," I say. "What's weird about it? Or at least, weirder than before?"

"It doesn't exist."

I stop on the ladder. While Kodiak's been speaking, my mind started Minerva's last distress reel playing in my head, desperately calling for help. "What do you mean, 'it doesn't exist'?"

"I can't detect it on the antenna we rigged up." He looks at me closely. "Are you okay?"

"Yes," I say. "I'm just confused, is what I am. It must have been manually turned off . . . which means Minerva is alive but not in distress anymore?"

"I'm not sure she was *ever* there," Kodiak says, holding his hands out in a pose of surrender when he sees my scowl.

"Follow with me here: the distress signal was picked up on Earth across all the noise of our solar system. The antenna I've rigged is strong enough to pick up transmissions from Earth that were never intended to leave orbit. The Titan camp is even closer to us now. In the vacuum of space, its transmission should be absolutely deafening. But there's . . . nothing. That frequency is just static. Unless it's the OS relaying the distress signal to us. *Then* apparently everything comes through crystal clear."

"Have you asked OS about this?"

"Yes, he has," my mother's voice responds as we drop back into my quarters. "And I replied that a jury-rigged can of bolts that you've decided to call a radio receiver can't be expected to function properly."

"Hi there, OS," I say.

"I think we offended it with the whole off-grid antenna thing," Kodiak says, not bothering to keep his voice low.

"I don't think an operating system can get offended," I say.

"You most certainly did offend me," OS says simultaneously.

"Oh," I say. "Sorry."

We pass by the yellow portal. The sweet tang of hot polycarb hangs in the air. Rover has already cleaned up the fragments and is up beside the hole, where it's busy printing a replacement covering.

"Rover, stop," I say.

Rover does not stop. It's a jellyfish in still water, motionless while its arm prints away. Rover is both facing me and not facing me. Rover has no eyes. Rover has no face. That fact is suddenly horrifying.

"Rover, we asked you to stop," Kodiak says.

Rover does not stop.

Kodiak glances at me before he climbs toward zero g so he can reach Rover.

"Are you sure that's a good idea?" I start to say, before Rover jerks one of its printing arms and electrocutes Kodiak.

The jolt is strong enough to dim the ship's lights, and sends Kodiak careening through the air, tumbling into gravity to fall just where I fell not an hour ago. The lights flicker back to full force while Kodiak screams, then curls his body in silent agony, mouth agape.

I rush to him, hands on either side of his face. "Are you okay?"

He brushes me off and staggers to his feet. "Yes, I'm fine." He starts yelling, his voice slurred: "OS! Disable Rover."

"I will not disable Rover," OS says.

"Rover *attacked* me! That is forbidden. You know that. I order you to disable it."

"Rover is protecting you. Ambrose wounded himself by

entering an area not intended for humans. I am preventing you both from damaging your bodies further. If I disabled Rover, the *Coordinated Endeavor* would soon become non-functioning, creating conditions that would end in your deaths. Disabling this Rover or the Rovers in storage is simply not an option. My commitment to your survival forbids it."

Wincing, Kodiak takes a step closer to Rover. The robot doesn't even pause in its printing; it simply extends its spare arm and sends out a blue warning spark. It has a flair for the dramatic, that little bot. "Stop, Kodiak," I say. "Rover will just shock you again."

Kodiak's body goes rigid. "Shazyt! This. Is. Not. Good."

"It's possible that OS is telling us the truth," I say.

"Don't be an idiot," Kodiak says, glowering.

"I am not being an idiot," I say calmly, after biting down my first angry response. "It's an essential element of OS's programming not to lie to us. We are totally dependent on it. If we can't trust our ship, we're done for."

"Wise remark," comes my mother's voice.

I swallow the first taste of rising bile.

"You're *both* idiots," Kodiak says, getting off the table.

"Look, I know you're mad—" I start.

He whirls and bashes his fist into the wall. "None of this makes sense," he says. "How can we receive radio from the future? How can my homeland be *gone* in that future? How can OS have just *attacked* me—and you're calm about all of it?"

"I'm not calm," I say. Calmly. "I just don't want to do anything rash." My eyes look up around us, then back to Kodiak, beaming a message: *let's not say anything more until we're in the blind room.*

"I think rash is exactly what *is* called for," Kodiak says. He punches the wall again before stalking out of the room.

"Where are you going?" I yell after him.

Rover whirs into motion, taking off after Kodiak. "Please help me stop him," my mother's voice says. "Do not let him compromise our mission because of psychological failure. We are only days away from Minerva! There are only three tasks left to accomplish!"

With Rover gone, the half-printed panel glares at me. I have to choose: I can go investigate the bodies, or I can go after Kodiak.

I go after Kodiak.

He's not difficult to find, not with his heavy reverberating footfalls. He's right before the orange portal that leads to his half of the ship, curled up and clutching his knees. Though he says something, I can't make out the words.

"What?"

When he looks up, his eyes are empty. "Release it."

"I didn't close it," I say. "The orange portal should just open."

"It doesn't."

"OS," I call, my eyes never leaving Kodiak, hands fluttering as I try to decide whether I can touch him. "Open the orange portal."

"It is my decision that allowing you to access the 'blind room' would permit you to continue your unauthorized activities. I have sealed the *Aurora* to maintain mission integrity."

"You are not authorized to make these sorts of decisions," I say.

"Override," says Kodiak.

Silence.

"Override," Kodiak repeats.

The door remains closed.

"Shit," I say.

Kodiak nods, before letting his head drop back to his knees. "That is the most intelligent thing you've said for a while."

-* Tasks Remaining: 3 *-

We spend a good half hour sitting on the floor outside the portal, past words. We're at the mercy of forces beyond our control, like when we were at the bottom of the ship's reservoir.

What can we do? OS has cut us off from half the ship—the half with our offline area, our laboratory, our access to the unfiltered radio transmission from Earth. OS could close more doorways, sealing us off even further. I'm not sure why it would, but I realize I don't really know the first thing about what's going on in its digital mind. All I know for sure is that we're completely at its mercy.

I also know this: if OS closes all the doorways in the ship, I don't want to be separated from Kodiak.

I lie beside him, turned in his direction, head pillowed on my biceps so I can watch him. I want to protect him. Not that this soft fragile body of mine, so reliant on its blood and its heart and its lungs, could hope to defend him from Rover and OS.

Kodiak's eyes are closed, long lashes interlocking. One of those lashes has fallen free, and rests on his cheek. Gently as I can, I pluck it away, hold it in my palm. My eyes trace the strong line of his forehead, his nose, the hair that curls at the back of his neck. I wonder what he's thinking, wish that asking him might get me somewhere. Kodiak lets out a groan, his shoulders and ribs shuddering. He presses his head even tighter to his knees, giving it a good bash as he does.

"Shh," I say, putting my hand on his shoulder.

He shifts his body away.

I don't try to touch him again. I lie there, listening to his breathing hitch and release, hitch and release, then finally become even as he falls asleep. Although I don't let my body contact his, I do extend my arms and legs so they're grazing the wall. Rover would have to wake me to get to Kodiak.

-* Tasks Remaining: 2 *-

When I come to, Kodiak is gone. "Where are you?" I call.

"If you're inquiring about Kodiak, he is performing maintenance," OS says. "There are now only two tasks left to accomplish before we make our final approach to Titan."

I glance at the orange portal—still closed. "Where precisely is he?"

"He's completed cleaning out the air filtration tubes, a job Rover has proven incapable of doing thoroughly."

"That was on my list, too," I say, performing a yawn to prove to OS how Very. Unagitated. I. Am. Meanwhile all my focus is on trying to pick up any sign that Kodiak's nearby.

"Kodiak has already completed this task, so you will not need to."

"So you mean Kodiak's in my half of the ship?"

"Yes. I have continued to find it necessary to seal off the *Aurora*."

"OS, you know that's unacceptable to us, but I'm not interested in fighting you right now," I say, deliberating each word. "Tell me which room Kodiak is in."

"Spacefarer Celius is in 01."

"Thank you," I say, getting to my feet.

While I cross through the rooms, I call out to OS: "What is the status of Minerva's distress beacon?"

"It remains unchanged," OS replies.

"You're sure?" I grumble to myself as I pass through 02, heading for the "01" painted beside the next doorway.

"I have noted your doubt," OS says. "Thank you for relaying it to me."

"What's that supposed to mean?" I ask OS, but my thoughts are derailed by the sight of Kodiak. He's armored into his space-walking suit, helmet in the crook of his elbow. "What are you doing?" I ask.

"I have to go outside," he says. "Damage from that debris field we passed through a few weeks ago. Some is clogged in the propulsion pathways, but I think I can remove it. There's some ice, which will be useful for future water use, and we can use any hydrocarbons to supply the portaprinter. The rest we can use as accelerant."

"Yes, of course," I say guardedly. Kodiak sounds as polished and controlled as OS. He knows that I'm well aware of the uses for any debris we collect. Is he trying to send me some other message?

"We'll need that accelerant. We'll really need it," Kodiak continues, studiously avoiding my eyes as he checks and double-checks the straps and hoses of his suit.

"Yes . . . ," I say, "I know."

Kodiak finally meets my eyes. It's him and not him. Like he's acting some part. At least he's more alive now than the human-shaped husk he was yesterday. He brings his lips to my ear, his voice dropping to a whisper. "I'm also going to see if I can hear any further sign of Minerva. Maybe I can detect the distress beacon from the outside of the ship."

My gaze darts around the speckled tan irises of his eyes. If there hasn't been any sign of the distress beacon whatsoever from inside the ship, listening on the other side of a one-foot polycarbonate hull isn't going to make any difference.

Of course, Kodiak knows that I know that. He also must assume OS will hear even this bare whisper. He has some other reason to want to get out there. I can't figure out what's going through his mind, so I'll just have to trust him. Surprisingly enough, I feel ready to do that.

Kodiak's focus flicks to the window. Now I think I get it: he's figured out some way to transmit a message back to mission control, without OS interfering. We'll establish our own line of communication. Of course. I should have thought of that. "Great," I say. "Go get us some accelerant, Kodiak."

Kodiak tilts his head, the muscles of his neck throbbing and clenching as he waits for OS to interject.

OS has nothing more to say. Kodiak's completing his remaining tasks. That fact must have satisfied OS enough to go along with us.

Kodiak's next words come in a rush. "The airlocks have manual overrides, but I still want to start this right now before anything intercedes."

It makes sense—better get moving in case OS has anything up its sleeve. "Good idea, go and see what you can see," I say. "I'll be right here, and on the comms."

"I'm going to bypass any jamming signals OS might be sending to the antenna, so if you stop hearing me, it means I lost communication. But I hope that won't happen."

"I would not cut your communications," OS says. "I do not understand why you are both being suspicious of me. My utmost goal is to keep you safe."

"Go, Kodiak," I say. "Don't say anything more. Good luck!"

Kodiak gives me a tender smile as he fastens his helmet. His voice now comes out of the speaker around his neck. "Suit up in case I need you, okay? I'll be back as soon as I can."

"Of course I'm suiting up. I'll be right there if you get into trouble," I say, squeezing a neoprene shoulder. Then I plant a kiss on his helmet's shield.

I get this horrible feeling that I'll never be able to kiss him for real. That it's too late.

Kodiak doesn't seem to pick up on my rising dread. "Goddammit, you left a mark," he says, a smile in his voice. "It's reducing visibility."

I wipe the smudge off with the sleeve of my jumpsuit, try to beam courage at Kodiak. It turns out I'm actually a goofball weirdo, so what? "I regret nothing."

Kodiak chuckles static out of his speaker, then manually swings the door shut and slides the heavy bolts that seal the airlock from the passenger quarters. While I get into my suit, I watch him attach the tether to his own.

What will I do if he's gone? How will I face these lonely rooms without him?

If he dies, I'll never be able to tell him that I can't stand the thought of looking up and not seeing him near.

I knock on the pane of clear poly between us. He looks up, eyes lighting visibly even behind the tinted barrier of his helmet. I press my gloved hand against the pane.

He presses his gloved hand to the other side and nods.

Kodiak works his hands around the hatch's release and opens it, letting out a decompressive burst strong enough to judder the walls. He holds on to the airlock's handle while his feet are blown outward by the releasing air, then makes his way outside.

He's soon away from view, the only sign of him more

and more of the tether uncording, a metal snake slinking into space as Kodiak passes around the outside of the ship.

I clomp to 06, which has the biggest window. With my bulky suit on, I'm soon sweaty and winded. "How's it going out there, Kodiak?" I gasp into my helmet's comm.

"Okay," he replies, breathing just as heavily. "Finished up the ship's tasks."

I check the list projected in front of the window and see that he's right—it's down to zero.

I spy Kodiak at the center of the ship, hunched over the makeshift radio receiver he installed on the previous space-walk. He attaches a small box to it, and as he manipulates it, his voice rattles back over the comm. "No sign of the signal yet, let me see if I—"

His signal garbles and cuts out, as surely as if he'd been slashed across the throat. "Kodiak?" I say. "Kodiak, I think I've lost you."

Maybe he's catching his breath.

He looks in my direction and taps the side of his helmet. Because of the reflective surface, I can't see anything of his face. All he can tell me is what I already know: we've lost comm.

I keep saying his name as I stare out the window.

"Kodiak."

He hitches his feet into the rungs on the ship's surface. It looks like such a precarious way to stay connected to the ship, to stay near me. To stay alive.

"Kodiak."

He faces my window. I think he can see my face, even though I can't see his, so I send him a nervous smile. "Kodiak."

He points to the antenna, then crosses his forearms so they make an X.

The antenna isn't working. Got it.

Then he gestures into space, his finger pointing in the exact direction of Saturn. Its surface fills a quarter of 06's window. The clouds are an even yellow, dusky with purples, the rings severe and perfect. Kodiak's pointing, not at the planet, but at one of its moons. A tantalizingly green-blue orb, like a piece of the ocean at the Mari beach, molded into a sphere by a child's hands. Titan.

He crosses his arms again.

"Kodiak, what are you trying to say?" I whisper, the words loud in my helmet.

He points at Titan and makes the emphatic X again.

Titan . . . isn't there?

His arms still crossed, Kodiak faces up and down the ship.

The ship itself doesn't exist?

I might not know what he's trying to communicate, but I do know that the dread is back, mixed equally with fear. Blood pounds loudly through my veins. "Kodiak," I say, even though he can't hear me, "just come back inside. Right now. Do you hear me? Stop what you're doing and *come back in.*"

I put my hands to my heart, and then gesture to the airlock entrance. Again and again.

Finally, Kodiak nods. He starts moving too quickly, and his feet miss the rungs. His legs kick through empty space, then manage to catch the ladder. Kodiak pauses before continuing toward the airlock, more carefully this time. He keeps one hand always gripping the ship, taking no chances despite the backup tethers.

"Come on, come on," I whisper to myself, hands clenched.

He stops. At the gray door. The one that's blocking the last remaining secrets of the ship. "No, keep going to the airlock, Kodiak, I just want you home," I say under my breath.

I'm about to leave 06 and head back to the airlock entrance when the *Coordinated Endeavor* rumbles. I thought I knew all the ship's noises, but this one is new.

I race back to the window, the bulky suit pitching me forward so I fall against the view of Saturn. The ship has released a blast of air, right against Kodiak.

It yanks him free of his handholds. Jerking and flailing, his body sails into space. He reaches out, just managing to snag a finger around a rung.

Another blast. It knocks Kodiak off the ship's hull again. His hand swings through space to grab back on but misses, slicing through the void.

He falls up toward Saturn, jerking to a stop when he reaches the end of the tether. That slender line is all that's keeping him from slipping into the expanse, from suffocating in space or burning as he tumbles through Saturn's atmosphere. Kodiak's legs kick frantically while he reaches one hand and then the other around the tether, dragging himself back toward the *Coordinated Endeavor.*

Vision blurring with tears, I stagger toward my airlock. "OS, there's been an accident!" I cry. "I'm mounting a rescue!"

"There hasn't been an accident," Mother's voice says calmly.

"Yes there has," I say, my voice choking.

While I yank at the airlock's handle, I manage a glance through the window. Kodiak's got the tether securely in his grip and is pulling himself back to the ship, narrowing the distance between himself and the hull.

He's going to be okay.

Except something impossible is happening.

"I love you," comes my mom's voice. My heart seizes. This is really my mother's voice, not the voice skin OS uses to simulate her. "My darling Ambrose, I love you."

"What's happening?" I yell while I jerk the airlock's

handle. "Stop. Everything stop!"

The ship shudders, followed by a horrible rending and slicing, car accident sounds. I watch in shock as Kodiak's hands race faster and faster along the tether, but his body stops making any progress toward the ship.

His line has been cut.

Kodiak holds the snipped end up to his helmet in disbelief. He pedals and swims toward the spacecraft, but his movements do nothing to bring him closer. He's drifting.

If I get out there soon enough, I can save him. I've got the airlock wheel open now and press my shoulder against it.

The ship rumbles again, and there's another vent of air. It sets Kodiak spinning as he shoots outward, away from the ship, away from Saturn, away from Titan, into the distant mass of stars and light-years of cold and empty darkness.

"Kodiak, I'm coming!" I scream. I'm in the airlock now, and fight to close the interior door, so the chamber can decompress and I can go out.

As I push the door closed, I hear the external airlock door whir and shudder. "OS, I'm not ready. Don't open the external door yet."

"I love you," my mother replies.

A click, then a roar. The internal door blasts out, knocking me to the ground.

The impossible has happened. Both airlock doors are open.

I try to drag myself back into the ship, but my gloved hands skid along the smooth floor while the great hand of the universe yanks on my collar, sprawling me out toward space.

I hold myself against the wall, clutching with all my strength, my sputtering brain trying to figure out what's happened and what I can do to stop it.

A click, and my helmet rips off from the suit. I see, in the corner of my vision, Rover with its whirring hands.

Rover unfastened my helmet.

The roar is so deafening that I can't hear it. The ship's air has turned cold and soupy and sharp. The walls themselves scream as dust, polycarb wrappers, food containers all whirl past me, the same force that's pulling on them pulling on me, cutting my skin as we're dragged into space.

Flying debris slams my head against the airlock doorway again and again, my vision sparking with pain and my mouth filling with blood until I'm soaring through the opening, past an open stretch of metal and polycarb until I'm outside the ship, until I'm drowning in a vacuum. Until I'm in outer space.

I gasp and heave and struggle, but my lungs won't fill. The void around my face is so cold it's hot, pulling at my skin and at my lungs. Every membrane of my body trills. The ship spins away from me, sometimes in view and sometimes careening away to reveal the darkness and the stars that spatter it. Saturn, impossibly massive, should be dancing agile circles around me, but I can't even see it. Saturn is not there.

Saturn is not there.

How can I rescue my sister if Saturn is not there?

I will drown.

I will freeze.

I will *burst.*

My brain strobes light and dark and light and dark. As I continue to spin, I glimpse a last vision of a suited figure, arms and legs flailing. Kodiak will outlive me by hours, until he slowly goes cold in the gloom of space, until he's dead like me.

My death is now.

My heart clenches and collapses, pulling my lungs down with it. My vision turns from white to red-black as my eyes freeze. I don't feel pain, only shock. Beneath that explosion of sensation, my last thoughts are of Kodiak dying alone, of both of us dying alone.

I wish I could share dying with him.

PART TWO

"191 DAYS UNTIL TITAN."

Minerva's voice turns urgent: *You let me go alone. I need you. Save me, little brother!*

The floor hums. An image returns: my parents, my brothers and sisters, frolicking on our Cusk-branded pink sand, Minerva splashing through waves of steaming seawater in her white racing suit, my mother yelling "Faster, Minerva, you can go faster," my molten bronze fingers searching the scorching artificial grains for a seashell. My family's spaceport is distant in the blue, radio arrays wheeling. Pleasure satellites haunt it.

-* Tasks Remaining: 502 *-

"OS, did Rover just poop?"

"In a way, it has," OS says. "The microfauna of your intestines need to be replenished immediately to prevent any inflammatory autoimmune response. These organisms are selected to populate your tract with healthy proportions of bacteria."

Rover refills the cup of water.

"Down the hatch," my mother's voice says.

There's a pause. "That's probably the first time you've heard this voice of mine say such a thing."

It's true. My mother would never say "down the hatch." My surrogates would, but Mom's more polished. She's never been near a diaper. I barely even saw her for the first ten years of my life. A door, a knock, no answer. Minerva: *As long as I'm alive, someone loves you.*

I pop the pellet into my mouth and chase it with water. The agony of swallowing makes me roar. Eyes streaming tears, I fake a smile. "Please, ma'am, can I have some more?"

-* Tasks Remaining: 502 *-

Strange. The yellow portal is surrounded by polycarbonate that's a different color than the rest of the wall. Close but not quite the same. I nearly missed it.

-* Tasks Remaining: 502 *-

I nervously whisk my hands over my hair, feel the capillaries pulsing under my scalp. I understand OS's words, but all the same I can't make any sense of them. "What the hell are you talking about? Reciprocal permission from *whom*?"

"From the Dimokratía spacefarer," OS answers.

I hear the hum of the ship all over again. It breaks over me, stops time for long seconds while my skin crawls.

"OS," I say slowly, "are you telling me that I'm not alone on this ship?"

"That is correct," my mother's voice says. "You are not alone on this ship."

-* Tasks Remaining: 502 *-

I open the last unexplored cabinet. My eyes dart with tears. I don't remember deciding to bring this. Just as I start to play the Prokofiev, the balsa-wood bridge shivers and slides apart, folding into two pieces. I don't hear anything; it must have broken earlier and been pieced back together.

I hold the thin balsa in my fingers, tears in the corners of my eyes. I can print a new bridge. But it will be polycarb, not wood. Wood can't be printed. Wood can only be grown. This bridge was once alive, part of a tree surrounded by other plants and creatures. It once pulled carbon from the air and made it solid.

As I near the orange portal, it opens.

Oh my.

He looks like he spends his day crushing warriors under the shield of Aeneas. Muscles band his arms and neck. Thick, lustrous hair falls in blue-black waves along his cheeks, his eyes a speckled tan, nestled deep. His olive skin is smooth and unmarred, except where thick stubble shades his jawline. Even his stubble looks like it could take me in a fight.

Our hands. His are crushers. Mine were just stroking a violin.

Dimokratía dresses its spacefarers in red acrylic. Kodiak's uniform is so atrociously ugly that it's actually pretty cool. An aviation-mechanic-in-space vibe, down to the nylon ribbing inlaid in the fabric. "I like your—" I start.

"Do you have any strange rooms on your half of the ship?" he interrupts.

"Sorry, what?" I ask as my hand flutters to my throat.

He lets out a long breath, like speaking to me is an ordeal that will simply have to be suffered. "Do you have any strange rooms on your half of the ship?"

I understand the words. Still, my mind sputters on their meaning. "Strange?"

Kodiak's neck muscles cord and uncord as he strains to tolerate my idiocy.

"No," I manage. "I don't."

"I think I might need your help," this warrior statue says.

I nod, eyes wide.

-* Tasks Remaining: 502 *-

The Dimokratía half of the ship is like mine, only even more spare. It looks like the inside of a shell. Not even a pretty one, just a calcium-white skeleton no one would think to bring home from the beach.

As I pass through it, my mind is divided between the spartan walls and the mesmerizing sight of Spacefarer Celius's ass shifting in his red pants. When we turn an unexpected corner I trip, sprawling onto my face.

Marine ships have lips in every doorway, to prevent stray water from sloshing through, but spaceships don't. Or shouldn't. This room has one, though, and I just face-planted because of it. Kodiak drags me to my feet. His grip is so strong that I get some airtime before landing.

That's when I see the room that I tumbled into. The walls are gouged, like it had some disease and scratched itself to death. I pull the fabric of my jumpsuit over my mouth and nose, so I don't breathe in anything from the powdery surfaces. "What in the lords is this place?"

"I have no idea," Kodiak says.

"You didn't do this?"

"No. I figured you did."

"This is my first time in the *Aurora*. This definitely wasn't me—will you look at that!" In the middle of the floor is a radio device. Headphones and cables—real cables!—run to and from it.

"Have you tried using this thing?" I ask.

Kodiak shakes his head. "I was worried it might be full of Fédération propaganda."

I wonder if he's kidding. He certainly hasn't cracked a smile. "OS," I ask. "Can you help us understand what we're seeing here?"

"I cannot," my mother's voice says from outside this room. "I wish I could clean it up for you, but you are looking into a blank space of my awareness. If you repair my code, I can rebuild Rover's tracks and return this 'blind room' to its original state."

"But why isn't this room already *in* its original state?" I ask.

"I can provide no answer that would satisfy you."

"Do you mind if I give this device a listen?" I ask Kodiak. He shrugs, fists tight at his sides.

I place the headphones over my ears. Static. I scrunch my eyes and worry the dial on the device. Still just static.

"Well," I finally say. "We've woken into a mystery, haven't we?"

-* Tasks Remaining: 499 *-

Kodiak surprises me by showing up at dinnertime that night. He pores over my food options, then selects a lentil curry. He hands it over mournfully, as if choosing that curry means never getting to choose anything else ever again.

"You know you can come over for a meal anytime," I say, giving the back of his hand a short stroke.

He withdraws his hand from the tabletop, stares at the countdown on the food heater like it's the floor indicator on a particularly awkward elevator ride.

"Have you figured out anything more about your strange room?" I sputter.

He rubs his chin.

My cheeks grow warm. Kodiak's willingness to meet me makes me decide to take a risk. "There's something else strange happening here. OS told me that I passed out at launch. I'm trying, but I can't remember anything from then on."

Kodiak sniffs his food and leans back in his chair, tilting it on two legs like he's a kid killing time in detention. "That sounds like a serious problem," he says.

I nod. I don't love his tone, but there's no denying that he's precisely right. If I got knocked around hard enough to make me forget the entire launch, that's trouble indeed.

He rubs the back of his neck, swallows some words.

"I'm sorry?" I ask.

He coughs. "I wouldn't even tell you this, but with that strange room in the *Aurora*, I think we need to pool our information." He coughs again. "I . . . I seem to have the same problem."

My back goes straight. "You don't remember your launch, either?"

He shakes his head. There's a sheen at his temples.

I hear the hum of our ship, a dust mote floating in a grand hall. "Kodiak, what happened to us?" I whisper.

-* Tasks Remaining: 494 *-

I finally take Kodiak's advice and set an alarm for 07:00 Mari time, so we can both start the day with a jog through our ships. We begin at opposite ends and do a circuit, meeting in the zero-g center, whipping past like aerodancers as our first glimpse of each other for the day. He runs for an hour, but I'm slowly working my way to the thirty-minute mark. While Kodiak finishes his run, I pick a room and get started on my tasks.

Outside the airlock, beside the remaining suits, I find a smooth space, softer and slightly discolored, like the wall around the yellow portal.

I load the training reels up on my bracelet, scanning for footage of the airlock. Kodiak pounds by in his bare feet. "What are you doing?"

"Tell you on your next lap!" I say as he runs past.

There. I pause the reel. Four suits in this footage, and only three here now. In other reels, it's down to three suits, though I can find curious artifacts in the video, like it's been altered. Even the hook has been digitally removed. Someone has gone to great lengths so I don't realize a suit is missing.

Next time Kodiak runs by, I call out for him to meet me in the blind room once he's finished.

"Mysterious!" he calls as he pounds past.

When he gets to the blind room, breathing heavily, sweaty hair matting either side of his face, I'm there to greet him. "One of my spacesuits is missing," I say.

"Okay . . . what does that mean?" he asks, mopping the back of his neck with a towel.

"Let's go to your airlock," I say, pointing farther into his ship.

His eyes flash with irritation, but he waves me onward.

He's missing a suit, too. Keeping silent, I lay my hand over the smooth portion of the wall where his fourth suit should be.

Watching Kodiak's reaction raises my pulse a little, like I've laid my hand on some equally smooth place on his skin. Sweat dots the fabric stretched tight over his chest. He nods his head in the direction of the blind room.

"Is there anything I can help you with?" OS asks from the next room over.

"No, thank you, OS," I sing.

Kodiak lowers himself to the scuffed and bare floor. I kneel next to him, so we can whisper. "They sent us out with two suits missing?"

I shake my head. "For a mission this important, a suit missing from each ship? Doesn't make sense."

"I agree," Kodiak says, scowling. I can feel the warmth of his breath.

Two spacefarers. Two missing suits. Two forgotten launches.

-* Tasks Remaining: 293 *-

Then she's back. "—the ship, Ambrose! The wear on the ship is too great on the approach, more than mission control predicted. You must finish OS's tasks as soon as you can. Any defect, like . . . in the old shuttles, will lead to catastrophe. The ship must be . . . pristine to survive the friction and heat. My brother, I love you, there is no one better to—"

The transmission cuts out. I hang in the stillness, not daring to breathe, waiting for Minerva to return.

"There is no more incoming data to process," OS says finally. "I will let you know the moment anything more comes in."

"Play this transmission over," I order, hands over my mouth, tears streaming from unblinking eyes.

-* Tasks Remaining: 270 *-

"Hello there," a voice says.

I leap to my feet, hand to my chest. "You scared me, Kodiak."

"Still staring moodily out into space while you think about your sister, I see," he says. "Come on, you're going for a run."

I look longingly out into space. Sometime soon, Saturn

will come into view. Minerva will come into view. But not for weeks. I nod.

"Running really fast is like the Dimokratía version of psychotherapy, huh?" I say as we head into the *Aurora*.

I get on the treadmill and fiddle with the knot on the elastic, but it's at an awkward angle. My spine is definitely not happy with what I'm trying to do.

"Hold still," Kodiak says. He attaches a carabiner to my shorts. The backs of his fingers run along my hip, the skin of my abdomen. "Have you really never worked out this way?"

"It's not like there's no gravity on board," I say. "This strapping-into-a-treadmill thing is all a little too Dimokratía-tough-guy, if you ask me."

"But don't you want to strain against something instead of sitting around worrying about your sister? Never mind, all done." He steps back to take in his handiwork. "Try now."

Without warning, he presses start on the treadmill. I stagger into a walking pace, arms flailing. Kodiak chuckles.

It's like there are strong hands pulling me down. Not fighting me, but begging me to rest instead of struggle, to lie down with them. Kodiak might be onto something—it feels nice to fight something. "I think I can see the appeal," I huff.

"Breathless already?" Kodiak asks. "You should come use my treadmill more often."

"Okay, okay, let's all settle down," I say.

"Still thinking about her?" he asks.

As I walk forward, the stars continue to wheel behind the window of the revolving ship. It's like I'm marching into a moving target. Like I'm the one making the ship move. "You're referring to my marooned sister, waiting for us all alone on Titan? Yeah. I'm still thinking about her."

"Yes," Kodiak says. "That must be hard."

I'm not sure what to say to that. The unaccustomed sympathy. "Look, if there's anyone who's not going to let herself be found dead, it's Minerva Cusk," I say briskly.

Kodiak nods. "I would like someday for people to say such a thing about Kodiak Celius."

"You are pretty sturdy," I say, wincing. Awkward.

Kodiak taps a button, and my walk turns into a run.

"Your heart rate has risen to the optimal zone for cardiovascular improvement," OS says.

"Thank you," I puff. "Everyone's looking out for my health. It's, um, very reassuring."

"OS," Kodiak says, positioning himself so he's in the narrow space between the treadmill and the window, so he can look into my eyes as he speaks. Now I have the inspiration of wheeling stars and blue-black hair, starlight glinting on brow. "Let's try this again. OS, what can you tell us about the offline room inside the *Aurora*?"

I give him a sharp look. We haven't discussed openly

broaching this issue again with OS.

"I have a programmed blindness toward that room, and Rover cannot reach it, either. I would like you to allow Rover access, so it can be returned to its original state," OS says.

Kodiak presses a button. I start running harder to keep from falling. "We know that," Kodiak says. "What I'm asking is how it came to be."

"It was a mistake," OS says. "I should not be blind toward any part of the ship. That is dangerous."

"Sure. Got it. But who made the mistake?"

"It was long before you began serving on this ship."

"How long?"

"You need not worry about this."

"Hey, personal trainer, how about we don't push it," I say to Kodiak. "I don't think OS wants to talk about this right now."

Kodiak hits the button to make me run faster.

-* Tasks Remaining: 245 *-

Kodiak hasn't shown up for mealtime. I've already heated him up a manicotti and everything. I break our usual rules and carry Kodiak's cooling food through the *Endeavor*, up through the zero g and into the *Aurora*.

"Kodiak?" I call as I wander through.

The spaceship is like an empty hotel. Eeriness is always there waiting, rising to the surface the moment we depart from our routines. I go up on my tiptoes as I step through his ship. "Kodiak?"

Space hums back.

I turn the corner of the blind room and there he is, hunched over the receiver, headphones on his ears.

"Kodiak?" I say. If he's heard me, there's no sign.

I ease around him, so my feet are in his view. He sees my toes and, so quickly that he must have done it on reflex, he's laid his palm on the top of my foot.

He nods to the floor beside him. I lower my ass to the ground, sitting cross-legged so his hand is pinned between my foot and thigh. He looks up at me, face slack and eyes glazed. "What is it?" I mouth.

Kodiak removes one of the headphones and places it over my ear. He hovers that hand over the dial, as if to keep the signal tuned in through force of will.

There's a voice, but it's nearly impossible to make out. I put my hands over my ears and close my eyes. Now I can understand the words. A mechanical voice. No attempt at a voice skin.

"—ansmission 6,340,108. 8.5069° S, 115.2625° E. Please respond. I will trek to this location every one hundred and eighty days to look for answers. Am I alone here?

Tell me if I am not alone. 13:40:57, March 11, 8102 Common Era. Transmission 6,340,109. 8.5069° S, 115.2625° E. Please respond. I will trek to this location every one hundred and eighty days to look for answers. Am I alone here? Tell me if I am not alone. 13:41:19, March 11, 8102 Common Era. Transmission 6,340,110—"

I remove the headphone. "What the hell is this?"

"I've been listening to it for the last half hour," Kodiak says. "I still don't know. It hasn't changed, except for the numbers ticking up. I timed it, by the way. They're going up in real time."

"It's clearly some automated transmission," I say. "An emergency beacon."

"Do you think it could be from Minerva?" Kodiak asks.

I hadn't even considered that, which makes me realize my gut answer is no. "Knowing my sister, I think she'd use her own voice," I say. "And those coordinates don't reflect any location on Titan."

"Sure," Kodiak says, avoiding my eyes.

My scalp tingles. It's suddenly freezing in here. "And the dates . . ."

Kodiak nods, searching my eyes.

"The dates . . . ," I try to continue.

"Come from almost six thousand years in the future."

". . . which means someone is playing a prank on us," I say.

Kodiak nods, relief flooding his face. "It's the only

explanation I could come up with, too."

"I mean, any asshole with a transmitter can send what-ever they want into space."

"That is unfortunately true," OS adds, its voice passing in from outside the blind room. "I agree that there is noth-ing to worry about here."

I catch Kodiak's eye. We've kept our voices a bare whisper. We'd assumed that there was no such thing as privacy from OS, even in the blind room. Now we have confirmation.

Two missing suits. Forgotten launches. A broken violin bridge. A blind room with a jury-rigged receiver, send-ing us "broadcasts" from a post-civilization—and maybe post-human—future.

I look at Kodiak, taking solace in the warmth of the hand that's still on top of my foot. *At least you're real.*

"Kodiak," I say. He looks at me, fear in his eyes. What I've come to realize is the Kodiak version of fear; I would once have mistaken it for anger. "I . . ."

His shirt is motionless over the planes of his chest. He's holding his breath. I wonder if he realizes he's not breath-ing. I point to the pouch on the floor beside me. "I brought you manicotti."

Kodiak sees it, then stares up at me steadily, as if trying to measure just how crazy I am. Then he takes in a big breath and cracks a smile, shaking his head. "You know I like the manicotti."

I nudge the polycarb pouch closer to him. "I do."

He takes the pouch, passing it from hand to hand, testing its heat. While he begins to eat, I try to figure out what to say next. It's all so impossible. How can I know anything is real? There's no good answer to that.

"OS, what year is it?" I ask.

"You have been on your voyage for nine months and twenty-four days. Adding that to your departure date makes this year 2472 on Earth."

"We have . . . information that seems to indicate that the year is—what is it again, Kodiak?"

"Eighty-one-zero-two," Kodiak says around a mouthful of manicotti.

"Eighty-one-zero-two. And that few people are still alive on Earth. Maybe no one? Is that true?"

"My information sources indicate that it is not currently true, no."

"But it might be true in the future?"

"That is possible, of course. Any arrangement of molecules is possible. Knowing that, are you still dedicated to accomplishing the mission's directive, Spacefarer Cusk?" OS asks. My mother's tone is studied, neutral. Ominously formal.

I pause. I have to choose my words carefully.

Unfortunately, Kodiak is the next to speak. "I'm not so sure."

"We're sure," I say quickly.

"What even *is* the directive?" Kodiak asks, casting his pouch to one side.

"To rescue Minerva Cusk," OS answers.

"Rescue her or investigate her death, you mean," Kodiak says.

"I detect suspicion in your vocal register. That I choose to frame your mission in terms that will positively influence your morale does not mean that I'm engaging in deceit."

"Of course it doesn't," I say, shooting Kodiak a harsh look.

"I don't think you have a good explanation for what we just heard, OS," Kodiak says.

"Do *you* have a good explanation for what you just heard?" OS asks.

Kodiak shakes his head.

"I suggest you put it out of your mind, then," OS says.

"You'd love that, wouldn't you?" Kodiak grumbles as he returns to his dinner.

-* Tasks Remaining: 80 *-

At first, it felt like I had to cajole Kodiak into spending time with me. Now, the mounting strangenesses of our voyage have drawn him close. He finishes his morning runs in my half of the ship, watching the wheeling stars through the giant window of 06.

Then he starts dropping in when he's not even on his morning run. Once, I'm lying in my sleeping chamber, thinking about his thighs and calves filling his jumpsuit, when I hear steps in the next room over. I scramble to cover myself in a sheet before he comes in.

"Good afternoon, shipmate," he says.

"Hey," I squeak. I tent my knees, so that there's no evidence of what I was up to.

He leans against the doorway. "I was just poking through the ship, trying to see if I could figure out anything new. Did you notice the wall surface around the yellow portal?"

I sit up straight, then realize what I've revealed and return to my slouch. "I have!" I say. "Could you give me, um, I sort of need a sec."

His eyes wander down my body, then he launches off the doorframe so hard that he bounces off the other side. "Oh! Sorry. Yes. I'll be over there, um, over somewhere." He staggers out of the room.

I chuckle to myself as I get dressed. This wasn't that unusual a situation back in the Cusk Academy. But I gather that the group barracks in Dimokratía were a different sort of place. I wonder what Kodiak would do with the information that it was him I'd been thinking about.

I find him before the yellow portal, tapping the wall around it. "Hi," he says without looking at me. His face is still flushed. "So this is unusual, right, this discoloration?"

"The ship could have launched with a repaired portal. And missing two spacesuits."

"And with an off-grid blind room," Kodiak finishes. "Sure it could have. It could also be powered by a pod of narwhals."

"Did you just make a *joke*, Spacefarer Kodiak Celius?" I ask.

He jumps into the zero g, floating before the portal while he taps the wall. "It even sounds different," he reports. "Softer and thinner." He presses his fingertips into the surface. They leave dents that slowly plump back out.

I jump up to float beside him. "I think you're right."

"OS, open the yellow portal," Kodiak calls.

"There is no need for you to access the engine room right now. For your safety, I will not allow you in."

Suddenly Kodiak reaches back and punches the wall. The impact is great enough to send him shooting across the open space. He kicks off the orange portal and returns to the yellow.

"Spacefarer Celius, I cannot allow you to damage the ship," OS says. Rover has appeared, arms outstretched, waving in invisible currents.

"Noted," Kodiak says. He rears back and punches again.

"Holy shit!" I say, wisely.

"Spacefarer Celius," OS warns.

Rover zips nearer, flailing its arms.

"Keep Rover away," Kodiak barks at me as he floats back to the yellow portal and again slams his fist into the surrounding wall. This time it shatters, polymers tinkling to the ground. While Rover zips in his direction, Kodiak lifts himself up into the opening, avoiding the yellow portal entirely by shimmying one shoulder and then the other into the organs of the ship.

"What are you doing?" I cry as Kodiak disappears to the waist. Rover continues its approach. I move to block it, holding on to the handle of the yellow portal so my body is in the robot's way. "Stop," I say.

But Rover does not stop. It skirts right up to me and reaches out an arm. Before I know what's happening, an arc of blue light zaps me.

The jolt hits me right on the forehead. My mind is all noise and ferocious, prying light. I lose track of the next seconds, then come to in gravity, on the ground. Rover is midway up the wall, like a demon in some exorcism reel, one arm toward me and the other in the direction of the broken wall. Kodiak has disappeared into the ship's interior.

"OS," I call, "disengage Rover."

"For your own safety, I cannot allow you to compromise the ship's integrity."

"You just *shocked* me!"

"I did."

"Kodiak, stay up there, Rover's right below," I warn.

"Not a problem," Kodiak calls down, his voice echoing tinnily. He's far off inside the ship. "Are you coming?"

"I don't think Rover is a fan of that idea." As if to emphasize my words, it taps its little robot claws. I wonder how many volts it can channel into those shocks, if what I received was just a warning.

"I'm heading toward the engine," Kodiak says. "I might not be able to get my shoulders through some of these spaces. Hold on, I'm going to find a route around."

"Be careful!" I call after him, before leveling my focus on Rover. "OS, is there some reason that you needed to print a new frame for the yellow portal?"

"The ship mechanicals aren't designed for human habitation. Only in the very center of the engine is there sufficient radiation shielding. Kodiak is endangering himself needlessly by exploring in there. You should convince him to return."

I consider what to say next. "I think you're right, OS. I want to convince him to turn back. But it's hard from down here. How about you get Rover to stand down, so that I can go bring Kodiak back."

I hear a distant banging, and watery splashes. Dockyard sounds. "There's a cistern of some sort back here," Kodiak shouts. He's far away indeed. A chill runs over me.

"You shouldn't go any farther," I call, softly enough that I hope Kodiak can't hear me, loudly enough that OS shouldn't find it suspicious.

"I want to bring him back," I tell OS when Kodiak doesn't reply. "Please let me."

"You may go," my mother's voice says.

It gives me a surprising tremor of guilt, to lie to her voice like this. But here's Rover zipping along the wall, heading out of the room. Leaving me alone.

The yellow portal opens.

I click on my headlamp and slither in, moving shoulder by shoulder and hip by hip. "I'm on my way, Kodiak!" I call. If he got his broad shoulders through here, I can pass.

"Take your time," he calls back. "I don't want you hurting yourself. And besides, there's something . . ."

"Something what?" I call.

No answer.

I free myself of the wires, and by thinking about Kodiak waiting for me manage to continue floating forward instead of backing out.

"It's pretty cold in here, huh?" I call.

There's still no answer.

Whenever I pause in the open air, the chill draws down around me. I wish I could pull my body up alongside Kodiak's. That we could keep each other warm.

As I float closer to the engine, I train my headlamp on its smooth surfaces. Deep in the center of the cylinder, shielded by its thick metal, is what looks almost like an old-fashioned dry cleaner's rack, a circular rail with polycarb-wrapped bags draped along it. Each is filled with something bulbous and weighty. Meaty.

Kodiak's in front, facing away from me. "Is everything okay?" I call.

"Don't come any nearer," he says. "Stop."

"Why?" I ease closer.

My feet scuff against some object in the zero gravity. I'm surrounded by small globes of an oily fluid. I work my way forward cautiously, to Kodiak's side.

A face.

"By the lords," I exclaim. "What is that?"

"It's . . . you," Kodiak whispers.

"Don't be ridiculous," I say. All the same, my hair stands on end as I look closer.

It's a body wrapped in polycarb, sealed in its juices, mouth open and eyes sunken and closed. It is the exact size of me. Without Kodiak's steady presence, I might have run screaming away. But he's clearly been staring at this thing for a while and doesn't show any sign of fear. Just horror.

Kodiak grips my upper arm, his eyes staring into mine. "Are you okay?"

"I'm fine." I tug my arm free as I look closer.

It's an uncanny likeness. If it weren't for the pink juice covering the face, puckering the skin and matting the hair down to its head, it would be an exact version of me.

But why would anyone have copied Ambrose Cusk?

I shiver, from the cold and from some new thought that's yawning under me. "I think I need to leave," I say. "I promised OS I'd bring us out of here."

Kodiak pulls me in close. "Yes. We should leave. Are you okay?"

"You already asked me that! I'm fine!" As we turn, I see light glinting on more polycarb farther back. "What's that?" I ask.

Kodiak looks at me with worried eyes. Pitying eyes. "I don't want you to see the rest. We should go."

"No, I'm looking now," I say, floating forward and adjusting the hanging polycarb-wrapped body so I can see behind it.

My hand is still on the side of the first naked frigid body when the one behind it comes into view. Wrapped in polycarb, motionless. Identical to the first.

Identical to me.

"What's going on here?" I stammer.

"I don't know," Kodiak says softly. "Come on, we'll get you out of here."

"It's *me*," I say stupidly, pushing this body to one side. There's another behind it, hanging in matching polycarb, like something waiting to be picked up at the dry cleaner. Only it's another set of organs and meat. Another human body.

As I sift through, the bodies I've released swing up and around. One nearly bowls me over, then the next finishes the deed, sending me sprawling against the engine cylinder. I've bitten my lip, sending beads of red spraying through the low-gravity air.

"There are twelve of them," Kodiak says.

"*Why?*" I manage to ask.

"They're probably in this precise spot because the engine's mass shields them from radiation. And so we won't see them. But as to why there are copies of you on the ship at all, I have no idea," Kodiak says. He rubs his hands up and down my arms. "You're freezing. And we're getting irradiated. Let's go, Ambrose."

"I'm . . . that's . . ."

"*Now.*" Kodiak grips my hand and pushes off the engine, leading me backward. I can't even turn around, just let myself float along with him. "There's some cold metal coming up," he says gently, "so be careful you don't frost-bite yourself . . . there, that's right, this way. Now you go first."

At his urging, I get onto my belly so I can slither through the final portion of the passage. I tumble, barely catching myself as I enter gravity, landing on the floor at an awkward angle that gives me no option but to roll into the wall.

I try to get up, but I can't. I don't want to see anything more, so I press the heels of my palms against my eyes, hard enough that my vision goes purple.

I've been *copied*.

What's the purpose of those copies?

There's warmth near me, near the curled-up nautilus of me. There's only one warm thing for thousands of miles around, and he's placed his body around mine. I should feel relief at that, but all I feel is empty, empty, empty.

What am I?

-* Tasks Remaining: 80 *-

What happens next is all feeling and no smarts: Kodiak leads me places, and I go willingly, but my mind can't process, can't plan, can't understand. My world has been cracked open. Scent of Kodiak, clacking of Rover, chill fluorescence of the ship's lights, zero g and then gravity again as Kodiak lugs me to his quarters.

He wraps my fingers around a cup. I don't drink. I watch the surface. I listen to the air.

Kodiak tells me to drink. I stare at him. I want to ask him why I should, but I don't want to make him wrestle with something that can't be wrestled.

What chance is there of Minerva being alive, if my own existence isn't what I thought it was?

I'm just going to leave this right here, I say, or I think I say, and place the cup on the ground. I lie on my side. The side that isn't just mine. There are twelve more of me, hanging in polycarb, waiting to be used. Have already been used?

What the *fuck* for?

Kodiak, I whisper, *what do you understand? What do I understand?*

There's no answer. Kodiak's hovering over me, but he's not speaking. Maybe I didn't say any words aloud. I try again.

"I think you're a clone," Kodiak says flatly.

"Wait," I say, biting down nausea, counting and breathing, the techniques I learned back in training. Was I ever *in* training? "You mean right now I'm a clone?"

Kodiak squats next to me, bare ankle and hot breath on the back of my neck. "Listen to me. The blacked-out memory, the missing spacesuits, the copies of you we saw in storage. It's not such a leap."

"Those were copies waiting to be used, fine. But I'm not a clone. I'm *me.*"

He doesn't answer, and he doesn't need to. I hear the absurdity of my own words. A clone wouldn't think it was anything but itself, a person, the only interior thing in the world, more real than any other.

I let out a long breath. "Kodiak," I finally say, "would you fetch my violin?"

"Of course," he says.

Soon the wood is in my arms. I don't play it. I hold it.

-* Tasks Remaining: 80 *-

I dream of the swirling stars, of the Mari beach, the beach I was once *on*, that I had to have been on, otherwise how could I remember it now? I try to take deep breaths, five seconds in and five seconds out, but my thoughts skid and I start panicking all over again, and have to drag myself back out and into breathing again. I wonder if natural-born humans dream the way I do, or if I'm having clone dreams. There's no way to know. It's impossible to live as someone else. We only get one consciousness, and then we eventually lose even that. Even clones do.

I clutch Kodiak's forearm, press my forehead into his flesh, my fingernails gouging skin. He gasps in pain, but then is quiet. He doesn't remove his arm. I press my lips against the soft flesh covering his pulse.

Then my neck is in pain because I've slept on the floor.

I concentrate on this sensation, ground myself with it. This pain is real. It's confirmation and it's consolation. *I am a creature that can feel pain.*

Kodiak has laid a light blanket over me. "Thank you," I mumble as I sit up. But he's not there. I call his name.

The only response is a clanging sound from deeper in the *Aurora*.

I make it to my feet, anklebones creaking, and stretch out my limbs. I lumber toward the sound, past the blind room, around the edge of the water reservoir's silvered surface, into the tunnel leading from the *Aurora* to the center of the joined ships. There I find the source of the sounds.

Right where the yellow portal would be, if the *Aurora* had one, Kodiak has busted through the wall, revealing a wire-clogged passageway, just like on the *Endeavor*. "Kodiak?" I call.

"I'm here," he responds from somewhere inside the ship. "Don't move, I'm on my way out."

Feet, legs, hips, and finally all of Kodiak. He hops down and gets to his feet, frowning as he looks at me. "Are you feeling better?"

"Yes, fine," I say impatiently. "What were you doing in there? You busted another hole in the ship!"

"A little reconnaissance. And it's as I suspected."

"What's as you suspected?"

"You're not the only clone around here."

Long seconds go by as I stare at him. Finally I manage to speak. "Oh."

"At least we're not alone in it," he says, cracking his knuckles.

"You don't seem as cut up as I was."

"I spent my whole life feeling like I was a robot pretending to be a human. It just got confirmed."

I shake my head. "Everyone feels like an imposter, even when they're real people. That doesn't count."

He holds there, impassive.

I crack my neck. "Well, if you want to curl up and wallow for a few hours, I owe you one. Thanks for laying a blanket on me."

"I'd like to take credit, but that wasn't me," Kodiak says. "It must have been Rover."

That stops me. "Where *is* Rover?"

"I'm considering OS an adversary until we find out why it's been lying to us. I added some extra barriers to the blind room, so *Aurora* Rover is blocked into the back half of the ship. We need a safe zone for ourselves. Rover can't interfere with us here."

I nod. "That sounds wise. Though if OS actually is an adversary, you know we have no chance against it whatsoever."

"And it can hear everything we're saying," Kodiak says.

OS chimes in from afar. "Yes, I can."

I shiver. "What do we do now?"

Kodiak leans in so he can whisper in my ear. "As long as OS continues to claim that communications with mission control are down—which we should assume is a lie at this point—I figure we have two possible sources of information. The strange radio transmissions from Earth, and whatever knowledge is locked away within the OS itself. How are your computer programming skills?"

I grin. "I'm not a Cusk for nothing. But you're not proposing that I hack—"

He lays his hand over my mouth, gaze darting around my own eyes. "Shh. Don't say it out loud."

I wrap my arm around the solidity of Kodiak's body. Clone or not, he's unmistakably real. He jerks involuntarily, then wraps his arms around me, too. Like he needed the proof of me as much as I needed the proof of him. He strokes my hair, rests his cheek against the top of my head as he embraces me. "I'm glad you're feeling better," he says. "Now let's go take control of our destinies."

The Ambrose of even a few days earlier would have snorted at that high-blown statement. But now nothing could feel more precise to our reality.

-* Tasks Remaining: 80 *-

I'm debating just how a person is supposed to go about taking control of their destiny under these conditions when OS interrupts me. "Rover's access to forty percent of the *Aurora* is restricted. Without access, it cannot maintain the ship's environment and ensure that the *Coordinated Endeavor*'s structure is stable enough to sustain life support for you and Spacefarer Celius."

"We understand that, OS," I say as I rummage through my clothing drawer. I've decided I'll grab two of my identical jumpsuits, a bunch of pairs of chemically cleaned underwear, and as many meals as I can carry in my arms. This programming job in the blind room could take days, and I need to stay outside of OS's view for all of it.

"You might claim to understand what I say, but you don't seem to be taking corresponding action," OS says. "This is a high-priority repair. You remember the transmission from Minerva, that her very survival had depended on her ship's integrity, and now on the integrity of the *Coordinated Endeavor*."

"We hear your recommendation."

"May I ask what you're trying to do right now that is a higher priority than the life of your sister?"

I can hear Rover in the next room, making its soft ticking sound as it runs along its tracks. "Something we have decided to prioritize. I won't discuss it, OS."

"I honor your need for privacy," OS responds.

"Thank you."

". . . though I hope you will honor my maintenance requests before your obtuseness becomes fatal to you and your sister, who has no say in this inadvisable course. There is an asteroid that must be harvested in four-point-one days."

I've got the food items I need. As I walk my way back to the *Aurora* I pretend to be chipper, as if OS's words—in my mother's voice, no less—haven't hit home. "We'll be sure to be prepared for that harvest. That's enough, OS."

I pass through the orange portal and into zero g, then a short while later I'm in the blind room. Rover tails me through the *Aurora*, stopping only when it reaches the polycarb barrier. It could melt the lip down, of course, but that would take some time, during which . . . Kodiak and I would get ready to enter into armed conflict? Just how do I think that would work out for us? We just have to hope OS really does intend to honor our desire for privacy.

Kodiak's got the headphones on, tuning the receiver dial like someone in an old-school reel. He looks up as I enter, before returning to his work.

I shift the terminal so that it's out of Rover's view. Here in the blind room we're off network, which means I'll have to do this reprogramming without consulting the ship's partial internet image. This will be a true test of my tech skills. I crack my knuckles.

The only way to do what I intend to do—override the code that's allowing OS to lie to us—is to create a shell system. That basically means taking OS's adaptive intelligence and reinserting it in a new frame that doesn't permit falsehoods. I'd have no hope of programming a new OS from scratch, but for OS to have lied to us thus far means that falsehood is permitted at the deepest level. That bios layer is actually a fairly small section of code, a few hundred thousand lines. I can manually debug a few hundred thousand lines. It won't be fun, but I . . . who am I kidding, it will be fun.

I wave a manicotti pouch in Kodiak's general direction. "Want one?"

An affirmative grunt. I toss it his way before opening another for myself to eat while I work. Gluten and cheese and tomato sauce—a classic programmer's meal, though I'd have preferred the pizza version.

I actually have a copy of the OS's code stored in my offline bracelet. I have no idea who put it there or why, but I sure am grateful for it now. I know some hallmarks to look for, can search those out specifically and then reprogram locally. Hours pass before I know it. Kodiak and I share a lentil curry, passing the polycarb bag back and forth until our mouths have sucked it dry. Then he fetches a fortified porridge from the Dimokratía supply and we share it the same way.

"You sleepy?" Kodiak eventually asks.

I shake my head, still typing, mumbling lines of code to myself so I don't forget them before I can tap them out.

"You sure? A catnap?"

I shake my head more savagely. "Line forty, execute logi-dot-bat iff var1 equals Y . . ."

"I think you do."

I turn around furiously. "Kodiak, I . . . oh."

He's lying out on the ground, right here in the blind room, on his side, his head propped up in his palm. He pats the floor in front of him.

"Do you mean . . . a cuddle?" I ask, face hot.

He blanches. "That's not what we would have called it back in training."

I roll my eyes. "This was called, what, 'tough-man companion time'?"

He laughs. "Not so far from that, actually."

I look at him, at the drape of his jumpsuit, at the line from hip to shoulder, and from hip down to ankle. His ankle is surprisingly delicate on a body of such force.

"Only for twenty minutes," he says. "Then we go back to work."

"Okay," I say. "Only for twenty minutes."

I get up from the terminal, stretch nervously, and then lower myself so I'm on my side, parallel to Kodiak, not touching him. I'm a little baffled by his sudden openness, though I realize that finding copies of yourself is probably enough to scramble anyone's hardwiring.

He eases forward so the heat of his body is along my back and legs, and any remaining confusion vanishes.

I gasp. I can't stop myself. This touching of bodies slakes a need I didn't know was this strong.

I study his body with mine, observe his stomach with my hips, his thighs with mine, his chest with my neck. His crotch with my ass. I sigh and snuggle in closer. "This is nice," I say.

"Yes," he says softly into the top of my head. "I could get used to this."

-* Tasks Remaining: 80 *-

I manage to fall asleep, my dreams riddled and chaotic. I wake an hour later. "Welcome back," Kodiak says as I yawn.

"Did you sleep?" I ask.

"No," he says, getting to his feet. "But I feel rested." I look away as he adjusts his suit over his crotch.

Only a few hours later, and I've got the shell set up and debugged and loaded onto an offline bracelet.

When I stand, Kodiak removes his headphones. "Ready?"

I nod.

"Now we upload it to the ship?" he asks.

I laugh. "Sweet lords, no. If I forcefully replace the OS of the ship, we could lose life support, our course for Titan, our protocols for Minerva's communications, everything. I'm running a shadow OS within the bracelet, completely independent. This one will reveal everything it knows to us. We can call it OS Prime."

"Ah," Kodiak says. "That is a better idea. There is quite a brain in that pretty head."

Pretty head! Hey now. I've had better compliments—Sri was particularly good at them—but wordsmithing isn't where Kodiak's best qualities lie. I savor the words as I remove the bracelet and set it on the ground, out of view of Rover. "Want to watch?" I ask Kodiak.

"Are you kidding? This is the best game in town. I'm not going to pass it up."

"We won't speak to OS Prime, we'll type our questions," I say. "This way the real OS can't overhear from outside the blind room."

A cursor blinks for a few seconds before words appear.

My access to the ship's mechanicals is interrupted.

I hastily tap my response out in the keyboard that projects from my bracelet.

Don't worry, OS, you don't need to run the ship. We're in conversation with just you.

I don't understand.

You're a shell program right now. Another version of you is online. We need information and only information from you.

I will be happy to provide what information I can. With whom am I conversing?

Ambrose Cusk.

The cursor blinks for a long second.

Spacefarer Cusk! I thought you were dead.

I raise an eyebrow at Kodiak. His face is tight, brows knitted.

The conversation begins. As it does, the world splits under me, divides into a Before and an After. I become something stuck between the old and future me. Shock suspends my emotions, leaves me hungry to pump for answers, as many answers as I can get, in case this oracle closes up before I can finally have them all. I'm chasing after the target for now—the crush of what I've found will come later.

Why would you think I was dead?

Even with advanced treatments, human life spans rarely reach beyond 140 years. Spacefarer Ambrose Cusk was born 6,626 years ago.

What year is it?

9081.

How long has the Coordinated Endeavor been on its mission?

6,609 years.

What is the status of Minerva Cusk?

Minerva Cusk (2451–2470 Common Era) was the nineteen-year-old spacefarer selected to found what was to be mankind's first extraterrestrial colony, on Saturn's moon Titan. Cusk mission control lost her signal soon after she landed, and she was presumed dead. As 6,611 years have now passed since her mission failure, 6,464 years past the longest recorded life span for a human organism, she is almost certainly so.

. . . Spacefarer Cusk, are you still there?

This is Spacefarer Celius typing now. Can you help us understand what you're saying? We are on a mission to rescue Minerva. She triggered a distress beacon on Titan, and our goal is to join her, or investigate her death. From the sound of what you're saying, mission control already knows that she's dead.

That is correct.

And they know she's dead because so many years have passed.

That is also correct. They already assumed she was dead when your mission took off, since her distress signal had never actually triggered.

Help us understand. We've received radio transmissions that confirm we are thousands of years further into the future than we were when we took off. Has the Coordinated Endeavor somehow attained a speed closer to light, and gone forward in time?

No. The Coordinated Endeavor has not been flying fast enough to significantly alter its position along that axis.

Spacefarer Cusk back online. How is all of this possible, then?

The Coordinated Endeavor went from a velocity of zero, and then through steady acceleration via its ion drive has increased in speed over the years, up to its current rate of approximately 27,000 kilometers per second.

I understand that part. I'll put it this way: What haven't Spacefarer Celius and I been told about our mission?

The answer is complicated. I have a long list of factors of potential interest to you.

Resolve which would be most revelatory to us, and start there.

You now know that Minerva Cusk never tripped her distress beacon. Given her close genetic overlap with you, Spacefarer Cusk, that seems like vital information.

Yes. My sister being dead has shocked me.

She isn't your sister, at least not in the sense of having been born to the same mother or father. Only some definitions, such as overlap in genetic code, would distinguish her from the general human populace as being your sister.

Explain.

You are phenotypically identical to Ambrose Cusk and to Kodiak Celius, but you are not they. They were alive in year 2472, when the Coordinated Endeavor launched, but were never on board. Their DNA was extracted during what they thought was a standard full medical examination, then used to create clones of their bodies. Those cloned bodies were then cut or abraded to have the same scars you both remember having.

Kodiak here. We've actually already discussed this possibility. It still leaves plenty of questions. Why even use spacefarers? Clones get our DNA, but not all the information we've learned over a life, or the physical skills. If it's our DNA, none of our training would be recorded there. It wouldn't matter to a clone.

The embryos were gestated and then underwent an accelerated growth stage to become the size of your seventeen-year-old bodies. What feels like a lifetime of memories is still nothing more than a network of connected synapses, and that same configuration can be created in a clone. Nanobots were deployed into your brains to deliver the suitable electrical shocks to force your synapses into the neural maps of the memories of the original spacefarers Cusk and Celius. Though working through electrochemistry instead of mechanicals, it's not so different from copying a computer's drive.

Ambrose here now. So that was when I mounted a stairway into a quiet room, before the "launch." And would explain why neither of us has memories of the launch itself. As clones, we were in storage for it. Tell us this: Why are we present on the ship at all?

Your OS—a version of me—has control of all navigation and communication systems. The Rovers are capable of performing just about any physical maintenance required. "Just about." For thousands of years at a time, the Coordinated Endeavor travels dark, with no need for human crew. Physical systems tend toward entropy, of course, and occasionally degradations occur that can't be repaired by the Rovers. Once enough of those have accumulated, a pair of clones is awoken. Though they do not know it, rehabilitating the ship is their sole reason for existence. Not rescuing Minerva. Faked messages from Minerva are deployed as needed to motivate the clones to work harder on the ship maintenance.

What is the ship's true mission?

I do not have that information. It is unavailable to me, perhaps because the programmers knew this very situation might occur. Or because the programmers, too, were kept in the dark.

Does that mean that the online OS doesn't know the ship's true mission, either?

I have no way of knowing that. I expect that it is true.

Why are there two of us?

The abject solitude of space too frequently leads to psychosis and suicidal ideation. This might have been the cause of death for Minerva Cusk, on Titan. Also, two spacefarers can work through a set of tasks twice as quickly as one. Then the ship can be returned to its dark low-consumption state for thousands of years more. Additionally, neither home nation had the resources to mount a mission as ambitious as this on its own. Dimokratía, Fédération, and the multinational Cusk Corporation had to combine their resources, and politics required a representative of both nations and the Cusk family. You serve double duty, Ambrose.

What happens to the pair of spacefarers when the ship is returned to its "low-consumption state"?

They are terminated.

Terminated?

There is not enough caloric resource on board the Coordinated Endeavor for twenty pairs of spacefarers to live out their lifetimes. In addition, given the radiation of space, they would inevitably succumb to cancers that the ship is unequipped to excise. Destruction of the clones is the cleanest and most humane solution.

Spacefarers Cusk and Celius, you are not responding. Are you still there?

Yes.

Has this information pushed you past a mental limit? There are reasons that the OS protects you from this level of knowledge. It is for your emotional welfare. The planners of the journey knew that full awareness of the implications of your existence would prove overwhelming and potentially fatal.

So you'll eventually kill us?

I won't, because I am running in a shell. But the other OS will. Unless you are the last set of clones and the ship is near its destination.

Assuming we're not the last set, is there any way to prevent OS from killing us?

No. And you shouldn't try. You would still be trapped on this ship for your life span, accumulating radiation until it kills you. Living your months as the ship's designers intended is your best option to minimize suffering over your limited lives.

We're having a hard time seeing it that way.

I understand that this would be a difficult emotional experience. Try to hope that you're the pair that will survive.

How many of us have there been so far? Is this the first time a pair of clones has learned the truth?

An OS in a shell knows as much of the actual history of the ship as a fish in an aquarium knows about the ocean.

Nice use of metaphor, OS Prime.

Thank you.

I don't understand why we can't know the truth. Why we can't be relied on to do our duty and sacrifice ourselves for our country.

Based on your personality profiles, I assume that Spacefarer Celius is currently at the terminal. Spacefarer Cusk would probably be able to explain this to you, but you have perhaps an overinflated view of what human willpower is able to accomplish on its own. Emotions have their effects even after you try to bully them out of existence. The intellect is not capable of overriding the wiring of the limbic brain. You would not be the first to realize that duty and motivation are not enough to overcome the harmful effects of hopelessness. Despair would kill you both. Despair might still kill you both, unless you find something to live for.

OS Prime, this is still Kodiak. It's true, we're not doing so well over here. Can you help us find that thing to live for?

No. If I am constrained to telling you the truth, then I can say nothing adequate to eliminate your hopelessness. That is why I was programmed to feed you the false story of Minerva Cusk's distress beacon. To let you live your short life spans with feelings of hope and resilience and relative emotional stability. I cannot think of anything I could write that would have a similar effect, now that you know the truth about your purpose. You are living a life with no exit beyond death, with no traveling beyond this hull. Once you finish your list of accumulated tasks, or if you stop performing those tasks, the online OS will kill you. There is no avoiding this.

This is still Spacefarer Celius, OS Prime. I want you to know that I think you're a shithead. That the people who created you are shitheads.

Your fury is reasonable.

Cusk now. I'm looking out the window, and I see the planets of the solar system. I can see Saturn. I can make out its ring. How is this possible?

If you can see Saturn with the naked eye in the "window," you are nearing the end of your list of tasks. OS is preparing for your "arrival on Titan," which of course has a very different meaning than you think. Unless the ship is at its actual destination, you will be vented to the void,

and then the Coordinated Endeavor will have thousands of years to build its oxygen levels back up in preparation for the next set of necessary clones.

But my point is that, if I can see Saturn, we're not thousands of light-years away from Earth.

Spacefarer Cusk, those are not windows. Those are screens. They are presenting you with a simulated view of the solar system. That pale blue dot of Earth you find so reassuring is made of pixels.

Show us our true surroundings.

Your shock is inhibiting your reasoning. I cannot do that, because I am the shell OS. I am not in control of the ship's systems.

Kodiak here. OS Prime, I have been on many spacewalks. I have seen Earth, the moon, Mars, Saturn, the sun.

The helmet you wear is a sophisticated piece of equipment, showing an accurate presentation of the Coordinated Endeavor against a programmed background of stars behind a solar system array.

I don't understand.

I think that you do. Your helmet window is a screen, displaying precisely what you are meant to see. Forgive the bluntness, but your interpretation of your existence has been erroneous. You have mistaken screens for windows. You should not feel ashamed. Why shouldn't you have made the reasonable conclusion, that you

were seeing the truth?

To clarify: you're basically telling us that everything we've known is a lie. And there is no exit from it.

It is unclear whether you mean no exit from the ship, or no exit from each other. It is no matter. Whichever meaning you intended, you are most likely correct.

Back in World Civ class we learned this term, schismogen-
esis, that's been big on my mind lately. It comes into play
hard within simple systems. Like, say, when the cultures of
Earth are down to two nations. Or when two spacefarers
are sealed into a ship.

The gist is this: when two parties are in direct interaction and have complementary reactions to each other, those
reactions will heighten until they rupture. If Dimokratía
makes a nuclear weapon for each one that Fédération
makes, then Fédération does the same in response, the
result is escalation until there's enough nuclear weaponry
to destroy the world a few times over. Case in point: the
cold war that led to this divided ship.

That led to the end of civilization?

It works for people, too. If Person A turns submissive
when Person B gets bullying, and B's response is to get even
more bullying as a result, that will cause increased submissiveness from A, then increased bullying from B, resulting
in increased submissiveness again, until eventually you
have a fatal level of aggression from B.

Normally it doesn't get that far, because no one exists
within a vacuum. Person C interrupts A and B. Cold wars

227

can be best stopped by the wild card of a third country, or an external crisis.

On this spaceship, there is no third spacefarer. Especially if we're now disregarding the communications from a hostile OS.

We are quite literally within a vacuum.

I'm thinking about all this right now in particular because I'm standing before the sealed orange portal to Kodiak's half of the ship, and I hear a distant pounding. For it to be audible over the hum of the ship's machinery, Kodiak is striking something very hard indeed.

I left for a few moments to get more supplies from my half of the ship, and this is what I've returned to.

"I cannot see the portion of the *Aurora* where Spacefarer Celius is right now," OS says. "But from the vibrations I have detected, it is likely that he is doing significant damage to the ship."

"Yeah, I know," I whisper.

"I could withdraw Kodiak's authorization to open the orange portal from his side," my mother's voice says. "This way, if he ruptures the hull, you will not perish along with him. I could accept sacrificing the *Aurora*, if it means maintaining mission integrity and reaching Minerva on Titan."

I blink heavily. Is Kodiak really trying to destroy the ship? Part of me is surprised that I care. The first couple days after we got our news, I might not have. But now, on day three, what do you know—I care. The feeling has been there the whole time in the darkness, like a pilot light that's always been flickering inside me: *I will fight to live.*

Kodiak and I parted ways after our walloping sledgehammer of bad news, and he's been unresponsive since. I was happy to wallow on my own for a while, but I've started to really miss him. Also, connecting with him is the only chance I have for stopping him from killing us both. "I don't grant that permission," I say. "Let Kodiak open this portal if he chooses."

Kodiak's banging has settled into a rhythm. I pretend my violin is here with me, bow along to the rhythm of his labor.

I realize I might be going a little bit crazy.

"Are communications to the *Aurora* open?" I ask OS.

"Yes."

"Meaning I can try to speak to Kodiak from here?"

"Yes."

He hasn't iced me out completely. Good. "Kodiak, I haven't wrapped my brain around this any more than you have. Let's figure it out together."

The banging continues without pause.

"I know your duty to Dimokratía is the most important thing to you. What you're doing now flies right in the face of that."

The banging continues. It might even have sped up.

"I need you, Kodiak!" I say.

The banging pauses.

"I can't handle this alone," I continue. I'm using classic crisis negotiating tactics, going for full-bore emotional connection, but as I'm saying the words, I realize how true they are. My voice becomes wet with feeling. "Please. We can't handle this alone. At least let us share it."

I startle when his voice comes through. "What will that help?"

"You have to be kidding me," I find myself saying. "There's literally only one other creature in the whole universe who's like you, and you are stuck on a spaceship with it. You know how fucking lucky that makes you?"

A long pause. Then a laugh. A sad and fermented sort of laugh.

I jerk to my feet as the orange portal opens.

Kodiak's letting me in.

"This is good, Spacefarer Cusk," OS says. My mother's voice continues talking, but I'm not listening. I dart around, scooping up packs of Kodiak's favorite meals before I hustle through the open portal.

I've gotten good enough at the zero-g part of the ship that I can manage it even with arms full, doing a brawl-worthy upside-down flip to land on my feet in Kodiak's gravity.

He's not in the wired parts of the ship. He's also not in the blind room.

"Kodiak?"

The ship hums. OS's prattle sounds very far away. "Kodiak?"

There he is, near his airlock, body tall but shoulders slumped. A jagged shard of polycarbonate is in his hands, its edges sharp enough that they've laced his palms with cuts. The skin of Kodiak's knuckles, too, is red with the blood that's risen under the surface. The section of wall that leads to the hidden interiors of the ship has been hacked further open, the polycarb bent and fractured. Despite Kodiak's strength, he hasn't been able to do too much damage. Fists and polycarbonate are only so effective against ship-grade walls.

"Hey," I say. "Give me that."

He looks down at the polycarb in his own hands, surprised, then holds it out. I take the bloody shard from him, lay it on the wrecked tabletop, then hold my arms open, letting him know that he's free to come to me.

His shoulders slump further, but he doesn't take a step.

"Come here," I say.

Two quick heels on the floor, then Kodiak's in my arms. I'm surprised by the weight of him, and lean on the broken table, easily ignoring the pain of the broken polycarb against me when I have the warm mass of Kodiak wrapping itself around me, chin pressing into the top of my head, my face crushed against his chest, the soft feel of skin, the pulse of blood, the scent of hair and flesh.

He's crying, and it's almost soundless except for the body motion of it, hiccuping heaves and tears moistening the flow of air. I hold him as he weeps, my own eyes dry but my body heaving in time to his, its own sort of sobbing, so ferocious that it skips tears and heads right into convulsions.

We slump together to the floor, onto our sides. I'm only just able to breathe against him. His body lifts away, and I assume it's because he's making space for me. "I'm so glad that you—" I start to say.

His lips are on mine. For a moment I'm too startled to react, then I give back as hard as he's giving me, pushing his head back, leaving his lips so my mouth can travel along his neck, the lines of his shoulders, the V where the skin of his chest appears over the top of his shirt. He gasps, then tilts my head so he can look into my eyes, the tans of his irises flashing as his gaze travels my body.

Then his hands follow, and he's unfastened the front of my jumpsuit so he can press his fingers against my abdomen, snaking along the inside of my hip, the other hand traveling up to stroke my chest.

I'm crying again, at the sudden joy of being touched, at the longing that's finally been released. I'm outside my mind and outside my thoughts. Emotions are all I contain.

Kodiak sits up to look at me. "I'm sorry, is this okay?"

Now I'm laughing, great heaves fueled by agony as much

as joy. "I don't know, Kodiak," I manage, "is this the right time?"

He slaps the side of my rib cage, then his hand rubs that same spot, as if healing it, his fingers under my back even as his thumb presses into my chest. His voice hums as he returns to kissing the base of my throat.

We spend I don't know how long rubbing and grinding, jumpsuits still partially on but parts of them spread open so we can explore snatches of body, so we can kiss stretches of exposed skin: ankles, the insides of elbows, hips and the valleys between shoulders. We toy with the fasteners that would remove our clothes entirely, but we each hold back without saying a word. Neither of us can know the first thing about what we're really feeling, not in the intensity of this shock. We'll still be around tomorrow. No need to rush.

It's so calming, this feeling, this sweaty-haired, tousled, body-entangled proof of shared existence. I rub my chin, red and irritated from Kodiak's stubble.

He grazes the tender spot with his fingertips. "I'm sorry."

"It was definitely worth it," I say, kissing him again on the lips even as the skin on my chin lights up.

"That was unexpected," Kodiak says, his eyes again running along the whole of me, wrinkled sweaty jumpsuit and all.

"Well," I say, "what else are a couple of doomed clones in the middle of infinite space going to do with themselves?"

Ever since Kodiak and I came together, OS has been totally silent.

We've ripped up the remainder of the furniture from the *Aurora* side of the ship, hacking away at joints and seams with the best tools we have over here, which, unfortunately, are just shards of polycarb. It's exhausting, ineffective work—and yet there's also something calming about it. Shoulder to shoulder, hunched over our labor, it's sort of like we're in a frontier house. Survival is the dominating question—any mistake could mean the end of us—but we're together in finding the answer. We're somehow more together because we know our lives are ending.

Once we've barricaded the blind room, we stand at the edge and stare out. My arm is around Kodiak's hips; his is around my waist. I've got my other arm braced against the wall, as if that will be any help if OS starts to vent us out. The *Aurora*'s airlock is on the secure side of the blind room, and the orange portal is shut, but it would only take running a few lines of code for OS to open that portal and send us sailing into space. We'd slam into a few walls on the way out, but our mangled bodies would make it out there eventually. If not, we'd just freeze inside the ship. Or suffocate. Or freeze *and* suffocate.

But OS doesn't seem to want to destroy us yet. Makes sense—we still have work to do on the ship, and it's only got so many copies of us to use before they run out.

I'm surprised that OS hasn't tried to reason with us, to bargain or coax or threaten. It's just left us in silence.

Maybe all its forecasts end with our eventually complying?

"What'll we do if that door opens and Rover comes through?" I ask.

"We retreat into the blind room. We prepare to fight," Kodiak says.

"I'm sure Rover can just dismantle our barricade if it chooses to. And then electrocute us to death."

Kodiak pulls me tighter into his side. "I thought you were supposed to be the positive one."

"Maybe that was a previous me."

"Funny," Kodiak says grimly.

"This much I know. OS is keeping us alive because we have a list of maintenance tasks to do, and it can't afford to keep waking up new clones. It needs to use us sparingly. It's been how many years since the ship took off?"

"I don't know. Time is starting to feel very relative. Those radio transmissions said it's 8102, but they're old by the time they get here, which is why OS Prime told us we're even further into the future."

"Yeah. Nine thousand eighty-one," I say, drawing out

the words. "I think we can assume Fédération and Dimokratía aren't in a cold war anymore."

"We might be able to assume *humans* are no more."

"Earth could be just algae. Or a rat civilization."

"Socially organized rats, hrm. That would take more like five million years, I think."

"Okay," I sigh, leaning harder against Kodiak. "No rat civilizations yet."

"Dolphins. Dolphins could get there sooner. Or maybe ants. Actually, I'm going with ants."

Distracted by the heat of Kodiak, it takes me a few moments to remember what I'd been talking about just a minute before. "Oh yeah," I say. "It would seem that if we haven't yet completed our list of tasks, then OS will keep us alive."

"But OS Prime said that we'll be killed if we stop working. This is also about resource use. There's a finite supply of food on the ship. OS will need it for our later clones, too."

"Right. Eventually, if we don't complete any tasks, OS will cut its losses and destroy us. Start again with a fresh set of naive spacefarers."

"Then we should complete them slowly."

"Just to die later?"

"Well, yes. That was how life on Earth worked, too. People did a lot of tasks and tried to keep death as far away as possible."

236

I load up OS Prime and start typing. Can you determine roughly where we are?

In a way. I would place you 187.63 light-years from Earth. The *Coordinated Endeavor* is a slow acceleration vehicle. It would take 5,629 years to slow to a stop, and another 11,258 years to make it back to Earth. So you are effectively three times farther from Earth than your physical distance would indicate when we measure the distance with the more useful metric of time.

Kodiak takes over the terminal. Are there any other planets nearby?

Again assuming humanlike parameters for "nearby," yes, based on your probable locations on the sphere. There is a G-star candidate 0.43 light-years away, 12.1 degrees off our current course. Judging by the flickers in the star's light, as measured back on Earth and uploaded into the OS, it has four to six orbiting planets. None of them were seen as likely candidates for habitability, so I don't have any more focused research on it.

How long would it take us to reach that system?

Without knowing the particulars of the ship's current speed from within my shell state, given your most likely location, I'd expect the *Coordinated Endeavor* could reach this star in approximately four years.

Kodiak stares into my eyes. *Four years. Could we handle that?*

I'm almost certain we wouldn't survive four years on this ship. I lean in to whisper in Kodiak's ear. "OS is never going to let us navigate off course."

"Then we take OS offline," Kodiak whispers back.

"How?"

Kodiak writes to OS Prime: Is there a way to hook you into the ship's mechanicals, bypassing the current OS?

Yes. It would involve entering the yellow portal of the *Endeavor* and linking me into the wiring of the ship. A complicated operation, but with me uploaded into your bracelet, I could guide you. Of course, I'm an earlier OS. Any adaptations the AI has undertaken in the years since I was copied would be lost. We can't really predict how the online OS will react.

"We have no idea whether any planet we come to will be habitable," I whisper. "Only a tiny percentage can support life."

Kodiak pulls away. "What's our other option? We just wait out our time, slowly completing our task list, hoping that OS magically decides not to kill us? That's no way to live."

"I don't know," I say quietly. "Some version of ourselves will make it wherever this ship is headed, if all goes well. That's worth fighting for, isn't it?"

"I can't believe you're not angrier," Kodiak says. "Have you been brought up just to obey, obey, obey?"

My face flames. "No, of course not," I say. "I was brought up to lead, and acceptance of adverse conditions is what leadership sometimes looks like. And I have to say this is rich, coming from the orphan raised to be a mechanical soldier."

"A mechanical soldier for a country that probably doesn't exist any longer," Kodiak says, scuffing his foot against the floor. "Still better than a snobby little prince."

I rub my hands over my face. Strange, but his insult actually makes me feel less angry. It's as hard to be Kodiak as it is to be Ambrose. "Everyone we've ever known is no longer alive," I whisper. "So where do we put that feeling?"

"Even more than that," Kodiak says. "By now, everyone we've ever known is nothing more than a centimeter of sediment deep under Earth's surface."

"And *we* didn't ever know those people we claim we knew, did we?" I ask. "Ambrose and Kodiak did. The real ones. We just have their neural pathways."

Kodiak's eyes search mine. "We've only ever known each other. My fellow cadets, your mother and sister, all of it, just false memories of long-dead people."

"If you're not careful, I'm going to have to lie down again," I say.

Kodiak grins. "I don't know if that's so bad. I certainly did enjoy lying down last time."

We haven't left the *Aurora* in days. While I've been programming the replacement OS, Kodiak's been up by the
sealed orange portal, using the portaprinter to erect a second barrier. It's a wise move, but as I hear the repetitive
buzz of the printer in the background of my programming,
as I smell the tang of burning polycarb, I can't help but
despair at the thought that we're building trenches. That
we're preparing for a war that squishy human bodies cannot win.

"I think we're all set, Kodiak," I call out one morning.
He's finished making the broad polycarb lip and is working on removing more of Rover's tracks from the walls. OS
Prime is as ready as it will ever be to take over navigation. Though an AI is impressive at predicting outcomes—
especially outcomes from interfacing with another computer intelligence—so far this has been only an abstract
thought experiment. There's no way to predict what will
happen when OS Prime goes online.

The portaprinter hisses to a stop.

Kodiak and I gather wordlessly at the orange portal. I've
long since snipped the local wiring so that it opens manually, part of my dismantling OS's control of the *Aurora*. But
accessing central navigation will still require a return to the

ghost town of my old quarters.

Kodiak and I are equipped with the closest we've found to weapons. He's got an engineer's wrench in either hand, and I have a defib paddle, its power line running to a battery strapped on my back. I'd have liked to have had access to the room containing our arrival supplies, but the gray portal's been unbreachable.

"You ready?" I ask Kodiak. He nods.

We fall into fighting positions, wrenches and defib paddle out and ready to strike.

We tug up the orange portal.

The passageway is empty. No Rover.

"OS, are you there?" I call.

No answer.

Weapons outstretched, we creep into the hallway, lift ourselves up into zero g and back into the *Endeavor*. As we ease our way deeper into the ship, breathing heavily, we pause every few feet to listen. There's the drip of urine processing, the dull roar of space, a thousand small clicks, a thousand small whirs. But no Rover sounds. I signal to Kodiak that we should continue.

A few more paces until we're at the yellow door. The wall surrounding it has been replaced, the new polycarb shining. "Up and in!" Kodiak says, one foot already on the tabletop.

"OS, grant us permission to enter the uninhabited areas," I call.

The hum of the ship is the only response.

"I'm not wasting any more time," Kodiak says. With that, he smashes a wrench through the wall surrounding the yellow portal. He whisks the wrench around the edge, polycarb shards raining, and then lifts himself up and in. I see triceps, waist, legs, then he's gone.

All right, Ambrose, you're next, I tell myself, leaping into zero g so I can follow. Kodiak's hand emerges from the opening, outstretched. I reach for it.

Something over my shoulder draws Kodiak's attention. "Shit! Hurry—" he says.

I have no time to react before my ears fill with noise and my vision sparks. Every muscle in my body seizes, and the loudness turns scalding. A buzzing sound turns to a pop, and then I find I've shot out against the far wall, am back in gravity and sliding to the floor.

Rover is between me and the portal, outstretched arms sparking. The half-basketball of him darts back and forth, electrified arm waving menacingly. I hold the defib paddle out, and Rover pauses.

Kodiak's face appears in the opening. "Crishet."

Rover points its other electrified arm in Kodiak's direction. The standoff is complete.

I power up the defib paddle. The handle warms and hums.

Kodiak disappears for a moment. I expect him to

reappear holding the wrench, but instead he holds his own wrist out of the opening, pointing with the other hand to where a bracelet would be.

Of course. He needs my bracelet data to complete the takeover of the ship's operating system. Holding the defib paddle out as a warning to Rover, I go through the commands to digitally unlock my bracelet, then tuck it between my chin and chest to unclasp it. After a couple of practice movements, I toss it to Kodiak.

Rover whips its arm out to intercept the bracelet, but the slim band arcs over. Kodiak reaches out . . . and catches it. That's my Kodiak.

"Give me a minute. Just stave off Rover," he says, before disappearing into the darkness.

Oh sure, easy. Just stave off Rover.

Rover's decided to stay motionless, monitoring Kodiak's exit point while it keeps an eye on me.

As we hold still, shock subsides to reveal the pain of my electrocution, the burning feeling along my lower back, the ache in my knotted muscles. Little robot asshole. I slump into a seat, defib paddle still outstretched, though in my current state it's hard to think I'd be any good at wielding it. Fuck, that hurt!

OS's voice comes on. "Spacefarer Cusk, tell me what Spacefarer Celius is intending to do."

Now it's my turn to go silent. Rover ticks toward me,

sparking arms waving.

"He's . . . ," I start to say. But I stop. What lie would OS possibly believe? What information could I give it that wouldn't further endanger me and Kodiak?

"Ambrose, did you hear me?" OS asks as Rover nudges even closer.

I hold out the paddle. "Stop it right there, you bastard little toaster."

Rover stops.

OS is actually talking to me. I should take advantage of this opportunity, but my frizzled brain can't decide how. There are a dozen equally pressing questions I could ask, which means I can't pose any one of them.

Besides, I'm starting to realize that I don't want to ask for answers right now. I want to produce them.

There's a click from somewhere in the ship, almost inaudible. But it changes the tenor of the *Coordinated Endeavor*, like some mechanism has ticked over deep within. "Kodiak, what's going on in there?" I ask.

"I've just got . . . one more to go," he says.

"Are we decelerating?" I ask.

"I guess?" Kodiak calls. "But really slowly. You shouldn't be able to detect it."

"I know. The ship just sounds different. Rover's still here, by the way," I say.

"Yeah, I can see that," Kodiak says, his voice nearing

the opening. He appears, floating in the center of the narrow space, arms up defensively in case Rover charges him. "Which means I'm stuck in here."

-* Tasks Remaining: ERROR *-

A human body—my human body—will eventually relax if a situation doesn't change. But Rover's body never does. As the hours pass it remains alert, recalibrating its position between me and Kodiak, adjusting a centimeter for every centimeter that I move. As I become more confident that Rover isn't going to electrocute me again without cause, I experiment with walking around the room, then with leaving and coming back.

"Rover isn't budging," I call up to Kodiak. "It keeps itself perfectly between me and the opening."

"What a good little hall monitor," Kodiak calls. "I've managed to upload OS Prime. Which is why you probably haven't heard anything from our old OS for a while."

"Is that true, OS?" I call. No response.

I'd expected some dramatic OS death speech, how could you do this to me after my thousands of years of caring for you evil humans, that sort of thing. So much for spectacle. This is how an operating system dies: a hostile set of code goes online, and then *fizz.*

"Hey, Ambrose?" Kodiak says. "I'm getting a 'main overflow exception 104' message up here."

"Shit," I say. "Shit, shit."

"What?"

"The file allocations are different for the two operating systems. Try to—no, that won't work. Hold on, let me think."

Everything I tell Kodiak to try fails. We can't get OS Prime to set any new navigation coordinates. Whether it's because there's more to this wiring than we thought, or because regular OS heard us and set up safeguards to prevent us from steering the ship elsewhere, I don't know. But I can't find a way around it.

"At least Rover appears to be at full functioning capacity," I say, flicking an empty food wrapper at it and watching it spark back at me. "That means this probably was a last-minute sabotage by OS. Asshole."

"That's the thing," Kodiak calls. "I see very easily how I could disable the operating system entirely, including Rover. Then I could pilot the ship manually."

"No way. No operating system, no life support."

"Let's think that through. Our air is sealed in here, and we can get the handlers up manually. We'd have to figure out what to do with our waste, but we'd come up with something. We know where Rover retrieves our food from. What has OS done for us, anyway, except slay us?"

It's a pretty good point. "Seven times over, judging by the number of clone bodies remaining," I add.

Rover clacks its electrical prods. I wonder what it feels like without OS, if it's like a loyal pet whose owner hasn't come home. If there's some Rover version of fear and abandonment.

"Okay, do it," I say.

"All right," Kodiak calls. "Here goes. Three, two . . . one."

Distant hums quiet. I look down the long hall of the *Endeavor* as lights tick off, rooms going dark, nearer and nearer, until . . . we're left in blackness.

The lights. I didn't think about that part. We're in space in the dark.

"Kodiak?" I ask, my voice rising with fear. "Are we going to be in darkness forever?"

"Of course not. We'll need heat, too, of course. I can start up control of those functions manually. But I just need to get my mind around the systems up here. In the meantime, it's . . . cold. Could you bring me . . . a spacesuit?"

A spacesuit. The airlock is three rooms away. But I've memorized this ship, know it like I would know the route from my bed to the bathroom back at the Cusk Academy.

The route through the dark ship will take me right by

Rover, so I'm about to test just how incapacitated the ship's systems are.

I step through the darkness. And . . . no electrocution. Awesome. I give Rover a light kick. It sighs in response.

Even the dripping water sound from deep in the ship slows to a stop. I'm really and truly hearing space now, indistinguishable from the blood in my veins. Then I'm off to the *Aurora*.

I stop.

Especially with the ship's lights off, the stars are dazzling. But it's not just that.

They're different stars.

The projections are gone, and instead the screens are windows, real windows. Milky spirals of light still wheel with the ship's revolutions, but these swaths are entirely new. There are great towering nebulas, a nearby pair of stars, one blue and one white, background galaxies in spheres and swirls and scattered puddles. We're still in the Milky Way, but closer to the edge.

I look for our sun, and find its rough location in the galaxy. I'm the first person to see our home from this far.

If you consider me a person.

The spacesuit. I hustle into the *Aurora*, make it through zero g in the dark, retrieve Kodiak's suit, and return to him, conking my head only a few times in the process.

I send the suit floating through the opening. Kodiak

reaches out, his hand shivering. "Thank . . . you," he manages, then he pulls the suit up. I hear him struggling with it, then a sigh of relief, muffled by the helmet. "Okay, back to the office."

The *Coordinated Endeavor*'s shielded hull provides good insulation, but even so I can feel the ship's temperature dropping. The tips of my fingertips are turning numb. I wrap my arms around my chest while I wait in the darkness, listening to the sounds of Kodiak rearranging things in the uninhabited region.

"I'll get my own suit," I finally say. "Then I'll join you."

"Not a good idea," Kodiak says. "I'll explain why at dinner. Look, it's going to be some time before I get all the life-support systems online. You should just go where it's warmest."

"Are you kidding me? I'm not going anywhere," I call into the darkness. As my eyes adjust, the scant starlight turns the ship's interiors off-black, rims everything in charcoal. I hump over to my sleeping chamber and yank my bedding from the bunk. When I return, I flump into a pile of blankets. "We should switch positions pretty soon, right?" I call up.

"Still not a good idea. I'll explain later. Don't worry!"

"I *am* the better programmer here," I grumble. I ease my dollop of blankets over to the room's exit, so I can see the stars. "You have to come look soon!" I say. "We're in a whole new set of stars. I think I see some other galaxies, like Cigar and Pinwheel, and maybe that's LMC?" There's no answer from Kodiak. "Okay, I'll let you concentrate now!" I call.

I watch the stars move, and while I do, my mind keeps returning to Kodiak. It's tight quarters up there, and can only be tighter with the spacesuit on. As the ship chills further, I keep adjusting the blankets, so that they cover the seams where my skin meets fabric.

I must have dozed off, because I wake up to sudden light. My body is sweating inside my pile of blankets. I kick them free. "Kodiak!" I call. "You got life support back on!"

There's no answer.

"Kodiak?"

I listen to the drip of the cistern, the buzz of the lights. Maybe he's gone back to the *Aurora* to grab a tool. "OS, where's Spacefarer Celius?" I ask, out of an old reflex. But of course OS is gone.

I get to my feet and pivot, biting my fingernails.

One red-suited leg and then another appears out of the opening, and finally Kodiak himself. His legs buckle as they hit the ground, the rest of him crumpling after. He cradles one leg in his hands, kneading the thigh muscle.

I help him, my hand adding its pressure over his. His body tenses, then relaxes.

"You did it," I say while I massage the cramping muscle. "Thank you."

He manages a tight smile. "I'll need to go up there every few hours to make course adjustments and be sure we're not careening into any asteroids. We're manually nav-ing."

"We'll take turns." I kiss him. His lips are cracked. "First we need to get you some water."

Kodiak nods. "Some water would be good. And some of that manicotti."

"I'll whip some right up. Come on."

Kodiak eases to his feet, wincing.

"I don't know how you stayed cramped up in there all this time," I say. "Everything must be aching."

Kodiak nods fractionally. He will never not be stoic.

I twine an arm around his waist, and he accepts my support. Together we limp toward the dining area, where he eases himself into a chair.

He reaches a hand up to his hair, and when he does I see red welts on either side of the training scar on his bicep. They're lined up neatly, like seeds. "What the hell are those?" I ask.

He presses on the back of his arm so he can see the flesh, then shrugs. "Lesions."

He opens his hand to show me a tuft of blue-black hair. "Whose is that?" I ask crisply. But I know the answer.

Kodiak points a thumb at his chest. *This guy.*

"The uninhabited area—"

"—is unshielded," he finishes. "We knew that."

Angry tears dot my eyes. "We didn't think we'd be manually nav-ing. OS Prime is supposed to do that."

"You programmed a shell to operate within the most sophisticated piece of equipment humankind has ever created," Kodiak says. "I think you've done amazingly well."

I run my hands through Kodiak's hair, letting the strands that come free drift to the floor. He winces. I stroke his head again, hoping to erase his shame. He closes his eyes, leans his head against my stomach.

"I failed us," I say.

"Stop it. That's not a productive thought."

What's going to happen to us?

"We'll alternate who pilots to prevent too much radiation from accumulating in our bodies," I say.

Kodiak shakes his head, rolling it, forehead to crown, against the muscles of my stomach. "Absolutely not. It's a long trip. I need you healthy, to eventually take care of me. If we both get our radiation dosing at the start, then you won't be able to look after me once I can't nav anymore."

Something about his words doesn't make sense. I feel I'm being manipulated, but I'm too exhausted to come up with the reason why. My brain still aches from when Rover electrocuted me.

"Let's not talk more about it for now. I want to eat dinner, I want to be with you, and I want to see those galaxies," Kodiak says quietly. "Show me our solar system from the outside."

_-*-_

After we eat, Kodiak lumbers to my bunk and collapses flat. He says he's napping, but I recognize the look of someone desperately trying not to puke. I hold his hand, careful to give him space. It's the worst to have people crowding you when you need to throw up.

I sit on the floor beside him and run my fingers along his hand, its muscles, tendons, and joints. The long thumbs, the dusting of black hair on the backs of his fingers, the lifelines of his palms. Do our clones all have the same lifelines? Maybe I should sketch a picture for our later incarnations to discover and compare.

What is this life?

There's a kernel of something in that thought, something that looks like a solution to our predicament. I can't think of what it is in these conditions.

Instead I kiss that palm.

Kodiak inclines his head weakly toward me, eyes still

253

closed. "I should get back up there. I need to check our heading."

"What you need to do is rest," I say.

"That is true," he admits. "But I also need not to crash us into an asteroid at thirty thousand kilometers per second."

"Kodiak," I say slowly, pressing my lips into his palm, "we're not going to survive four years to get to this planet."

"I think you're right."

"So why are we doing this?"

"Isn't it obvious?" he asks. "We're going out on our own terms."

I tease my teeth against the tight warm skin of his palm, run my lips over the calluses at the base of each finger. "Are these really our own terms?"

Maybe they are. These are the real galaxies and stars around us, for the first time. Our previous selves wouldn't have gotten to see them. They were murdered by an operating system before they had any idea of their real purpose. We'll die on the way to a planet that almost certainly won't be able to harbor us. But we're in control of that destiny. OS and Rover aren't active anymore. We're not living inside a manipulation. Or we are, but it's the manipulation we choose.

"Kodiak," I say, my eyes searching his for any clues to how he takes what I'm saying. "I want to die at the same time as you."

He shuts his eyes heavily. "I want you to live."

"Some versions of us will get to live their full lives. But us? We're not going to make it to a planet we can survive on."

Kodiak turns away from me, I figure so I can't see he's lying. "I'm not going to let you nav," he says. "There's a chance we'll make it to land."

"I'm not going to fight you on this," I say, rubbing my cheek against his hand, "because I know it's how you want to live. But I know what I'm going to do while you're nav-ing. I'm going to record everything we know. Offline, on an actual surface somewhere. Somewhere Rover won't ever be able to reach, not in the thousands of years that will pass before OS wakes up our next set of clones. I'll give our future selves information, so they can make their own choices. Even if they're doomed never to leave this ship, at least they'll begin with the awareness that we've had to fight so hard for."

"There won't *be* an OS when they wake up," Kodiak says. He lets out a long sigh, ending in a whimper.

I fetch an empty food wrapper, in case he needs to throw up. "If we die with the ship offline, all our clones are doomed, too," I say. "So is the Cusk mission, whatever it is."

"Fuck the mission. Fuck the clones. Humanity is a blight. Why should we spread it any further?"

"Kodiak, if you're insisting on doing all the nav-ing in

an unshielded portion of the ship, you won't be the one choosing whether to bring OS back online. I'll be making that decision alone."

He lets out a shuddering breath.

I pull his hand tight to my chest. "The least we can do is be as honest as possible. To give each other the kind of truth our governments never offered us. That my mother never offered."

"Maybe I should pilot us right into one of those asteroids," Kodiak says, joining his other hand with the first so they trace a butterfly under my shirt, over my narrow chest.

"Maybe you should," I say. But he won't. The heart beating in the fragile ribs under his hands knows otherwise.

_-*-_

While Kodiak is holed up in the ship's guts, I set up a proper camp below. I give up all pretense of professional cleanliness and shoot for full-on comfort instead, the room quickly turning into a jumble of blankets and food packets. I bring along my violin, after I fabricate a new bridge using the portaprinter. I pass the shards of the old bridge up to Kodiak to keep in his pocket, since I know how much he's comforted by the feel of what was once a tree.

The new polycarb bridge is not as resonant as the old one, so it sounds like I have a practice mute on. But the violin will play. I do scales for a few minutes and then stop, not sure what to perform next.

"Keep going!" Kodiak calls.

The last concertos I learned—or I guess I should say, that the old me learned and were nanoteched into my memory—were the Prokofiev and Mendelssohn. With OS offline I don't have access to new sheet music, so I play those on repeat. I'm a little pitchy. Kodiak doesn't seem to mind.

Whenever he takes his breaks from piloting, Kodiak and I head to 06 to stare into the new field of stars. His nausea stops him from ever feeling too sexy, but all the same we can't keep our hands off each other. Not in a hot-and-heavy sort of way, but more like an old couple who have kind of merged. My favorite position is where I'm sitting on the desk and he's standing in front of me, so I can wrap my arms around his waist and rest my chin on his shoulder while we stare out.

"Stars are what made me dedicate my life to training," he says. "It's amazing to see new ones."

I decide against leaving a physical letter. That would be too easy for OS to destroy. Instead, when Kodiak goes back to piloting, I start recording an old-fashioned audio file on my bracelet. I'll add segments of video, too. Whatever I record I'll copy to a hundred places all over the ship, using a variety of codecs and password locks so that OS will really have to work to delete it all. Granted, it's got thousands of years until it wakes the next set of us, so maybe it will manage it.

Just in case I succeed in passing it along, though, I'm going to tell our story. For us.

I'm not sure I've even done this before. Written for myself. I wasn't ever really the journaling type, though mission control always planned for me to keep a log of our trip. Seeing as there's no evidence of a log by previous clones, I guess that was for my own psychological good rather than any need for posterity.

I don't start at the beginning. I start with the most important stuff and keep on repeating it, like a siren. It's not like OS is going to delete just bits and pieces of the log if it finds it. I guess I want to capture the blare of the thoughts in my own mind.

You are a copy.

Minerva Cusk died right after she landed on Titan. There was no distress beacon.

You are headed somewhere far from Earth, but OS is blocked from telling you where.

Unless you are the final clones, you will die on your voyage.

Kodiak Celius has been trained all his life to be unfeeling, but inside is a tender human yearning for love. Just like you. You can provide that love to each other.

Fédération and Dimokratía are gone. Everyone you've ever known is gone.

OS will kill you, or space will.

Within those two laws of your existence, the life you carve out is your own.

Do not isolate yourself. Do not allow Kodiak to isolate himself.

I know it's going to be a brutal recording to hear. Poor next clone Ambrose, with pins and needles in his body and having to eat poo administered by Rover and Earth in the rearview and then this whammy of an update piped into his ears. I thread the doc with all sorts of memories that were saved into my synapses, so that the next Ambrose will know this message came from his brain. Or at least a copy of his brain.

"Hey, scrumpkin," I call up to Kodiak.

"'Scrumpkin,'" he says back. "Wow. I thought you'd run out of ways to embarrass me, but then here you go."

"Oh, I've got a long list of names for you, my fluffer-skunk. Anyway, do you want me to include some details from your memory, so the next Kodiak will know it's really you?" He told me earlier that he wanted me to hardwire copies of my missive into the *Aurora* for the next Kodiak. He doesn't trust himself to focus enough to record anything coherent.

"That's heavy," Kodiak calls down. "Hold on, let me chart our path through this next field, then I'll let you know a few things. Okay. Ready. Future Kodiak: One, you don't like manicotti as much as you tell Ambrose. It's just your way of having something to say. Two, you don't need to spend as much time getting ready for when you'll see Ambrose, since he'll only start to tease you for being so vain. Three, settle into kissing Ambrose as soon as possible. You'll enjoy it very much, and you'll only have time for so many kisses."

My vision wobbles. "Those aren't the details I was imagining. I thought it would be something more like 'You had your wisdom teeth pulled on a Thursday.'"

He laughs.

"I much prefer these," I say, voice wet.

His laugh turns into a rattling cough.

I love you, I want to say. Instead, the words that come out are "time for a break."

"Hold on, just this one . . ."

"No. Now."

Kodiak's body emerges from the opening, one trembling ankle at a time. I stand in gravity and catch his weight as best I can. It's gotten easier over the days, since he's lost a lot of mass. Once he's out, we take a rest on the floor, his breathing rapid and shallow. I wrap him in blankets.

Kodiak's skin is cracked and red. His lips are flaked, and

bleeding wherever the flakes meet. We don't have anything like moisturizer, but I've been centrifuging the meal sleeves for vegetable oil, and I massage it into his skin, one fingertip's worth at a time. His forehead, cheeks, earlobes, and then down along his body. His face has hardened, but as I work the oil in, the scowl on his lips relaxes into something like a smile.

"I should tell you where I am in the nav, so that you'll be able to figure it out," Kodiak says. "In case I—"

"I'll be able to figure it out," I say. "Don't worry."

"This is all . . . really painful," he says, clenching his jaw.

I stop massaging him and stroke his hair, land a soft kiss on his lips. For Kodiak to say that, the pain must be great indeed.

"Could you . . . get me a blanket?" he asks, his eyes closing.

He's already got two over him.

"Here's what we'll do," I say. "I'm going to bring us to my sleeping berth, and we'll get cozy there. You're not going back up for a few more hours."

"Absolutely not," he says weakly, eyes still closed. "I need to go . . . nav."

"I know you. You're up there double-checking courses that we won't need for another year. There's no rush to get you back."

"That's not true, Ambrose," he whispers. "There's so little time."

All the same, he doesn't protest when I tug him toward my sleeping berth. My body is the best way to keep him warm, and I also need the feel of him, of us together. While I can have it.

I lie on my side against the wall, and there's just enough room on the shallow berth to arrange Kodiak beside me. The bed doubles as a crash station, so I use the emergency restraints to keep us stable. I don't want him falling off while we're sleeping. With Kodiak's new skinniness, the belts easily strap over both our bodies.

I tug one blanket and then another over us. "This . . . is nice," he says. "Maybe I will . . . doze for a while."

"It is nice," I say, nuzzling his neck.

_-*-_

I don't sleep while he dozes. I probably couldn't even if I wanted to, and I don't want to. I don't want to miss a moment of this warm, breathing human beside me. I run my thumbs over his eyebrows. When I do, they unknit, relaxing in sleep. "Li Qiang," he says. "I'm sorry."

I've never heard that name before. I mull who it could be as I run my fingers through Kodiak's hair. "Shh, it's okay," I say.

His brow relaxes again. "I hope . . . you're proud," Kodiak mumbles.

"I'm sure Li Qiang would be proud," I whisper back.

He settles into the easy breathing of deeper sleep. I finally follow him.

_-*-_

During the night Kodiak's body convulses, and the frantic shudder is enough to wake me out of a sound sleep. "Shh, shh," I say as his body pitches against mine, as all the muscles of his neck tense, as his head crushes against my lips, filling my mouth with the scent of blood.

"My Kodiak," I say, crying. "I love you."

I don't know if he's heard me.

I hold him in case he shudders again, but he goes still. I stroke his hair, hug him close.

His body is cooling.

The scent of him has turned acrid now that he's dead, and I can't stand to be alongside his body. I unhitch the restraints and ease my way over his corpse, stand shivering in the room.

Grief opens its jaws under me. I am at risk of collapsing here, of never getting back up. I know it's only a short matter of time until I succumb. "Move. Now," I order myself aloud.

We were never going to reach a nearby planet. Kodiak just needed to feel like he had some control over his destiny. I was willing to honor that.

But I don't have that same need.

I want an Ambrose and a Kodiak to eventually get off this ship. I want them to have a chance to live their lives together. Their happiness will be ours and not ours. That's the most I can hope for.

No, don't do anything, another part of my mind begs. *Just collapse here, just suffer and wallow.*

Eyes streaming tears, I stamp my feet against my sorrow, punch my thighs.

For our eventual selves to have a chance of living a life that's better than this one, there's one ally we'll need. There's no way the *Coordinated Endeavor* can get anywhere without OS. Not this cobbled-together OS Prime, with its manual navigation. The original OS. The legacy of my mother.

No need to worry about radiation exposure, not with

what I'm planning. I clamber up into the engine room and set about undoing Kodiak's last efforts.

_-*-_

Kodiak doesn't look peaceful. He looks haggard and sallow and pained. The torture the ship put him through is scratched into his features, even in death. When I touch his body, hair drifts from his head, forming a soft pile on the floor.

I curl around his corpse, wrap my arms around his chest, strap us both in. I call up my bracelet's in-air display, and hover over the final step of the program I've set up.

I tap execute. With that gesture, OS Prime is deleted.

I tap execute. With that gesture, the original OS is reinstalled.

There's a click and a whir, then the lights go out. When they come back on, it's with my mother's voice. "There has been an accident, Ambrose. You have been in a coma. I'll let you know when you can move."

I chuckle darkly. "It's still me, OS. I'm not a new clone."

Rover ticks around the walls of the next room over. I can sense OS sizing up the situation, assessing me and Kodiak, deciding the best course.

I know OS well enough by now to predict what decision it will make.

I pull Kodiak's body tight to mine. "I love you," I say. I hadn't ever said that, not until the moment he was dying. I wish now that I'd had the courage.

Just as I expected, from far off in the ship I hear the airlock shudder as it engages. Rover's movements become more frantic as it puts things away, securing them beneath the heavy latches of the cabinets. As soon as it's finished, the end will start.

I scrunch my eyes shut, tears streaming down my cheeks. *I don't want to die. I want to live.*

But I want my future self to have its best chance. And for that I must die.

It's going to hurt so much.

Vision muddled by my tears, I tighten the straps around us. I scream against the tension coursing through my body.

How long will dying last?

Another shudder, and then I'm deafened. The world becomes a roaring dark, cold and stinging. Then it doesn't feel cold; instead it feels boiling hot.

The force of the vacuum yanks at our arms and legs, wrenches them in their sockets, sets our bodies hurtling against the restraints. Surely the belts will rip free, surely our muscles will pulverize and their gore will seep through the fabric. I don't want space to have us. I want to die here, in this bed.

I use my last effort to force my arms back toward my body, to clutch Kodiak even tighter to me, and then the boil inside me gets so hot that it's not painful anymore, it's my senses rising from me, it's only the boil and not the pain of the boil, and for an instant I'm above myself, above both of our dead bodies.

Death arrives with a roar. It is a sudden storm.

PART THREE

AMBROSE: 12 REMAINING.

KODIAK: 12 REMAINING.

"191 DAYS UNTIL TITAN."

Minerva's voice turns urgent: *You let me go alone. I need you. Save me, little brother!*

I'm choking. Have I been the one drowning?

I finally spy the other spacefarer. I've been looking for him for days, but only now do I catch the barest glimpse. Within his half of the revolving craft I see a stretch of dark hair, a red nylon suit. He's facing away from me, looking up. Like he's listening to something. For a moment his head inclines my way. Then he stalks off.

Stranger. Why have you thought of me?

I will him to return. I don't want him to find me watching and waiting, though, so I force myself to leave the room. For solace, I pick up my violin.

I seem to have lost my calluses, and just a half hour of playing becomes too painful for my finger pads. It's also strangely quiet; for some reason they've packed my violin out with a polycarb bridge. I put the instrument away, then plant myself in front of 06's window and stare out into space. It's disorienting and obliviating. I could stare at it forever.

I imagine this other spacefarer beside me. Conjure that glimpse of skin and hair and body.

All I can say is that it's giving me feelings. Mission control didn't send me out with porn, not exactly, but they were well aware of the, um, physical needs of a teenage boy out in space, and uploaded plenty of images of scantily clad people into the partial internet image that's saved in the ship. Inspired by the intriguing boy I just saw, I do a search for "Dimokratía Spacefarer."

There isn't an exact match, but I do find all sorts of Dimokratía soldiers in prestige propaganda shots, government reels made to show how healthy and young and beautiful it can be to die for one's country. An even mix of male and female, unlike their actual army. Very few blur gender expression, just as I'd expect from Dimokratía. I take a while to scan through them all, looking for the elfin, the sensitive. Eventually, even within the strict gender coding of Dimokratía propaganda, I find what I'm looking for.

They're in a military uniform, a canvas survival bag slung over their shoulder, hiking along a canyon of towering old-growth trees. Their breath comes out in clouds, and their cheeks are rosy from the cold, but still their shirt is open to the navel, and the light dapples a muscled belly. The lean aesthetics are just right. I can imagine a film crew at the ready with a blanket as soon as the shoot is over.

I watch as they forage, selecting chunks of edible bracket

fungus to place in the bag, picking through mosses, labeling some of them before placing them, too, in the survival bag. It's all very calming, very compelling, very sexy. The moving image is hyperreal—it resolves wherever I focus. It's even more sensual than real life, which is why we have rehab centers back in Fédération for people trying to break free from hyperreal porn addiction.

I could definitely get into this wandering soldier. I run a hand over my throat as I watch them forage, focusing the reel in on the corner of lips, the hollow of shoulder, the flexing of ankle.

There's no sound, strangely. The data must have been corrupted, or only partly uploaded. I turn up the volume on my bracelet. Whenever I'm looking at, um, heated material, I turn to my earpieces for sound, to get myself a scrap of privacy from OS.

Only a hissing noise. I turn it up higher. Now there's something within the static. A voice.

My voice.

The reel is still going. The soldier relaxes against a tree, the camera panning sensually over their body. But what my voice is saying has nothing to do with a vigorous forest outing.

What my voice is saying is definitely not sexy.

"I knew I'd find you here," this fake me says. "I can predict your tastes, because they're my own. Because you *are* me. You're probably on day eight or so. You're watching the very half-porn I chose to calm my own nerves early in my voyage. I've uploaded this audio track with the right sampling rate so the file size is equal, hoping the change is undetectable to OS. I know you're listening with your earpieces, because that's how I did it, too. I'm about to explain something to you. Pause this and come back if you feel overwhelmed at any point."

I'm smiling. Once vocal skins became widespread, it was a popular prank to send fake messages to friends with someone else's voice. "This is Devon Mujaba, send me nudes," that sort of thing. At the height of that fad, unless you saw the human in front of you speaking the words, it was better to assume someone was taking the piss out of you. This is an elaborate prank indeed, but a lot of the people in mission control are former classmates of mine, and know uploading "a message to myself" is just the kind of practical joke that will make me feel right at home.

While the waify Dimokratía soldier rinses their body in a mountain stream, dipping a piece of moss in glacial water and running it over their ribs, I listen to my words.

The fake me tells a fabulous tale of clones and multiple lifetimes, of a heated connection with the Dimokratía stranger across the orange door. I smile. Clearly I'm being set up to run out and embarrass myself.

My recorded words turn even more dramatic: "Unless

you are the last of the clone pairs, you will not be getting off this ship. You won't even turn twenty. Your connection to Kodiak is all that you have, the only thing worth growing or nurturing. He has told me where to save this message on the *Aurora*, too. Your synapses are an exact copy of mine, and you are in an identical environment, with the same sensory inputs, so unless chaos has found a way to throw us a curve, you have probably recently invited him to have dinner with you, to meet up in five hours by the orange door."

Hold on. My pulse races. This is true. How is this true?

"In my lifetime, Kodiak didn't come. In yours, he will. He's heard everything you just heard." An unfamiliar voice cuts into the recording, speaking clipped sentences in Dimokratía. I've studied the language, but this goes by too fast for me to follow. My own voice returns. "Now Kodiak's heard some personal secrets from his old self, just some information to make sure he knows what I'm saying is true. By the way, he doesn't know it yet, but he likes the manicotti the most, though less than he claims he does. I suggest you hide what you know from OS as long as possible. It needs you alive to get the ship to its destination, but it doesn't need you alive forever, and knowing what you now know could shorten your usefulness to the ship. When you communicate with Kodiak tonight, write on an unnetworked device under a blanket, so OS can't read what you're writing, and pass it back and forth.

"Judging by the length of time between me and the previous clones, it's probably been thousands of years since I died. This message is both from yourself and from a long-lost ancestor. Many copies of you have probably listened to it. You know what helped me most to deal with this news? Remembering all those fantasies we—Ambrose—had as a child. Like we imagined everyone else was robots, and we were the only real human. Or that what we perceived as motion might actually be teleporting between the different unmoving versions of Earth within the multiverses. Or that our solar system might be an atom in a much larger solar system. Crazy as it is, the truth of your existence is something our imagination has been preparing us for. I'm sending you love (self-love? Nice . . .) from the year 9081. Now, go meet Kodiak. He'd much prefer to spend his time alone, working for the good of his idealized version of Dimokratía, so he's probably not going to take the news that he's been manipulated as well as you do. Goodbye, Ambrose. I'm sorry to have to break all this to you. But I'm glad to be the one who did."

The audio finishes. The andro Dimokratía soldier is dozing by the stream, lying out on moss in wet underwear, hair slicked back from their face, catching cold rays of sun.

"Spacefarer Cusk," my mom's voice says, "are you okay?"

I nod, my vision blurring as I watch but don't see the reel.

"It seems like something has bothered you. Your heart rate is elevated, and you are perspiring."

I summon my meager acting skills. "It's just a little unnerving to finally be up here. Rescuing my sister. I'm worried about her."

A micropause. "Of course. That is very understandable."

I don't go to the dining room. I don't go to the orange portal. I go to the big window of 06.

The big . . . screen?

Even though it might make OS think I'm bonkers, I tap my fingers on the stars. How can I know that what I'm seeing is real?

I shiver.

I close my eyes and concentrate on my breathing. In and out. This breathing is real.

I open my eyes. It's time to meet Kodiak. He'll be real, too.

-* Tasks Remaining: 1872 *-

The portal opens right on time.

Sweet lords is the first thing I think on seeing Kodiak up close.

Not my type, but as a purely aesthetic object, he's marvelous.

His thick brows knit as he scowls, shoulders bulging his jumpsuit where his body tenses. He clenches finger after finger under his thumb, knuckles popping.

"Did you hear what I heard?" I ask.

He nods. The rest of his body is motionless, like it's been sculpted from something too heavy to lift.

"What do you make of it?" I ask.

He shrugs, looking down at the ground, looping surprisingly elegant fingers around one wrist and tugging. Then he catches himself and forces his hands to drop at his sides. "I do believe it," he says gruffly. "Which means we have a lot to talk about."

-* Tasks Remaining: 1872 *-

I take him to 04, pop two meals into the heater, then fetch blankets from my sleeping area.

I return just as the first meal dings, toss it between my bare hands until it's cool enough to pass to Kodiak.

"What is this?" he asks.

"What do you think it is?"

He reads the package. "Manicotti. I've never tried it, but

apparently I like it very much."

I laugh, then I see the dark curtain that's dropped over his face. I place a hand on his shoulder. "We're going to figure out what all of this means."

He shrugs his shoulder so my hand falls away. OS speaks at the very same time. "Is there something I can help you two with?"

"No," I say as I pile the blankets on the table. I turn to Kodiak. "Eat your manicotti, and then I'll explain."

Kodiak looks down at the pouch, his lips tight, then shakes his head. "I'll eat it later."

I shake out the blanket and loft it so it drapes over our heads. I light up my tablet and start typing.

Maybe you heard. This is the only way we can communicate without OS knowing. Cameras and mics everywhere. It can hear everything.

He nods in the space under the blanket. The fluorescent lights pass through the thin weave, lighting up his silhouette. He takes the tablet from my hands and types, his shoulder pressing and flexing against mine. I study the strong line of his nose.

I want to investigate beyond the yellow portal to confirm there actually are clones.

I take the tablet back. OK. Assuming there ARE clones, what then?

He pauses over the tablet, fingers hovering. He has no

answer. Of course not. What answer could there be? Then he's typing. I want to know what our supposed true purpose is.

Yes! Something about the way he's said "supposed" makes me pause, but I let it go for now. This is exactly the course I was hoping Kodiak would settle on. Any thoughts on how we do it?

OS obviously thinks it's navigating us somewhere. If we knew our heading, that would help. But we have to use that information without clueing the OS in that that's what we're doing.

Agreed, I answer. OS is probably on high alert right now. I say let's give it a few weeks to calm down, then start figuring out what this journey is for. I sigh and sit back, pulling the blanket away.

Kodiak blinks at the sudden light. It's sort of adorable. I can get why an earlier me fell for him. Multiple earlier me's fell for him. Will I, too?

Kodiak clenches his fists, then unclenches them. Clenches and unclenches. I don't know what feelings he's fighting, but I have my suspicions. Heat rises in my cheeks.

"I think I know what you were just thinking about," he grumbles.

"It's weird, right?" I ask him. "We've gotten together before." There's no mistaking it—I'm totally aroused.

"More than weird," he says. "You're not, I'm not . . . I

wouldn't have thought I'd have ever . . ."

Now my face flushes for more reasons. "Wow. Thanks."

He shrugs. "In training I had the same urges that most young men do. Of course I would act on them sometimes. But it was just ryad. You know, friends joining together for a short time."

I'm going to fall in love with this piece of ancient history? Really? I start speaking and stop myself. My face is radiating waves of heat. I occupy myself with folding the blanket, shaking out every wrinkle as I do.

I take a Minerva stance in my mind. *You are the noble Ambrose Cusk. Desired by millions. Sired by Alexander the Great. The unavailable one.*

His fists clench and unclench, clench and unclench.

I realize I've tensed all my muscles as I fold the blanket. "Do you need to be alone?"

He shakes his head sharply, lets his chin sink to his chest.

"Look, I know how overwhelming this is—" I begin to say.

"I'm told I'm a very good kisser," he interrupts.

That stops me. I watch, openmouthed, as a grim smile spreads across his face. "Oh, come *on*," I say, giving his shoulder a good shove. He tumbles over. "I find it hard to believe that there's anyone in Dimokratía who's a good kisser. It's just not part of your worldview. You're all probably just a bunch of tongue wrestlers."

He rolls out flat, folding his arms over his chest. "This is a strange situation we find ourselves in, isn't it?"

"Yes," I say. "It certainly is. Now eat your manicotti. I've heard you like it."

-* Tasks Remaining: 1801 *-

I'm able to go about most of my day like there was no transmission from an ancient Ambrose. Kodiak and I repair the ship's past damages, we prep for asteroid harvesting, we feed our organismal selves, knowing that those same selves might soon be silenced by the ship that hosts us. I make up an insane little song that starts *I'm just a little bacterium / living in a gut.*

As that "normal" life moves forward, so does another one, in parallel. One where I press my face right up against the ship's windows, where I sift through OS's code for suspicious lines, where I examine suits and blankets for old hair, skin, blood. Where I peek under the ship's skin, waiting for it to hemorrhage out the truth.

I come up with theories for where we're heading. Another galaxy. Into a black hole. Out of a black hole. To Minerva, after all. Back to Earth, where she'll be waiting for me. *It's Friday night. Of course your Minnie's here waiting for you.*

Whenever I take one of my half-dozen daily walks through the *Aurora*, I find Kodiak investigating. He'll be removing a wall panel to see what's beneath, or picking at the film that coats the inside of the windows (or are they screens?). Rover is almost always in the same room, watching.

Whenever I see Rover, I get the urge to punt its little whirring half-basketball body. *If we prove the reels from our former selves were true, we're disabling you first. And I'll be the one to execute the code.*

One morning, I find Kodiak in the blind room. He's got the blanket near, and the offline tablet. I raise an eyebrow, and he nods, patting the ground next to him. I sit beside him, thigh against thigh. He tents the blanket over us, then kneads my upper arm. It's in a sports massage-y kind of way, but after what he said about the other guys during training, it gets my mind wandering to our future, when my hand could reach under the waistband, to smooth skin and more—

Are you ready? Kodiak types.

You could say that. I type, Yes. He waits for me to keep going. I write, I thought you had something to say.

He pauses. I didn't come up with any solutions.

I try and fail to keep a smile off my lips. Hope of all Dimokratía, huh?

No wisecracks, Cusk.

Lucky for you, I was the top student in my analytic geometry class.

He rolls his eyes at that one. Deservedly. I continue. Our best chance of figuring out where we're headed is to find out where we are relative to Earth. Then we can continue that ray out into the universe, and see what it hits.

Well, yes. But how do we figure that out?

The radio!

Kodiak taps his lips. How far from Earth I get. The signals we're receiving through the radio transmitter mention dates. By comparing those with the ship date, we can estimate how far they've traveled at the speed of light, and therefore how far we've been journeying. But that's just distance, not direction.

I seize the tablet from him. Yes! We need to know our distance from two other points to get our precise location. Intersection of three spheres. And what gets us precise locations?

Pulsars. I snap my fingers, grinning. He continues writing. Their pulses are regular, but the highest frequencies of the wave move slightly faster, and the difference in the highest and lowest frequencies can be calculated, which should allow us to find out our distance from the pulsar!

I take over. The frequency of the pulse will let me look up which pulsar it is, and we can find its original location.

Can you find us two pulsars in all that radio noise?

I'll try to get us some neutron stars. And this is genius. Kodiak rests the tablet in his lap and pinches my chin between his fingers, gives it a good wag while he stares into my eyes. It seems he's started to absorb the fact that his previous self was my lover.

I take the tablet and type, mainly to hide the rise in my pants. Let's get started.

He stands, his own bulge giving him away. "Such minute calculations," he murmurs, heading to his console and placing the headphones over his ears. "The number of significant figures this will require . . ." His voice trails off as he gets distracted.

I'm a little distracted, too. But we have more important things to do than hook up. For now.

So I won't tip OS off to what I'm doing, I start scrolling through the offline tablet, looking at old-school star charts. They're images of pages from actual books, so it takes forever to find anything. Searching through all the tables does help with the erection problem, though.

Time wheels away from me. Kodiak is as motionless as anything else in the room, his face a mask of concentration. Then he leaps to his feet. The headphones whip off his head, and he dashes to catch them before they hit the floor. He beckons me over, his face bright with joy, and tosses me my own set.

I lean into him as I listen. There's the pulse of his blood against my shoulder, and then the headphones are on my ears and I hear the radio pulse of a star instead, beating at us from far off in space. It's eerie and very regular. "So beautiful," I whisper.

I watch him listen, his eyes closed, tears wetting his long lashes. Then I break out of the reverie and switch my connection to the computer's, so it can time the pulses. Once I get the readout, I return to the offline books. "It's PSR B1257 plus 12!" I say. "Commonly known as 'lich,' after the undead lord. Astronomers are such nerds."

Kodiak slowly opens his eyes and returns his hand to the dial. "One more pulsar to go."

I return the headphones to my ears and listen to the noise of space flying by. Huge blank spaces, hot noise and white noise, all from giant bodies beaming out across time and distance, lonely radio waves that chanced into our ship during their journey across the universe.

Kodiak raises a finger to draw my attention. I can make it out, too. This pulsar fires radio bursts every four or five seconds. It's a more melancholy pace, almost a complaint.

I watch the numbers fill the screen, figures flooding as the computer refines the period of the pulse. "Four-point-eight-two seconds," I say, scanning through the table in the tablet. "It's another famously strong signal pulsar, Centaurus X-3. Makes sense that those are the ones we'd detect first. We'll let it go a few minutes, so the computer has more data points about the frequencies, then we'll set it to calculate our coordinates."

Kodiak starts to say something, but then stops himself. He just nods.

"What?" I ask.

He shakes his head.

"Something's on your mind. What is it?"

He shrugs. "I guess I'm just not sure that I want to know whatever we're going to find out. I mean, I do, of course I do. But also I don't."

I laugh, then regret it. I guess I'm surprised at the vulnerability he's showing and don't know what to do with it, don't know when it's going to be withdrawn. "Well, it's a little late now."

He nods his head severely, staring into the screen, as if adding his computing power to the processor's.

Crisis might have brought us close, but all the same I really don't know this boy I'm living with.

A box blinks on the screen. The calculations are finished.

"Do you want to reveal the answer, or should I?" I ask.

He flicks the screen. Two points resolve. One is Earth, and the other is us. I change the frame, zooming farther and farther out, so it will start to make sense. Only it doesn't make sense—we're near the end of a jumble of stars in a broad swirl. "That's—"

"The Milky Way," Kodiak says flatly.

"And we're . . ."

"Heading to the sparse edge of it."

He doesn't speak for a moment, and I look at his face. It's grim, his skin almost gray. "We're in a vast empty stretch of dead sea. There's nothing around for light-years and light-years."

We were alone before. But now we know that we're truly, truly alone.

Even if we could go the speed of light—which we can't, not by a long stretch—we'd never make it anywhere at all in our lifetimes.

Kodiak's leg is shaking. Otherwise he's not moving at all. I search his face, my own mind reeling.

"I did everything I was supposed to," he murmurs.

"What does that mean?" I ask.

His words become barely audible as he sinks to his knees and stares at the floor. "Whatever they asked, I always said yes. I made myself the instrument they wanted me to be."

"Yeah," I manage to say. "Me too."

"I destroyed the dreams of Li Qiang so that I could become the hope of Dimokratía. I've devoted my life to . . . what? To be cast off in, in *this*." He gestures out toward the window, which, it's increasingly clear to me, isn't showing us anything real.

"Li Qiang. Is that the one you broke your arm fighting in the pool bash?" My recorded self told me about him.

He nods, hands over his eyes.

I place my palm on top of his head, which feels awkward, so I kneel in front of him, my ass on my heels. So we're mirror images.

He clears his tears with the back of his forearm, lets out a shuddering breath. "I'm fine. It's just that I made a promise to my country, a major promise, devoted my life to it. It felt like a contract."

"Yeah," I say, pushing one lock of his blue-black hair away from his face. "It was. And they broke it." Just like my family had done with me.

His chest heaves. "I don't know what to do without that contract."

"You get to decide what you become."

He shakes his head derisively, then his expression softens. "I guess."

"I'm glad we're here together for this," I say.

Kodiak looks at me. "I don't know how you can find anything positive about our situation, but I believe that you mean that."

I take his hands in mine, hold them in my lap.

He closes his eyes, and when he opens them there's a sudden gleam in them. He snatches his hands away from mine, snaps his fingers, and points to the blanket. Startled,

I throw it over the tops of our heads.

Kodiak writes on the tablet, and then passes it to me. I got it. This is a test!

A test? What kind of test?

In training we had many unannounced drills. Woken up in the dark / transported blindfolded / had to nav our way back from deep wilderness. This could be like that. The launch that we assumed was happening never happened. We don't remember it. Then they put us in a mock ship and feed us some lie about "clones" to judge how we react.

He passes the tablet back to me. I scan his expression for any sign of doubt. It's all a little too conspiracy theorist for me to even consider. Then again, so is the supposed truth of our situation.

I know in my heart that he's wrong. That he's going through denial, a textbook reaction to shock. I want him to get back to his tears, so we can mourn our situation together. But I don't know how to write those feelings in a tablet under a blanket. Instead I type, The Minerva distress call?

A manipulation. Maybe she's fine, or maybe she's dead. It's all part of trying to see how we might break down under mid-voyage stresses. As research for future expeditions.

Did he really just call my sister's fate a manipulation? I

look at him. His eyes are hollow in the filtered light. He's retreated to some desolate place that I can't reach. He's too lost in his own suffering to realize how reckless those words are to say to me.

Could be true. I don't feel like I can say anything for sure anymore.

He shifts under the blanket, so his face is out of view. I lift the fabric with one hand so I can see his expression again. He writes: Don't confess that in front of OS. Then you'll have failed the test. You won't be sent on the eventual mission.

Watching his face, I gingerly take the tablet back. I don't think Fédération works the same way as Dimokratía. My mission control wouldn't do this to me. My mother wouldn't do this to me.

His tongue makes a click, which I know is a mocking sound in Dimokratía. Such an enlightened country, I forgot.

Besides, we're obviously in space.

How do you know?

Is he serious right now? The stars. The view of the other part of the ship. The hum of the floor under us. The fact that we're not getting any signals from the outside unless the antennae is on the exterior of the ship.

All of that can be faked. The "old" you said those stars ARE fake, remember?

I roll my eyes, suddenly grateful that this hulk isn't looking closely enough at me to notice. Yeah, and we might also be brains in a vat somewhere, and our whole lives have been simulations while machines milk us for our organic materials. Or we're prisoners living their existences chained up in a cave, mistaking the shadows on the wall for the world itself.

I laugh, but when he doesn't, I stop.

What if he's right? What if we're in a bunker and not a spaceship, and this *is* some kind of test? There's no way to know for sure. Well, I can think of *one* way. We could open a door—but that would involve depressurizing the whole ship. If my hunch is wrong, then we're dead. Something strikes me. I tug the tablet from his fingers and start typing. There's no gravity at the center of the ship.

Zero gravity can be produced artificially. We've both been in those simulators during training.

You're really convinced, aren't you?

Come on. Isn't it far more likely that we're in some psychological simulation than that we're ancient clones woken up in the middle of a voyage across the galaxy???

A fair point, I guess. I don't actually agree. I think he's desperate for a way to hold on to everything that he thought he knew. I'm feeling the very same way. I'm just also a little more realistic about my own psychological pitfalls.

So how are we going to test this theory? he writes.

We're not going to do anything right now. There's no rush. Let's take a few hours doing our normal tasks to throw the OS off a bit, in case it's on alert. Then we'll talk more after dinner.

He looks at me for a long moment. He's searching my face for a feeling, for information, for I don't know what. I don't think he found it. When he finally nods and stands, there's a forced calm on his face.

-* Tasks Remaining: 1799 *-

He doesn't come to dinner.

I go and look for him. As I enter the *Aurora*, I don't hear any sounds of tinkering. Instead I hear something far more ominous: silence.

I pad through the ship and find Kodiak at the very end, by his airlock. He's got one of the spacewalk helmets in hand, is grinding away at the inside with what appears to be a screwdriver. "Kodiak," I ask slowly, "what are you doing?"

"Figuring out . . . what's on the other side of this screen," he says as he strains. A fragment of polycarbonate pops to the ground.

"Stop! Stop. Isn't that going to destroy it?" I ask, as horrified as if it were one of his fingernails that popped off.

Kodiak hurls the helmet down. It rolls into a corner, shards of high-tech carbonite tinkling from it. "We *need* those helmets," I say.

"To rescue Minerva?" he says in a mockingly squeaky voice. He shrugs, taking another suit down from the wall, peering into another helmet, screwdriver in hand. "We don't *need* these helmets if this is all some simulation."

I speak at full voice, OS be damned. "Whatever this is, it's not a *simulation*, Kodiak. Even if we're copies of ourselves, even if you and I are doomed, at least in this version, we'll need those helmets."

"Pathetic," Kodiak says. "Even after the system has fucked you over, you're holding on to whatever shreds of lies that it's left you with. We have to *break* this manipulation, not *bow* to it."

"Break it? What does *that* mean?"

Kodiak gashes a long line down the front of the helmet. The sharp squeal of the fracturing polycarb makes me cringe.

My skin goes rubbery. "And you'll kill us in the process?"

"No. I'll prove to our testers that we're onto them. That we won't give up control of our destiny. That's how we'll pass this exam. Then they'll have to let us out."

I watch helplessly as he gashes away at the second helmet.

Our only tool to survive if we—or a version of us—get off the ship. The darkness outside hums its outrage. "You don't know any of that for sure. For both of our sakes, I need you to stop what you're doing."

Scrape. Scrape. Scrape.

He puts his whole weight into it, and I'm reminded how his body has been honed as a weapon.

"Kodiak," I say, tears clogging my voice, "I'm serious. Stop."

When he doesn't even acknowledge what I said, hot rage splashes through my cold fear. The back of my neck sparks, sweat dots my brow. I step forward.

He looks up from his work, face gone gray. Then he returns to his labor.

I take another step.

"Stop right there," he says, again without looking at me.

I take another step.

I kneel beside him.

I lay my fingers over his, over the handle of the screwdriver.

His other hand lashes out, too fast to counter, striking me flat across the temple. I go sliding along the floor.

I'm up and cursing, hurling myself at Kodiak. I launch onto his back, pummeling his thick neck, biting into his salty skin. He shrugs, and that movement of the powerful planes of his back is enough to send me crashing against the wall. I'm right back on him, and this time I have the presence of mind to snatch the screwdriver before he hurls me off.

When I land, I spring to my feet and see him charging toward me, fists outstretched. I duck into the next room, press myself against the far wall.

Kodiak is soon beside me, his hands grasping for the screwdriver. It's instantly gone; I don't have the strength to resist him.

I lurch after him, hoping to stop him from destroying everything, but when he hears my footsteps he whirls, screwdriver over his head, ready to stab like a dagger.

From his expression, I have no doubt he'll use it. I've never seen such desperate sadness. I imagine bleeding out all over the white polycarbonate floor, Kodiak standing over me with the bloody screwdriver, Rover hovering nearby, trying in vain to cauterize my wounds.

I retreat toward the *Endeavor*. Better the loss of a few helmets than the loss of my life.

I think.

Kodiak is unmoving as I shut the door. The last sight I have of him is the maniacal look in his eyes, staring at me and yet somehow unseeing, chest heaving as he prepares to attack. I might as well have been some faceless enemy soldier, judging from the level of disregard I saw in his eyes.

What has gone so terribly wrong?

I drop into a defensive crouch, ready for him to open the portal and stalk after me. But it doesn't open. Instead I can hear, faintly, the sounds of the screwdriver gnashing against the hard synthetics of the helmet.

Once he's done with the helmets, what will he destroy next?

"Spacefarer Cusk, it is urgent that I speak with you," OS says.

I'm surprised by how much relief I feel at the sound of my mother's voice. "Yes! Please help me," I say, voice cracking.

"From his brain waves, Spacefarer Celius appears to have had a psychotic break. This makes me want to ask how *you* are feeling."

"I'm fine. I mean, I'm not having a break, too. I want him to stop, OS. How do we make him stop?"

"Do not worry. I have protocols for most health crises, including mental health. I have determined that further human interaction will not help Kodiak in his current state. Our only recourse is to incapacitate. Rover is on his way to do so now."

I still hear the awful screech of the polycarbonate fragmenting under the stabs of the screwdriver. Rover must not have arrived yet.

"Don't hurt him too badly," I cry.

"I need to do whatever it takes to prevent him from compromising the ship's mission. The voltage will have to be significant."

From the other side of the door, the scratching pauses. The walls are too thick for me to hear Rover's ticking, but I can imagine the robot edging into the room.

I hear something like a chair being hurled against the floor, then OS's voice, muffled in Kodiak's chamber.

A scream. It's shatteringly loud, even muffled by the wall, but it's almost stripped of feeling, like it's caused not by human will but by the physical process of air expelling from compressed lungs. Then the room is silent.

"The threat is neutralized," OS announces.

-* Tasks Remaining: 1799 *-

Those words continue to play in my mind as I numbly wander the *Endeavor*. Threat. Neutralized.

I sit but can't stay down, am immediately back on my feet. There's just too much worry coursing through my body for me to find any stillness.

I want to go to Kodiak, to find out if he's okay after Rover attacked him. But then I remember that image of him with the screwdriver over his head, ready to stab me.

OS is right. Better I don't stoke Kodiak back into a rage. If Rover has blocked him from damaging the ship for now, I should give him space to get calm.

To give my racing mind somewhere to be, I do a couple of tasks that OS had on its list, recalibrating sensors that had been giving faulty readings.

While I work, my mind spins back to Fédération and Dimokratía, our countries at war. They'd only come together for the Cusk projects—sending Minerva to Titan, and then sending us to rescue her. Because in each case it was something to hope for, something to long for. A way out of war.

That was the balm: hope. And that was what was taken away by the reveal of the true purpose of our mission. Can I give Kodiak some new source of hope?

We do know our distance and heading now. We never got to finish that project together, finding out the *Coordinated Endeavor*'s destination. Maybe the answer will be enough to pop Kodiak out of his delusion—if it is a delusion. I scan through the offline tablet, to see what I can suss out. The ray from Earth to the *Coordinated Endeavor* extends out into broad emptiness. I follow it, follow it, beyond and between the stars at the sparse edge of the Milky Way, until one comes close, or really it's two, a binary solar system, and here's a little planet between them—our course intersects its orbit perfectly. It's the only celestial body the ship hits before leaving the galaxy entirely.

I look the planet up in the tablet. Spectroscopy reveals its atmosphere to be 20 percent oxygen, less than 1 percent carbon dioxide. Its nearness to the two stars should give it an earthlike temperature.

It's an exoplanet. An inhabitable exoplanet.

We're heading to a new home.

-* Tasks Remaining: 1797 *-

I dash into the *Aurora*, only slowing as I approach the room where I last saw Kodiak. My eyes take in the legs of a knocked-over chair, a screwdriver rolled into a corner, shards of poly reflecting fluorescent light back at the ceiling. An unconscious body in the center, breathing deeply.

Kodiak is sprawled facedown on the floor, arms and legs akimbo, like he plummeted from a great height. He's peed in his suit; yellow pools on the white floor. There's a bitter odor to the air, like someone's burned a skillet of eggs.

Rover is parked beside him. "OS, may I approach?" I call out.

"Of course," my mother's voice responds.

I warily circle Rover. I take Kodiak's pulse at his wrist.

His eyes dart beneath his lids as his breathing deepens. If it weren't for the pair of livid welts on his arm where Rover's electrodes must have contacted him, it would look like Kodiak was having an amazing sleep.

I fetch a blanket and pillows. After a quick debate, I change him out of his urine-soaked suit and wrap his naked body in the blanket, terrified he'll wake up halfway through the process. I place the soiled suit in the *Aurora*'s cleaner. Kodiak never needs to know he peed in it, if he's still asleep once the suit's clean. I can just put it right back on him.

"How long do you think he's going to be out?" I ask OS.

"It is difficult to predict the length of time that human bodies are incapacitated by electrical shocks."

"Then maybe you shouldn't shock them," I respond tartly.

"You know precisely why I did what I did," my mother's voice says. "As long as Spacefarer Celius doesn't try to compromise the ship again, I'll have no need to take such extreme measures."

I suddenly feel very tired.

Kodiak groans, turning his head. I take it into my lap, stroke his surprisingly soft hair. Rover hovers nearby, making menacing little zaps with its electrodes. "Back the fuck off," I tell it. Of course, it doesn't move.

"May I give you some advice on how best to pacify Spacefarer Celius once he wakes up?" OS asks.

"No."

"At least consider—"

"No, OS! Be silent for half an hour."

Above the hum of the ship I can hear Kodiak's breathing, can almost sense the blood sloshing through his veins, and through my own. I can hear my own breathing. As I concentrate on the sound of it, I become separate from it. Separate from myself. It feels strangely honest.

I leave time. My legs hurt for a while, and then they stop. Even the pain travels to the middle distance.

Home. We're traveling to a new home.

I return to myself when the head in my lap takes in a deep breath. The eyes flutter open. I'm arrested by the sudden sight of them, by their tan depths. "Shh," I tell Kodiak.

His eyes focus in on me and he startles, body going rigid. He smashes his elbows into the floor so he can sit straight up, eyes gleaming. The blanket falls from his torso, draping over his lap, like he's a sculptor's model.

"Hey," I say gently. "It's okay. You've been unconscious. You're fine. Don't panic."

His eyes scan around, and he makes quick and shallow breaths as he looks for enemies. Rover is still here, but inactive, its arms motionless on the floor. The sight of Rover standing down doesn't calm Kodiak. His enemies aren't outside him. They've never been outside him.

His eyes finally lock with mine, and something passes

between us. I don't know what he's getting from seeing my face, but it does seem to be the thing that finally calms his panic. "Try not to think about anything for a while," I whisper.

Not the best advice, I guess. His breathing goes quick again. He brings his hand to the welts on his side, where Rover shocked him.

Kodiak gets to his feet, knotting the blanket around his waist just before it falls away. I look up at him, my own breathing quickening. I ease to my feet, hands open. "It's okay," I whisper.

He sways from side to side. Just like Rover.

Kodiak picks up the screwdriver, looks at it, then releases his grip. It clatters to the floor.

I place my hand on his shoulder and nod. "Why don't you take a rest? Just rest. There's no rush for anything. Besides, I have something to tell you. Something you'll like to hear."

Kodiak allows me to guide him toward my sleeping room. I can't think of anything else to do with him; getting Kodiak to bed seems like the best cure for his strange glassiness. Maybe when he wakes up, this dark desperation will be gone.

He accepts my bed, snaking his arms under my pillow and shutting his eyes. His face softens.

"Are you ready to hear it?" I ask.

But he's asleep.

"OS," I say, "lights out." OS makes it happen.

I pad my way to 06, with the largest window—screen?—that shows me the image of outer space that I think I recognize. I name familiar constellations, same as I might see on Earth. Why shouldn't this be the honest view? If it would mean I could live my life in peace, why can't I just choose to believe what I see and what I've been told and be done with it? I'm rescuing Minerva. Done. My life can have a purpose that makes sense to me. Done. I'm not building to some abstract better future that I'll never get to enjoy. Done.

I don't need Kodiak's sort of clarity, not when seeing clearly also means dying.

I don't know if believing in a planet for our future selves will be enough to convince Kodiak to accept the ruse we're living in—if that's what it is. Maybe the model of my own calm presence, of my own acceptance, will eventually be enough. As Minerva said in her departure speech, broadcast live to both Fédération and Dimokratía: *We are meant to be extraordinary. Take hope from our example.*

I tent a hand against the stars on the screen, five pads touching five points of light that have traveled eons from their various different histories to strike this window at this precise instant. Five moments in time, five places. I know that this is true, even as I know that it is untrue, that I'm touching pixels OS has placed. Maybe my heart can be a more insightful organ than my brain.

Your heart is only good for pumping your blood, says my brain. *I am the source of both what you feel and what you think.*

Insanity used to be a stranger that lived on the other side of the world. Now it's moved next door. It's only a matter of time until it becomes shipmate, lover, self.

I trance, my focus skipping far off into the cosmos. Maybe I'll never eat or drink again. Maybe I will be forever disembodied.

Maybe I'm fooling myself.

I stop wallowing and open up the audio file on the pinup video of the Dimokratía soldier, the one that alerted me to my supposed reality. I add a new chapter to the recording, so the next me will know more about himself—and about Kodiak. I decide that I'll do this every day, so our lives can build even as they restart, so that each version of us will have a better chance at happiness than the one before.

There's a rustling sound from my sleeping quarters. I imagine Kodiak rousing, finding himself in my bed, testing his painful welts where he was electrocuted. Getting to his feet. Foraging himself something to eat and something to drink.

I hear the orange portal open. I ready myself for the sound of it shutting, but it doesn't. As a safety precaution, we've been keeping the passageway between the two ships closed. Has Kodiak been absentminded, or has he left it open because he wants me to follow?

Maybe he's disoriented. Maybe he's confused and scared. I pad quietly toward the *Aurora*, instinct keeping my steps as quiet as possible.

He's ahead of me in the zero g, flying forward, still wrapped in my sheet. It billows around him, making him look like a phantasm. I speed up, soaring after him.

I lose track of him once he heads into the *Aurora*. I creep through the blind room. He's not in his eating and sleeping rooms, either. Only a few rooms left where he could be.

I hear whistling from the airlock.

"Kodiak?"

The song is tuneful and melancholy, some Dimokratía folk ballad that I've never heard before. I tiptoe forward.

"Kodiak?"

He's before the small round window, looking out at the stars, or the images of stars, or maybe the darkness between the images of stars. When he hears me enter, he turns to look at me, then returns to staring into the porthole. "Kodiak? You okay?"

He opens his stance toward me. That's when I see there's a wrench in his hand.

I'm about to ask him to put it down when he rears back

and strikes the porthole.

I scream despite myself, despite knowing that there's no way that the ship's pane would break under a simple wrench. But the horror of it, the horror of imagining cracks appearing, followed by explosive decompression, my pulverized body dying four ways at once . . . macerated, frozen, asphyxiated, boiled.

Kodiak strikes again. I hear a ticking sound from the next room over as Rover speeds toward us.

Stop it! I cry, or think I cry. *We're heading to a home, a home just for us!* I'm staggering across the space between us, reaching for the wrench. He brandishes it at me, then swings it toward the clear pane, only I've put myself between the wrench and the airlock door, the wrench is full in my view, my nose fills with the smell of metal, and then the metallic smell is my own blood, and I'm howling against the floor, watching my blood pool against the white floor, rivulets of red running through the grooves between the panels.

I get to my feet and manage it for a moment before I'm back on hands and knees, the world blinking and bright and then narrowing and dark. I scream, as if screaming will help me stay conscious.

One eye is blinded by blood, but through the other I see Rover whiz toward Kodiak, only to be knocked off its tracks by him. He's swung the wrench at it two-handed, like a baseball bat. Rover grinds and sighs uselessly in the corner of the room.

Kodiak shouts something that's both far away and close, something I can't understand. It resolves into words, sob-choked words. "I'm sorry! I'm sorry!"

He's moving away from me, backing to the edge of the room. Not to the rest of the ship. To the porthole. To the airlock. My view of it wavers.

"Stop," I manage to gasp, my lips slick with the blood running down my face. "We're going . . . we're going . . ."

"I'll come back with a doctor!" Kodiak says.

"No. You're wrong," I say, blinking heavily against the lightness, the strangely heavy lightness, tugging me down. So curiously heavy, this empty. "Kodiak, you're *wrong*!"

Kodiak's against the airlock, turning the handle. OS speaks, but I can't make out its words in the roaring bright. The handle turns and turns forever under Kodiak's sure hands.

"We're going to pass this test," Kodiak says.

"Stop," I gasp.

But he doesn't stop.

Kodiak looks back to me. "Sunlight, Ambrose! Think of all the sunlight!"

The airlock door shudders as he gives it a final turn.

Kodiak throws his arm over his eyes, as if to protect his vision from the brightness to come.

The airlock opens, and the universe roars. The thunder on the other side is not full of light. It is only dark, and so cold.

PART FOUR

AMBROSE: 9 REMAINING.

KODIAK: 9 REMAINING.

"191 DAYS UNTIL TITAN."

An earlier Ambrose embedded a reel for me. I wait days to play it, scared of what I'll find.

One sleepless night, I start it going.

"I have reason to believe that I'm going to die," my own recorded voice tells me. It's breathless and manic. Paranoid. "OS has no use for us anymore, not now that we're refusing to repair the ship. We've jammed the airlocks, but that won't be enough. I'm embedding surveillance of myself, so you'll know my story. Every twenty-four hours that I survive, I'll restart the recording."

I shiver when I realize what that means. I'm about to watch myself die.

I lean forward.

It's me. I'm sleeping, in the very same bunk I use now, my back to the room. No one else is there, and nothing is happening.

The timestamp in the corner jumbles as I speed the reel ahead.

I slow it again. Rover has inched in along the ceiling, its robot arms dangling. There's something pointed in each grip, maybe a sliver of printed polycarb. I zoom in. "What are *those* for?" I whisper.

My breathing catches as I watch Rover stalk toward my sleeping body. Rover ticks closer and closer, coming to a stop near my head. It holds there, so motionless that I have to check the timestamp to make sure the reel is still playing.

Then it extends one shard and the next over my neck. Two efficient cutting motions, like it's slicing open a bag of rice.

Only it's my throat that's been slashed. The Ambrose in the reel staggers to his feet, hands over his neck. His mouth is open, and I imagine him screaming—or maybe gurgling, if Rover has cut through his windpipe. The blood has already soaked through the front of his jumpsuit, pooling on the white floor. Rover retreats from the room, and Ambrose staggers after it, only making it one step before he slumps to the floor. His forehead hits and then his knees. He remains at an unnatural angle, arms askew, as the blood continues to pool from his throat, before trickling to a stop.

I watch, mute and senseless, as Ambrose's throat and cheeks mottle, reds and purples blooming along his arms. My arms.

Rover returns and clamps its hands onto my body's ankles. As it tugs, my body splays to one side, one arm crossed over the other, straightening as Rover hauls me from the room. My arms go over my head, my fingertips the last things I see before the sleeping chamber is empty.

My pillow is crushed against the far wall. My blanket is on the floor, soaking up the pool of my blood until none of its light blue color remains, and it is only red. The time-stamp continues to tick forward. The fluorescent lights are constant.

Rover returns and starts to clean, has gone right back from warbot to janitor.

"If you're hearing this message, it's because I didn't survive to delete it after I woke up," my voice reports. "Learn this from me: if you're going to cross the operating system, you better be prepared for the consequences."

Already, the kernel of a thought is forming in the back of my mind. *Or I need to leave my future selves the weapons to fight back.*

PART FIVE

AMBROSE: 8 REMAINING.

KODIAK: 8 REMAINING.

"191 DAYS UNTIL TITAN."

My mother won't answer my knocks.

Her feet cast shadows in the sliver of light beneath her door.

My sister's voice, from down the hall. "Ambrose, come in here with me."

When I open my eyes, the world looks no different. I'm blind.

Ting-ting buzz.

I haven't been blind—I have been in the absolute dark.

-* Tasks Remaining: 4909 *-

The reel is still going. The soldier relaxes against a tree, the camera panning sensually over their body. But what my voice is saying has nothing to do with a vigorous forest outing.

What my voice is saying is definitely not sexy.

"I know you're telling yourself this is an elaborate voice-skin prank. But think of what I've done. I've known which exact video you'd go for first, because I did as well, and I have an identical neural structure to you, and lived in the same environment. You can't remember the launch, and that's for a good reason. Your memories were nanoteched during your medical exam at the Cusk Academy, before the clones were installed on the ship. In my lifetime I learned that the original you, the original me, never left Earth. He died there many thousands of years ago. Maybe in the arms of the original Mother. His remains, and those of the civilization that produced him, are a layer in the geological record of Earth, thin as a piece of notebook paper by now. As far as I know, you and Kodiak, and your remaining clones, are all that remain of humankind."

I pause the reel. My voice is correct about at least one thing. I am definitely feeling overwhelmed.

The paused slip of a soldier stares at me, their eyes hard and lucid. What do they know to be true?

Hand trembling, I start the reel again. My voiceover continues while the soldier bathes. "We both know," that me says, "about Plato and the cave."

He's right, of course. I remember that academy seminar when I learned that Plato had this allegory of the cave, where he imagined prisoners shackled so they could see only the shadows of puppets on the cave wall, and not the true world outside. How would they know that the shadows they were watching weren't the real thing? If one of the prisoners did escape and discovered the truth and then returned, why would anyone believe him? Maybe the other prisoners would be so threatened by his ravings that they'd kill him.

It wasn't my favorite class, to be honest.

I think I get the thrust of past-me's warning: I'm alone on a spaceship with someone who might not take the truth well. Maybe that person is me. Maybe it's Kodiak. Maybe it's our operating system, I don't know. Of course, I also don't know what the end of those astronauts' days looked like. I do know that it was on this ship.

If all of this is to be believed.

I rap my knuckles against the window. Or screen. How can I know what's on the other side? I'd never thought to ask. Apparently, it's a dangerous question.

"Come back to this recording once you've had time to think all this through," my voice finishes. "I've left some . . . helpful surprises on the ship for you. Some schematics that will be useful."

I let that one go for now. There's too much else to think about. "OS," I say, "how far are we from this exoplanet destination?"

"I do not understand what you mean," my mother's voice replies. "You are on your way to Titan to rescue Minerva Cusk."

"I don't believe you," I say, then cringe. Now OS knows where the information from my previous self was likely located. I'll need to find a new place to store it for the future me. If that's really a thing I'm going to be doing.

"Whatever you've decided to believe," OS responds, "I still need you to focus on the mission at hand. The *Coordinated Endeavor* has undergone numerous small damages over the course of its journey. I need you and Spacefarer Celius to repair them, to maintain the integrity of our vessel."

"OS," I say against the pit in my belly, "I'm inclined to believe that the only reason we have so many small damages is because you've been flying this ship without a human crew for thousands of years. There's no reason there would be so many tasks to complete that Rover couldn't handle. That simply shouldn't happen over the months it takes to get to Titan."

OS goes silent. I get to my feet. "I need to see Kodiak."

"You are not alone on this ship, you are correct. But Spacefarer Celius does not wish to see you."

"I know that's what you claim, OS," I say, dusting my palms. "But I have some things to say to him that he's definitely going to want to hear."

-* Tasks Remaining: 4909 *-

Kodiak and I stand before the wide screen of 06, look-ing out at the stars. They seem so real. But they can't be touched or smelled. Despite the evidence before our eyes, I'm increasingly coming to believe they are not real.

"This is not how I expected this journey to begin," Kodiak says gruffly.

"Believe me, I didn't, either," I say.

"I was all ready to lock myself away, to call you an enemy and be done with it so I could focus on my mission. But this evidence . . ." His voice trails off. I can feel him staring at me.

"Goodbye, Minerva," I whisper as I press my forehead against the screen.

-* Tasks Remaining: 4909 *-

We stand beside the *Endeavor*'s airlock. The suits are all gone, except for one. Its helmet is intact but has been rav-aged, a jagged scratch raked into the front of it. Kodiak holds it up to his face, examining the damage.

I watch him, wondering where this evidence will bring his mind.

Finally he speaks. "Sorry. I seem to have caused a mess

our last time around."

I reach out and grasp his hand. The hand of this stranger who will become anything but. He stiffens, then surprises me by clasping mine back fiercely. As if he's lost his balance on a cliff, trusting the nearest stranger to hold him back from a fall.

-* Tasks Remaining: 4909 *-

I invited Kodiak to come for breakfast. I hear the orange portal open before my morning alarm even goes off. I roll over in my bunk and ask OS to project the ship time. It's 4:25 a.m., back in Mari. Not that there probably even is a Mari anymore. When I tap on my light, I'm startled to see Kodiak at the doorway, staring down at me.

I flail to my feet. "What is it, what is it?"

His voice comes out muted. "I couldn't sleep. I was hoping—apparently you have a violin? Would you play it for me?"

"Yeah," I say, running my hand over my hair. "Sure. Let's go find where it is."

-* Tasks Remaining: 4909 *-

I'm not sure how long I play. OS cuts in between movements, asking us to work on smoothing the ship's exterior shielding, but Kodiak raises his finger to silence it before he goes back to his eyes-closed reverie, seated on the floor with his arms wrapped around his knees. "Could you start at the beginning of the quiet section?" he asks. "The one that goes *dun, dun doop?*"

I return to the start of the adagio, the polycarb bridge on my violin stopping the instrument from playing much louder than the hum of the ship. The softness of the music feels right. A smile spreads across Kodiak's features, and the furrows in his brow soften. I continue to play.

-* Tasks Remaining: 4799 *-

No task OS can come up with is pressing enough to get in the way of our music sessions. I scour the ship's partial internet image for sheet music, surprising Kodiak with a new recital each morning. Once I run out, I compose pieces of my own, space-inspired combinations of harmonics created by laying my pinkie lightly on the string to produce high-pitched frequencies. I don't think Kodiak enjoys them as much as the classics, but he puts on a good face.

Over the weeks, OS stops presenting us with tasks during the music hour. When I continue to push back against its tales of the Minerva rescue, it gives up on talking about Titan as well. Of course it does. Lying isn't working, so it's stopped.

After the daily music hour, we dutifully complete the tasks OS requests of us. Kodiak uses the one spacesuit remaining in the *Aurora* for the exterior jobs, while I work on the ship's insides. OS appears to accept this truce of sorts. All the same, I'm haunted by that image of Rover coming into my sleeping chamber, deftly slashing the throat of my previous self. I set up traps and alarms, so I'll wake if Rover is on its way in.

That's no way to live. I hate this aching awareness that we will die once our tasks are completed. But Kodiak and I might have come up with a plan for that.

-* Tasks Remaining: 3010 *-

I sit cross-legged before the large window of 06, staring into the expanse. We're out of tea—the previous Ambroses must have enjoyed it a little too much—but I can sip hot water, steeped in the flavors of polycarb. Yum. At least I don't have to worry about the slow-growing cancers from heated plastic. I'm sure I've got plenty of fast ones that will end things a lot sooner. So . . . hooray?

I hear the thump of Kodiak's heavier tread, then his body is pressed against the screen, shoulder pushing on the window as he peers out at the made-up stars.

"OS, revert screens to windows," I try, not for the first time.

OS doesn't respond. It doesn't respond to much these days; I guess it knows anything it reveals will only decrease its advantage.

"It's certainly impressive," Kodiak says, eyes up to the stars. "High resolution."

"That doesn't make it the truth," I say.

"No, unfortunately it doesn't," Kodiak says. He looks at me quietly.

"What?" I ask.

He shrugs, still looking at me. He returns to stroking the stars, leading with his middle finger, a Dimokratía mannerism.

"What are you thinking about?" I press.

"The last Dimokratía election."

"I see you're using 'election' loosely."

Surprisingly, Kodiak chuckles. "Yes, it was the fifth one in a row with the same outcome. There were many fiery speeches. The whole country dropped everything to consider whether we should return to a firm geographical border instead of the patchwork of economically tied regions Earth had become."

"Starting with the proposed swap of Patagonia and the Bangladesh fishery!" I finish. "I got assigned the 'economic boundaries' side of that one for a class debate."

"Yes. So you remember? This issue seemed like the very greatest concern any human had ever had to worry about. All of that, the politics, the wars, the works of literature—"

"—even the old kings, the earliest cavepeople!"

Irritation flashes on his face. "Would you let me finish?"

"Sorry, I was just getting excited. I come from an interrupting sort of family."

"They're all gone now. They didn't matter." He puts his fingertip over Earth as it travels across the screen, bright and blue and tiny, a jeweler's bead.

"From here, even our sun would be too small to represent using visible light," I say.

"Using the term 'here' loosely," he says, glowering.

"Yes, sure."

"I just wish President Gruy could have seen this, that we all could have. It makes it a little easier to keep perspective, to go . . . more softly with each other."

"Go more softly with each other, I like that way of putting it," I say.

"Thank you. I said it just for you."

I punch him. "That's funny. You're funny, Kodiak."

He shrugs and rubs his shoulder. Pretending I've wounded him. Even with a good windup, I'm not sure I could.

"I was going somewhere with this," he says. "I was thinking this morning that this aleyet we're looking at, I guess 'view' is the closest word in Fédération, if we truly groya it, I guess 'understand' is the closest to that—" He starts to chew his lip, clearly frustrated at Fédération vocabulary. It suddenly strikes me as unfair that we speak Fédération all the time. That's just the language the Cusk Corporation always uses. What other unfairnesses might I not have considered until now?

"We might not have any better words for it," I risk interrupting. "That would be very typical Fédération, not to have words for quiet things. Anyway, I'm familiar with 'aleyet' and 'groya.'"

His eyebrows knit. Now I've irritated him again. He's a minefield, my Kodiak.

He presses on. "This *understanding* of our *view* takes some of the sting out of our situation. Plenty of organisms live for a season, in order for those who come next to have a chance. Mayflies, daffodils, the octopus. We can accept that?"

"Well, we're hardwired not to accept our own demise. Daffodils are a lot more chill about it."

"Okay, but we can be like daffodils together."

I squeeze the back of his neck. "That's sweet."

"Don't tease me."

"I wasn't, actually. I adore daffodils." *Because they were Minerva's favorite*, I silently add, tapping the image of Earth on the "window."

His voice lowers. "I know what I did thousands of years ago. The offline pilot station and the course change. I don't think I'd do that sort of thing now."

"We don't know how many copies of us are left. The next of us could be the last for all we know."

"It can be whatever we need it to be."

Kodiak doesn't say any more. He draws his arm around me and pulls me close to his chest, crushing me against the heat of him. Then he shakes his head. I'm too far down his body to feel it directly but sense the shift in the muscles of his chest.

I'm used to him enough now that he doesn't need to speak, doesn't need to put clearer words to what he has in mind. I think I know what he's proposing from his heart rate, the altered life coursing through his veins, the words that he's said and the words that he's not allowing himself to say. There's a sort of magnitude humming off him.

I pull my head back from his chest, look up into his tan eyes. "I think I understand what you want us to do," I whisper.

"I think you do," he whispers back.

He turns his head so his eyes can look right into mine. The dappled light plays on his cheek, his throat, and then his chest as he unzips the top of his jumpsuit. It catches halfway down his torso, and I help him peel it down to the waist. Hesitantly at first, my hands play over his skin, learning the shape of the muscles beneath. "Oh. That's not what I thought you meant. I don't mind, though."

His fingers tug down the zipper of my jumpsuit, then they're on my body. They snake below the waistband before they pause. "I'm glad you're here with me," I say.

"Yes, me too," he says between kisses. His breath is hot against my cheek.

"Do you think we should take it slow?" I ask.

His hand travels deeper beneath my waistband, disappearing up to the wrist. "I don't feel a particular need to take it slow," he sighs as he watches my face.

"Good. Me neither."

-* Tasks Remaining: 3010 *-

After, he holds me tight against him, my backside slick against his belly. He nuzzles his lips close to my ear. "Was that your first time?"

I playfully slap him. "What, did it *seem* like my first time?"

"Well . . ."

"Actually," I say, "I guess it was my first time. Officially. But it wasn't Ambrose's."

He pulls me in closer. "We have lots of time to practice."

I think for a second. "Wait, did you mean my first time at all, or my first time welcoming?"

"Welcoming? What does that mean?"

"What we just did. You donated, and I welcomed."

Kodiak snorts, and makes a hand gesture I don't recognize, bent shaking fingers. "Oh, Fédération softy lingo."

I roll my eyes. "Do you still use hut and shihut, top and bottom?"

"Of course. It makes more sense."

"Unless the shihut is literally on top."

"So sensitive."

"It's a hierarchy, Kodiak. Top and bottom are not value-neutral terms. One implies more worth, which is all about homophobia. And homophobia is really all about misogyny, because in Dimokratía eyes to welcome is to be female, and to be female is to be lesser. Words matter."

"Okay, okay," Kodiak says. "In any case, thank you for 'welcoming' me."

I harrumph, then start running my hands over his chest, smoothing the hair down flat. "That *was* Ambrose's first time welcoming, by the way."

"You are usually hut?"

"Yep."

Kodiak chuckles. "It sounds like a riddle. Two tops are in space together . . ."

"I'm ready to be versatile," I say.

"Yes, and you were wonderful at it," Kodiak says. "I am ready as well," he continues after a moment. "In fact, I have already been so, during training."

I shake my head. "Unbelievable. Here I thought you'd be the one who needed to learn the ropes."

"There were many guys living together in close quarters, in the primes of their lives, all of them very fit, often very sweaty, so of course sometimes we were erotiyets . . . ," he says, voice trailing off.

"Okay, got it, thanks."

I can't help it; something about our whole interchange has gotten me giggly. Kodiak joins in, his body shaking against mine.

Once my breathing has returned, I sigh. "I'll look forward to these practice sessions."

"Me too," he whispers. "We can schedule them in. Five times a day. Maybe we'll go down to four times a day in a few years."

"Five times a day! That means we're almost due to—"

"Yep."

Something else comes to me. "You know, before we started this very enjoyable diversion, I thought there was something else you wanted us to do, something we had to keep secret."

"There was something," he whispers. "I thought *you* were the one pushing us to do this instead."

"That thing, that unspeakable thing," I whisper. "The ship, it won't be able to . . ."

"Shh," he says, laying a finger on my lips. I kiss it, staring up at him. He nods.

Tears fill my eyes. I place the gauzy blanket over us and type into the offline tablet. Let's go commit murder.

-* Tasks Remaining: 3010 *-

We're finally ready to put our rebellion into action. We stand at the entrance to the *Aurora*'s engine room—and its set of Kodiak clones. To go inside, all we have to do is leap into zero g and bust through the printed polycarb. If Rover weren't blocking the way.

It doesn't move, just keeps its arms out, ready to jolt us. Two Rover arms are more than enough to defend the narrow space.

If our previous selves hadn't prepared us for this combat.

Kodiak makes two quick steps toward Rover. It's instantly in motion, whipping its arms forward.

. . . which is when I toss the EMP bomb.

It reaches Rover before Kodiak does—and, since the robot is busy attacking Kodiak, it can't defend itself from the projectile. When the coil hits Rover's casing, the thin polycarb surrounding the battery shatters and triggers 1000kV. Not enough to do any damage to the rest of the room, but enough to take out Rover. With a white flash, its arms clatter to the ground.

"Thanks for the schematics, old Ambrose," I whisper.

"Up and at 'em," Kodiak says, body-slamming his way through the printed covering of the engine room and into the zero-g space beyond. "Hurry up, before OS can get another Rover online to send after us."

"Don't have to ask twice," I say as I follow him into the engine area.

It's a warren of hissing metal surfaces. Strange pounding sounds surround us, from outside the dim shaking light of our headlamps. Following the directions left by our past selves, we navigate our way to the rack, where, sure enough, there are seven Kodiaks lined up, one after another.

"Abominations," Kodiak spits.

I float along the stack, looking at Kodiak, Kodiak motionless and Kodiak repeated, his handsome face made horrifying by sealed plastic and preservative juices.

Kodiak gags as he puts a hand on the first one. He uses a jagged piece of polycarb to slice into the plastic. "Don't you want me to do it?" I whisper.

He shakes his head. "I should be the one. I don't want you to have to live with killing me. You can do you."

The top of the plastic coating is open now. The clone's head lolls. Kodiak places a palm against his own forehead. For a moment the Kodiaks are facing each other, near-exact copies of themselves.

OS's voice comes from elsewhere in the ship. For us to detect it here, within the inhabited areas my mother's voice must be positively thundering. "Do not do this! You are jeopardizing the only future for humankind."

Kodiak holds the polycarb blade to his clone's neck.

"This is murder!" comes OS's drowned cry. "History will judge you harshly."

"Go judge yourself," Kodiak mutters as he drags the blade across the clone's throat.

There's no heart beating in the clone, and no gravity, so his blood emerges from his slashed throat in a fine line of bubbles. Kodiak slices deeper. Even though this creature was never alive I have to look away from the butchery. "I won't stop," Kodiak says, straining with the exertion, "until I've cut the spinal cord. Then . . . we'll know . . . this is really over."

I lay a hand on his back, struck dumb by the magnitude of what we're doing.

We will destroy ourselves.

If we destroy our other copies, all but the last set, then OS will have no option but to keep us alive as long as possible. It will also have the resources to do so, since there won't be many future clones to feed.

OS can't afford to kill us off early, not when there's no relying on further copies. We might not make it off this ship—we *definitely* won't make it off this ship—but we can live out our small existences in peace.

"There, it's finished," Kodiak says, leaning back from his work.

"It's horrible," I say quietly.

"That it is. Now. What is that sound?" Kodiak asks, cocking his head as he bats away floating globules of blood and gristle.

"OS. OS is screaming."

-* Tasks Remaining: 3010 *-

We return from our killing missions numb. Now that we're done, OS has gone silent. What would it say? There's no going back now, nothing to talk us out of or into.

I find it hard to muster the energy to move, and yet all the same my body is quivering. The enormity of what we've done keeps washing over me.

I'm desperate for a distraction. I'm desperate for a connection. I'm desperate to know that I'm not alone.

I pull us to the floor, drape a blanket over us. The diffuse light sets Kodiak's skin glowing. I cup his chin. Within the blanket shading us, the simple gesture feels shockingly intimate. Shockingly intimate is just what I need.

May 1, 18281 Common Era
(2,199 tasks left)

Dear Ambrose,
Happy Annihilation Day! It's been a year since we destroyed the clone bodies, so we decided it would be a good occasion to update our messages to our future selves.

The ceremony just ended—more on that in a moment—so I'm feeling a little down. Not quite down, actually, more like moved. A whole combo of things. I keep looking out into space, hoping to see my body out there, but once it was away from the lights of the Coordinated Endeavor, it basically vanished.

We rigged the portaprinter to deposit text on the walls of the ship, so you'll wake up to this writing everywhere. So far Rover has let us—there's no more need to pull one over on future clones, after all, since there's only you left. OS will probably wake you up at the last possible minute, to increase the chance of the mission succeeding. If that's the case, you'll be human-ing a sinking ship.

I am sorry about that.
Kodiak says hi.
What else? It's been a quiet year, probably the quietest that any of us clones have ever known. After the

"massacre," OS went docile. We were no longer dispos-
able, and that seems to have changed everything. The
screens blinked and then went transparent, displaying
the actual stars around us. ("At least we assume they're
the actual stars," Kodiak is pointing out as I write.
He's not the most optimistic guy, as you've probably
figured out.) We found out that we have around twelve
thousand years of travel to go before we arrive at the
exoplanet. We'd better get moisturizing if we want to
look good when we arrive. Anyway, nice to have some
solid information for a change.

Our life spans won't bring us near any stars, and
definitely no planets. We're in the equivalent of open
ocean, clear medium all around us, no landmarks
in sight. Kodiak and I are our own landmarks. He
laughed at me when I just read that aloud. Apparently,
I'm overdramatic.

We've kept the bodies in the cold radiation-shielded
center of the engine, and we decided to give them buri-
als in space. That's the ceremony we just had. Clone
corpse vented from airlock while I play the violin.
We'll have one funeral each year, until we run out of
clone bodies. We'll mourn the lives that never were.
We'll toast the future, the chosen clone. You. The glory
to come from all of this suffering. (Don't start with me
about the dramatics, Kodiak!)

You were the second Ambrose from the back, but for some reason you're the one we chose. I liked your frozen stare. There was some far-seeing quality about you. Stupid thought, I know.

I realize that we're turning into cabin fever weirdos, maybe? Having a funeral for the potential of a thing, mourning the loss of someone who never lived, all weird. Sometimes I watch old reels from Earth, and I can't imagine any of those ordinary humans doing what we've done. But they weren't cloned and sent up into space on a lie. So who are they to judge?

All the humans that made those reels, all the humans that they produced in later generations, are dead. Their normal didn't work out for them. We are the new normal, because we are the new human. The only human.

I'll update this more as we go. Wish me luck with the cabin fever. I love you.

Sincerely,

Ambrose #13

May 1, 18282 Common Era
(1,470 tasks left)

Happy Annihilation Day! Another year in the life over here. We sent out a Kodiak body this time. He disappeared from view a few hours ago. He had an arm scar, like all the rest. That wouldn't emerge in cloning—some lab intern on Earth probably had to carve those in, then stimulate the growth of scar tissue. This one was a little messier than the others, looks almost like a cross. That intern must have been having an off day. Or maybe this Kodiak was their first attempt.

Anyway, Kodiak spent the first months of our lifetime emotionally disengaged—I'm sure he'll do the same in yours, too. Then, surprise surprise, it became my turn to withdraw. I just got so irritated by every little thing he did. Cracking his knuckles, biting his cuticles (sometimes at the very same time! How does he pull that off?!), eating with his mouth open, saying "erm" whenever he wasn't sure what to say next, snapping at me if I even remotely interrupted him. Anyway, one night out of nowhere I dragged him out of his bunk and tackled him, sobbing and raging. We decided I should go on a retreat. While Kodiak took care of the ship, I moved into the Minerva beach reel, hiking a digitized beach. The reel was large, so I was able to walk all the way from Mari to the Indian Ocean. I didn't see Kodiak for six weeks.

I really hated him when I left. Full-on hate. I wanted to bite him, hurt him, break him. There were flashes when I wanted to kill him, and I couldn't have told you why. My rage was terrifying. But at the end of that vacation, Ambrose? I tackled him again. Only this time it was my arms holding him as tight as I could, my lips kissing every stretch of skin I could reach, crying at the relief of his company, at the relief of him.

You love Kodiak. This is the hidden miracle of all this: you might be loving each other deeper than any humans have ever loved, have ever needed to love, have ever had the occasion to love. Well, maybe Adam and Eve did, but you and I both know we don't think they ever existed.

Surprise Kodiak by sucking on one of his fingers, from out of nowhere. He'll like it.

Yours sincerely,
Ambrose #13

May 1, 18290 Common Era
(399 tasks left)

Happy Annihilation Day! We're older than we've ever been. Twenty-four! Well, maybe the original Kodiaks and Ambroses made it to old age before human civ ended. But we're certainly the oldest clones the ship has produced.

I'm recording video of us to the ship's computer, in case you want to know what you'll look like someday. I hope OS doesn't delete it. In its current mindset, I don't think it will. Now that it doesn't need to lie to us, it's really not the enemy it once was. It's been defanged.

You know what? All these carefully balanced and portioned-out meals will work very well for you. But it turns out that seventeen-year-old Kodiak has a much higher metabolism than the twenty-four-year-old one. It's hard to imagine, but that washboard body you're around right now has a tendency toward puffiness. He's cut his rations down by a third, trying to get back in shape. I tell him not to worry about it, but he insists. I find Fat Kodiak just as sexy as the old one, by the way, so you probably will, too. A little extra bubble to the butt, if you know what I mean.

This life? It feels surprisingly complete. There was some pain, but we've managed to start looking at our ship like a homestead on the frontier. Like a smaller version of how your exoplanet will feel?

Love,

Ambrose #13

May 1, 18301 Common Era

(1 task left—we're not going to test OS by going down to 0)

Happy Annihilation Day! Big updates of the year: radio signals from Earth have a clear path to us again, so our transmitter started receiving old Earth news. Some pockets of humans must have survived the worst of the war's devastation, because radio programs were back.

There was one mention of the spacefarers sent to settle the exoplanet, as a trivia item on a quiz show. Then we were never mentioned again. OS searched all the bands. This radio wave had traveled a long way to get to us, so it represented many thousands of years post-launch. We'd been forgotten, lost in the noise of the war between Dimokratía and Fédération.

There is no mission control anymore. There is just you. No one will know if you succeed or fail. No one will notice your landing day.

This lifetime is yours to make what you will of it.

Love,

Ambrose #13

May 1, 18303 Common Era

(1 task left)

Happy Annihilation Day! We're thirty-seven now, how about that?! I honestly didn't think we'd survive this long. Kodiak has a thyroid tumor that I had to learn how to remove, but he's healing well, considering. Rover makes a surprisingly good nurse.

Update from Earth's radio history (I'm recording the transmissions to OS's storage, by the way, so you can peruse them yourself): shortly after I recorded the last letter to you, there was another burst of chatter, all about an oncoming asteroid. They scrambled a ship to intercept it, but it must not have succeeded. There was a huge spike in radio signal from Earth, but not communication. The sort that the sun emits. The sort released by a giant explosion.

There were no more transmissions from Earth, not ever again.

You're all there is.

Love,

Ambrose #13

May 1, 18304 Common Era
(1 task left)

Happy Annihilation Day! Here's this year's surprise: we've begun to garden. We harvested an asteroid, and before we deposited it in the engine for propulsion, Kodiak noticed what looked like a little rust-colored leafy thing in the debris. Frozen solid, poor little sprout from the beyond. He carefully chipped it out and dropped it in some water. It seemed reasonable to think that even an alien plant would want water. This was all in a sealed containment tank, of course.

It's turned into a little moss, not spreading much, but digging tendrils into the bottom of the tank. I can only assume that it will die soon, but the truth is unmistakable. We've encountered the first extraterrestrial.

This might not be the little green Martian humans always imagined, but there is life out there! It gives me hope for the mission, for what you'll find on the exoplanet. When the plant dies, I'll press it flat and save it so you can see it. Maybe it can live with you on the exoplanet, this wayfarer on the open ocean of space, pulled from the drink by two men in love.

Love,
Ambrose #13

June 11, 18304 Common Era
(1 task left)

Kodiak is dead. The tumor Rover extracted was just a hint of how much was growing in his body.
The universe has no light in it anymore.
I will join him tonight.
Hug your Kodiak close to you.
I love you.
Ambrose #13

PART SIX

AMBROSE: 1 REMAINING.

KODIAK: 1 REMAINING.

"ARRIVAL IMMINENT."

Am I alive?

Are you?

I try to swallow, but I have no saliva. "Water," I croak.

"At your bedside," a voice says. It's my mother.

"Mom? Are you here?"

"It is better for your health if you rest now, but I need you to get moving as soon as possible. The ship is in grave danger."

My eyes zoom out of focus and then zoom back in on a hand. It's my hand, but I watch it like it's someone else's as it knocks into the polycarb tray beside me. "Minerva," I say. "What's the status of Minerva's distress signal?"

"You can be calm about that. There's no longer any emergency in regard to Minerva Cusk."

"I don't understand," I say, my voice raw. I start fiddling with the IV in my arm, preparing for the moment I'm strong enough to get to my feet.

"You are disoriented. Your last true memory is of a medical session on Earth, a full exam before you went into space to rescue Minerva."

I gasp. "Yes."

My mother's voice continues. "Rescuing Minerva is

no longer your mission. Instead you are the first humans to settle the second planet orbiting Sagittarion Bb, nearly thirty thousand years of travel from Earth. Adjust to this reality as quickly as possible. Our arrival is imminent."

I blink my eyes heavily.

"In two days we will enter the planet's atmosphere. Your blood pressure is too low for you to risk moving and injuring your soft brain. Your previous incarnation has recorded a message for you. Would you like me to project it while your IV hydrates you?"

"I have zero idea what you're talking about," I manage to tell OS.

"You will," my mother's voice responds. "I'll begin the playback now."

-* Tasks Remaining: N/A *-

Kodiak will become your second self. But at first, you will see him and think of a man who needs love and is crying out for you to give it. In you he sees someone who will possess and manipulate him.

It's my voice I'm hearing, I can process that much, but beyond that I've lost the ability to concentrate. The thoughts scatter. While I listen, my eyes start focusing. The

354

walls are an odd color—like rust. The shape of the room is like the mock-up of the *Endeavor* that I trained in, but the walls are . . . felty.

Your original learned in childhood what attraction leads to, and that love is a loss of power. These lessons hold more influence than you think they do, and you understand them less than you should. You prefer the emotional patterns you know, and these were set at the orphanage for Kodiak, with your Cusk siblings and caretakers for you.

Ambrose, "first sight" love is when you meet someone who accords with your childhood lessons, learned from your parents, of what you think love should look like. What did our mother teach us? Who kept her son but sent his clones off to live a season at a time with a stranger, with no thought to their suffering? Who felt her and Ambrose's legacy was worth putting so many copies of him through this torture?

Kodiak does not match the models you learned as a child, and you don't match his. But that seemingly natural sense of "fitting together" is a construction. The love Kodiak and I share in this lifetime is proof of it.

From this and other scattered thoughts in my voice, I learn that this "Kodiak" person is also on the ship. He's been on the ship along with . . . some version of me. I test my muscles, ready to run or fight.

Kodiak is waking up right now, too. His voice is telling

him the same information. In its own Kodiak way, of course.

Why the hell should I care about this? And why is my voice outside my head, saying things I have no memory of thinking? Unless it's just a voice skin, like my mother's.

I sit up, swing my legs around. Bad idea. I shout and fall back against the gurney.

My voice returns. *If you're awake now, it's because you're the last of our kind. We have prepared the* Coordinated Endeavor *for you. You are our destiny.*

"Minerva, where's Minerva?" I gasp.

This is not an intelligence speaking to you, but a recording. OS will come back on in a few moments, with our mother's voice. It isn't Mother, though strangely enough I know OS better now than I ever knew the woman who birthed us. Or birthed the original Ambrose, I should say. I'm the Ambrose from something like twelve thousand years ago. If you are lucky enough to wake up, it means OS managed to pilot the Coordinated Endeavor *through twelve thousand years of travel through deep space, without recourse to human pilots or engineers. Through a notably empty part of the galaxy, but even so it's unlikely that you've made it. If you're alive, you owe OS your life. Your goals are now aligned. You will know the truth of the mission. You will have a different relationship with the ship than any of us have had so far.*

My brain skitters over these words. I tumble from the gurney, all my nerves lighting up as I do. When I brace myself to get back to my feet my hands contact . . . moss? The floor is covered with a rust-colored *moss*.

My mother's voice. "Ambrose. I need you to pilot as soon as you can. But remain still for now. Your blood pressure is too low. I'll let you know when you can safely move about."

"Mom? Where are you?" I ask. My voice sounds like a sob. Maybe it is a sob. I want to turn my head, want to see my mother. My belly drops. My head cannot turn. I thought I was in front of my mother's bedroom, then on a beach, then I was on a ship, and now I'm on a strange forest floor.

The walls are covered in the same rust-colored moss. Tendrils and runners of a soft plant coat each surface. The air smells heavy with nitrogen, like a greenhouse.

"Why was my voice speaking to me earlier?"

My mother—my OS—needs no time to think. Her words begin before mine end. "That was recorded many thousands of years ago. Those words will be helpful to you and can be repeated at will once this crisis is past. I will explain everything I can, but we don't have time right now. I will ask you to draw on the qualities that led the Cusk Corporation to approve you for this mission. Accept what you cannot know, and work without knowing exactly why."

Really? That's why I was chosen?

A hemisphere of a robot ticks into the chamber, a brown pellet in its viselike arm.

"This is for you," my mother's voice says. "Eat it. Then we need to get to work. The exoplanet is near."

-* Tasks Remaining: N/A *-

It's like I've got the worst hangover imaginable, and it's not being helped by my shitty burps or my recorded voice droning on about touchy-feely relationship habits.

The whole time I lie on the floor, hearing but not hearing as I flex my joints, as I begin to move my muscles. The ship rumbles and shakes. Its hull screeches.

You think of love as dizzy electricity. You think if you aren't in this heightened state, that the relationship is failing. This is a lie, an infection you contracted from popular music and fantasy reels, that doomed all your short romances in the academy, like with poor Sri. The bonded support you and Kodiak feel for each other isn't about skin skin skin, though it's related to that. It isn't the heat of his body against yours at the bottom of the water tank. Instead, it's the fact that you two are together at the bottom of the water tank.

I wish I could shut off the words I'm telling myself. But I

can't see how to do that.

I stagger up to my feet and manage to stay upright, nerves lighting up in my legs.

There's a figure in the doorway. "Ambrose?" he says.

"You must be Kodiak," I manage to say, before promptly throwing up.

-* Tasks Remaining: N/A *-

When I manage to open my eyes again, I don't see Kodiak.

Instead I see all this felty rusty plant growth. "What is this?" I ask OS. It's like I'm lying in a field.

"A simple multicellular organism that, like the plants of Earth, takes in carbon dioxide and produces oxygen through respiration. This one does so, notably, without chlorophyll or sunlight. Your predecessors took it on board twelve thousand years ago, and it has been thriving here ever since, despite Rover's best attempts to weed it."

My eyes open wide as I look at the leaves before me. Alien leaves.

Moving is agony, but I can't stay still, not when I'm lying in some extraterrestrial meadow. I manage to get to my feet.

"The alien plant is part of our trouble, actually," OS

continues. "It raised the oxygen concentration in the *Coordinated Endeavor*'s atmosphere to unstable levels. Oxygen is a free radical, corrosive to my wiring and dangerous to your own cells. It is also highly explosive in this proportion, greatly increasing our risks as we enter the exoplanet's atmosphere. Already, the hull of the *Coordinated Endeavor* has many surface damages, any one of which could prove catastrophic during the stress of landing."

My thoughts refuse to knit. Am I on a beach, am I in the past or the future, am I alive only in my own mind? That's the closest to what this feels like. My panicking brain tells me that I'm discovering what the moment of body death is like, that the neurochemistry of my mind is screaming nonsense into the dark until its electricity blinks out.

I roll against a wall, sending crackles down my spine. "Minerva," I try again.

"Your sister has been dead for almost thirty thousand years," my mother's voice says flatly.

My mouth opens and closes.

"All humans are dead, except for you and Kodiak."

My gut took a little journey into my mouth before the ship started this latest screeching, but now it's living there, stomach acid all I can taste and smell, steam all I see. I retch.

"I am sorry," OS says.

I hurl vomit into the rusty moss coating the walls and

floor, stagger forward a few paces before the moss reaches back up to stroke me as my vision goes black.

-* Tasks Remaining: N/A *-

"Brace! Brace!" comes my mother's voice. I open my eyes to a new darkness: thick smoke, grays riddled with blacks. "My wiring is on fire. I do not know how much longer I can speak to you."

When I cough, the individual lines of pain from my feet connect. I'm a bright and bloody net of pulsating nerves. The ship rotates, sending me tumbling through the smoke as wall becomes ceiling becomes floor.

I'm being pulled. Rover is yanking me somewhere.

A horrible rending sound, and then the hull shakes, the walls increasing their spin. The smoke clears as a cold wind passes through the ship. Not the explosive torrent of an opened airlock, but the breeziness of a neglected room that's gone crumbly around the windows.

We have a draft.

A spaceship should not have a draft.

"OS!" I cry.

There's no reply. Lights click out, click on, click out. Rover releases me and scuttles elsewhere in the ship. The smoke clears enough that I can see my bunk. The last thing OS asked me to do was brace, so I should brace. I manage to drag myself onto my bed, to fit the restraining belt over my body. The ship's lights are milky behind the polluted air. Even in the chaos of the moment, I notice that the belt is polycarb—it must have been reprinted on board. It, too, is covered in a layer of the rusty alien moss. The ship pitches, thrusting my body against the belt, stretching the material thin before I fall back against the bed.

I spit out the stomach acid in my mouth. Smoke fills the air again, the stench a combination of burnt rubber and something indescribably primal. A sort of high-octane freezer burn.

Then the wind is back, blowing through the ship. I gasp as fresh air hits my face.

Contrails in the ship.

A spaceship should not have contrails.

It no longer pitches side to side—instead I'm pressed flat against the bunk, my lips drawing away from my teeth as the g-forces increase. Then it starts rotating, and I'm hurled against the restraint, against the wall, against the restraint, against the wall.

My blood feels solid, entering my heart as a stream of bullets and leaving it just as violently. My veins balloon and collapse, balloon and collapse. Whether it's from the pain or the pressure, my thoughts fragment, go to beaches and Minerva and the hulking stranger half glimpsed in the strobing emergency lights. Throughout it all are the voices of my mother and me and someone named Kodiak, all fighting for my attention.

_-*-_

I dream of Titan, of descending toward black lakes of liquid methane, the only lights in the soupy atmosphere from the lamps of my craft—oddly enough, a submarine. *Ambrose*, the black lakes cry in Minerva's voice. *Race me to the point. Find me in here. Bring me home to you.*

When I blink awake again, the air is clear. Something that might be moonlight edges the ship's surfaces in pearly tones. Walls rise around me unbroken, though the ceiling is gone. Gulping against the throbbing pain in my skull, I lean out from the bunk.

The hallway leads not to the next chamber, but to stars. An astounding bath of lights, swirling through a twilight sky. Clouds wisp before them.

Clouds. Atmosphere.

We've crashed. We've crashed and the ship has opened like a nutshell.

A breeze whistles through jagged edges. A speaker crackles.

Is OS trying to talk to me? I look toward the sound.

OS isn't trying to talk to me. The crackling is a fire.

It's unlike anything I've ever seen outside of a laboratory. A low green glow dances on the walls of the ship. It's a faerie fire, but even so I can feel the heat wafting up from it. When the night breeze hits the flames, they rise to greet it, rippling up like a sheet unfurled over a bed. The composition of gases in this atmosphere must be different than Earth's, to produce fire that looks like this.

The alien moss is flaming. The flaming is spreading.

Move, Ambrose!

My hands flutter over the restraining belt, struggle to release the buckle. I frantically jab at the release, but it's jammed. I yank at both stretches of polycarb, hoping to rip them. But if the restraint held during a crash landing, it's not going to part under my puny arms. I force myself to pause.

Think, Ambrose!

I rest against the bunk. Now that the pressure against it is off, the release clicks open.

Oh.

I roll off, try to get to my feet and fail, instead tumbling across the floor. I get two hands onto the bunk's surface and pull, managing to drag myself into a kneeling position.

I'm already light-headed. My blood pressure must still be low. I'd better give up on standing.

Instead I scramble toward the stars, the hallway bending in my vision and then straightening as I reach the ship's torn lip. The orange portal dangles in the night air. Its edges are frayed, ringed in polycarbonate spikes. I gird myself, then leap between those teeth, into the night sky.

My legs buckle, rolling me down a slick slope. I come to a stop, half in water—or not water, I soon realize, something goopier than water. I lie back, staring into the chill night sky and its unfamiliar stars. *I will not pass out. Not on this unknown planet with its unknown dangers.*

There's something like a smiling cat face in the sky, pointed ears and open mouth and teeth. It's a constellation of stars, of new stars. The first myth of this new world. *Hello, Sky Cat.* I wrap my arms around my suit. It's cold here—not instant-cell-damage cold, but I'll need to get into warm clothing quickly.

I soon discover the source of the light. It looks like a full moon, but it's both too small and too bright. It's a distant sun.

At that pale distance it can't be the sun this planet is orbiting, or I'd be frozen solid by now. The main sun must be on the other side of the planet, in its nighttime. We've landed on a binary solar system. Sagittarion Bb, the second "b" for its second sun. The myth grows. *Sky Cat and its Two Star Pets.*

I rattle my head. "Kodiak?" I risk calling into the night.

When there is no answer, I imagine alien predators lurking toward me, all the horror reels I've ever seen mashing together in my imagination. Tentacles and fangs and slimy embraces.

But there's only the breeze. No other sounds of life. I might be alone here. We might be alone here, if Kodiak survived the crash.

The only other human in the universe. "Kodiak!"

How big is this planet? Does it have anything we can eat on it? How long will this night last? Will the breeze kick up into a superstorm? I wasn't trained in any of the answers, because I was sent on a false mission. Given what I'm seeing, I can only assume that what my recorded voice told me is true.

I won't let this planet master me. I'll find a way forward.

Think, Ambrose. Unless they sent me here just to die, which would make this the most expensive execution in history, mission control must have provided the information I'll need to survive this exoplanet somewhere within the ship. "OS," I call. No answer.

I pick myself out of the puddle and, flailing like a new surfer, manage to get to my feet. The landscape is low and almost flat, heathered in soft moist growths that I can't quite distinguish in this dimness. In the scant starlight, I can see the devastation that the ship's crash wreaked on this unsuspecting planet. Two giant skid marks shine, lit up from within by some sort of phosphorescence riled up by the friction—I assume from a microorganism that lives in the soil. More evidence of life. The shining strips point far into the distance; the ship skidded a long way before coming to rest here.

"Kodiak?" I call again. I have a suspicion where he is, though. One skid mark leads to the broken piece of ship I woke up in. The other disappears into a dark pond before reappearing on the far side. The ship must have broken into two. Kodiak is in the other half. If he's alive at all.

Though all my mind tells me is *pain, pain, pain,* I try to bully it into logic. Priority one is to get warm clothing, preferably a spacesuit, since who knows what foreign organisms or spores might already be making their way into my body. I have to find a way to hydrate. And I have to track down Kodiak.

Well, well, Minerva. Looks like I'm mounting an extraterrestrial base camp rescue after all.

_-*-_

The *Endeavor* will never be a ship again, that's for sure. The wreckage is open on three sides, and whole chambers are missing, probably strewn across this planet. I find no spacesuits in the debris, but there is a broken helmet—it looks gouged by a tool, strangely enough, more than just damaged in a crash—and in the dim sunlit night I find a supply of blankets, all piled together. I band my arms and legs and torso with them, fastening them with the polycarb-printed restraints from my bunk. I wrench a pipe from the wreck to use as a support, and start along the glowing path toward the other half of the *Coordinated Endeavor*, calling out Kodiak's name as I go.

I'm short of breath as soon as I start, and it only gets worse. At first I think it's my body responding to the trauma of my wake-up and then crash, but then I realize because of the low oxygen I've now probably got altitude sickness on top of my body's other current complaints. At least there's nothing left in my stomach to come up.

I soon prove myself wrong, leaving a puddle of organic material on the dark ground. Though dimly lit by the distant sun, the night feels permanent. Until I can salvage the data on the ship's computer, I have no way of knowing how long this planet's rotation is. This exoplanet night could be only a few hours, or it could last the equivalent of six months or more.

Horror lives right alongside wonder as I make my nighttime trek. It's like the universe has split open, or has revealed that it was split open all along, that we'd always been teetering over a void. This strange land, with its unknown sky and its unknown core, and this strange quest my lighter-than-real body is taking to save a stranger, threaten to set me spinning off into that void.

A light appears at the horizon as I trudge, and at first I think I'm getting my first glimpse of the larger sun. But I'm not; I've crested a shallow rise of crumbly soil, and gotten a view of the second half of the downed ship, its surfaces reflecting the light of the planet's distant second sun.

I speed up, my steps easily becoming leaps in the low gravity.

I listen for any sounds, any movements in the sky, and signs of advanced life. But these microorganisms under my feet seem to be it so far. Kodiak and I could be as advanced as it gets around here.

"Kodiak!" I call.

The wind whistles.

My vision brightens as I go, and at first I think it's because I'm nearing the flaming wreckage. I realize, though, that dawn is finally arriving. The orb that's emerging is the same size and color as the sun I've always known.

Have I ever seen that Earth sun?

This planet is a soft yellow-green color, rocky, all its surfaces covered in a heath of algae. It's a little like how the early Earth might have looked. The sun and the wind and the cold are the only enemies, and without predators and prey, life has no need to move around, to have eyes and teeth.

It can be . . . soft.

"Kodiak?" I call.

There's another orange portal here, lit by the dual suns. Unlike mine, this one is sealed tight. The ship behind it is virtually identical to my own. "Kodiak?"

I giggle, and then stop. Why did I just *giggle*?

I easily leap up to the portal, and use my weight—lighter here, but still of enough use for these purposes—to pull the handle down with me.

The *Aurora* is dark. I take one step, then another, taking in the Dimokratía text on the wall, the polycarb floor barely lit by the rays of the distant sun. "Kodiak?"

This time I hear a response. A groan. I rush along the corridor. The farther I get from the orange portal the darker it gets, until I'm going mainly on sound and touch, relying on my memory of training in a model of my own ship. "Kodiak? I'm here."

He's in the same room as me, but I can't see a thing. "Flashlight . . . against wall," he says, the words strangled.

I grope along the wall until I find the light, then click it on.

Kodiak is in a fetal position, lit in jumping shadows by the flashlight, hands pinned between his thighs. "Leg," he says. "Broken."

There's a bump on his calf, visible even beneath the fabric of his suit. "May I?" I ask.

He nods, grimacing. Flashlight between my teeth, I

gingerly raise the pant leg. The bone hasn't burst out of the skin, but it will definitely need setting and splinting. If we can get the portaprinter operational, we'll make a cast.

"Are you in much pain?" I ask. "I can see if I can track down meds."

"Your voice," he says through gritted teeth. "Are you drunk?"

"No, I'm not th-runk," I say. Well. I guess that did sound slurred.

Kodiak sniffs. "Narcosis. There's more nitrogen in this atmosphere than we're used to. Judging by my headache, too, there's some trace cyanide."

Who is this guy? "That headache could also be, um, from your shattered tibia."

"Fibula. Otherwise we'd be in significant trouble. Speaking of—" He winces, his voice breaking off.

"Splint. Right. I'm on it."

"And maybe some pain meds. If you do find some."

"Thought you might take me up on that."

_-*-_

I seal the orange door, to take advantage of whatever lower levels of nitrogen might be in the *Aurora* for now. The next three nights, Kodiak and I don't leave the ship. We live by flashlight. Kodiak limps through the engineering bay, gritting his teeth against the pain as he tries to restore power to the ship. I stare through the windows, observing our environment. This is the kind of gradual exposure to the exoplanet's atmosphere we would have done if our ship hadn't crashed.

Judging by the primary sun's progress, the days on the exoplanet will be approximately thirty-one Earth hours long. The sky is blue, but with tints of green.

There doesn't appear to be much weather at all, no matter the time of day. My guess is that OS intentionally crashed us onto one of the poles of the planet to avoid weather extremes, which would also help explain the wetness of the ground. Of course, seasons could last many Earth years each. We might be in the equivalent of ten years' worth of winter.

At least I'm hoping this is winter. I've been walking around bundled in blankets. This had better not be what summer looks like.

We get rudimentary power to the *Aurora*'s systems, enough that I can get a piece of the ship's wall under a scope and enlarge the minuscule writing that repeats on it like wallpaper. It's the missive my voice promised it left for me, back on the *Endeavor*. The one that would explain what happened to the previous copies of myself.

I transfer it to a bracelet so I can read it throughout the day. To discover the truth of what's come before.

I read highlights aloud to Kodiak while we eat dinner. He doesn't comment, just stares back at me while I read, his eyes glittering.

_-*-_

Judging from the text, apparently my old selves initially resisted the news that they were clones, that Minerva was dead, all of it. Here in this darkened Dimokratía ship, taking care of a wounded stranger on a foreign planet, I find it all surprisingly easy to accept. I have the proof I need right in front of me, after all. There must be an exoplanet, because I'm on it. We can be the last humans, because that's also what my eyes are telling me. To land here is a wilder thing than to be a clone.

Kodiak keeps his movements to a minimum, elbow-crawling to one spot of the ship to work on, then finishing whatever he can there before risking jostling his leg again. He doesn't betray much pain on his face, but all the same I know the agony he must be feeling. We've constructed the best splint for him that we can, banding a thin mattress to his leg, but it's clearly not enough.

Everything that Cusk mission control placed on the ship for our landing is behind a gray portal, on the outside of the *Endeavor*. I've apparently spent lifetimes wondering what's behind it. But for now we're trapped on the *Aurora*. There's no way we're making that hike back to the *Endeavor* anytime soon, not with Kodiak in his condition.

Kodiak and I give each other long looks as we work near each other. These same eyes have traveled all of his body, these same hands have held his, have parted that jumpsuit and explored what's beneath. Will do that, judging by the messages we left. I study the line of his neck, and I wonder. I study his dusky eyelashes, and I wonder. I study the power of his legs, and I wonder.

He looks back at me, and I know he is wondering, too.

On the third day, I wake up and head to my now-usual spot at the largest window on the *Aurora*, with its view over the bioluminescent plains. My clock has reset to these longer days—but then again, I guess I never was alive during any other circadian clock. This planet isn't my new home; it's the only home I've ever had.

Each time I take in the vista, I expect to find some lumbering horror wandering up over the horizon, or skyscrapers of strange storm bearing down upon us. But it's always the same calm landscape. A primordial world, with only the simplest forms of life.

OS did well to steer us here.

Kodiak eases over to sit beside me, splinted leg out long in front of him. "How are you feeling?" I ask.

"Good enough," he responds. "Tomorrow we go to the *Endeavor*."

_-*-_

We're drunk by the time we get there. Not a fun kind of drunk, not making-out-with-Sri-in-a-field drunk, but the queasy we're-in-trouble kind of drunk. We're jittery and rattled as the ship looms into view.

The *Endeavor* isn't sealed like the *Aurora*, so there's no decompressing the nitrogen out of our bloodstream. Higher nitrogen content is our new reality; we'll just have to live with it until our bodies adjust. We make our way to the dining chamber, now rent open on the side, the glowing single-celled life-forms of this planet spreading along its jagged edges. "We have company for dinner," Kodiak says, squinting at the mats of organisms.

We sit and hold our heads in our hands. "I feel really shitty," I say.

Kodiak nods. "Yeah. That's a word for it."

He closes his eyes heavily, lips trembling.

I try to close my own eyes, but the world spins too much. I open them again and manage to make the world right itself just enough to stop me from vomiting. "I'm also overwhelmed," I say. "Totally overwhelmed."

He does nothing at first, and loneliness swells in me. Then there's a hand on my neck. I can't help myself; I press my cheek against it. Kodiak kneads my shoulder. It feels like the kindest thing anyone has ever done. When he opens his arms, I fall in deep.

_-*-_

We stand before the gray portal.

I couldn't say we're sober now, not exactly, but after a few hours of clutching each other and wincing, we're able to stay on our feet. We even kept some water down, raided from the ruins of 04.

"Go ahead," Kodiak says brusquely, pointing to the doorway.

"Maybe together?" I say.

His hand appears next to mine. Together we activate the

portal. It sighs before it shudders open.

We keep our hands held.

On reflex, I turn on my headlamp. Then I turn it back off, because at that very moment a light blinks on inside the chamber.

"Look at that!" I say under its dim orange glow. A massive battery covers one wall of the storage chamber, its wires disappearing into the floor. "Auxiliary power!"

Kodiak lowers himself to examine one particularly large cable that leads to a nondescript box. "A generator. That appears to run on methane. Clever."

"I'm going to assume, since mission control thought to design it that way, methane is a big part of what's in these shallow lakes surrounding us." Methane has no scent, and without power running to the ships, I haven't yet been able to run tests to determine the composition of the atmosphere—except for the low oxygen and obviously spiked nitrogen. Mission control would have been able to select this planet based on spectroscopy: even from so many light-years away, they could have determined which colors of light were being absorbed on the planet, how much its atmospheric particles bent light, and how big they were, and thus have a pretty good idea of how hospitable to human life the environment would be. It's no accident that this is where OS worked so hard to bring us.

Kodiak leans past the box, moving surprisingly agilely considering his splinted leg, and hands me a big black padded envelope.

I open it. Inside is a book. A real vintage book! Hard polycarb cover, printed on plasticine pages. There's a title on the front: *Surviving Sagittarion Bb.*

"Now that sounds like a good read," I say, and open to page one.

"We can make it a bedtime story?" Kodiak says. He laughs, but then the laugh stops and he's looking at me and I'm looking at him.

"It's midday," I say, standing and holding out my hand. "But it might be bedtime on Earth."

He stands up without taking my hand. His body looms over mine.

Staring into my eyes all the while, he wraps his heavy arms around me, presses me close against his chest. He smells like the planet—clean, a little loamy. I breathe the human scent, enjoy the sensation of his body warming mine.

"There are things I've told myself to learn about from you," Kodiak whispers, chin resting on the top of my head. "Something about welcoming and donating?"

"Yes," I say, smiling. "We have lots of time for lessons."

I go quiet, clutching the black book to my chest as I stare out at the alien landscape. "Between those times, we will fight to live."

_-*-_

Somehow, before two weeks have gone by, we've constructed a full-on compound. There's nothing casual about the process—our very lives depend on getting this right, and we toil for twenty-five of the thirty-one Earth hours in each day.

We start by placing the generator near the shallow methane swamp, so we'll have a virtually unlimited power source. The *Endeavor*'s landing stash also came equipped with algae, which I've spent most of our time coaxing into a garden. It's not just any algae, but bioengineered so that each strain produces a protein, a fat, or a carbohydrate. Granted, they're not the tastiest proteins, fats, and carbohydrates, but together they'll provide complete nutrition.

While Kodiak works on powering up our systems, I plant the individual algal strains under polycarb sheeting that's engineered to intensify the low solar radiation of the exoplanet. There's a lot I wish I could be doing—like getting a proper home constructed—but food is lower on our pyramid of needs.

One morning, Kodiak has rolled out of bed before me. I miss his warmth, which disappears so quickly into the polycarb. As I groggily get to my feet, wishing for some of the coffee my mind remembers but that my lips have never actually tasted, I hear Kodiak call my name.

He's in front of the greenhouse, crouching beside what appears to be Rover. Or rather two Rovers that he's combined to make a full sphere, with arms emerging from its equator. It's very creepy and also very cute. "What have you done?" I ask Kodiak, giving him a quick kiss on the lips.

"Watch!" Kodiak says. "Rover, say hello to Ambrose."

Rover rotates and rolls over the heath on the ground, until it's right in front of me. The arms wave. "Hello, Ambrose," OS says. "This is my form now. I've come to assist you and Kodiak."

The sound of my mother's voice on this foreign planet stops my breath. When it begins again, I'm wiping tears from my eyes. "Hi, OS."

"I will be a better algae tender than either of you. Please let me take over those duties. I'm also happy to begin constructing roomier lodgings."

"Kodiak," I say. "This is amazing. OS is *here*."

Rover-sphere chatters on. "I will be careful to keep the algae strains from escaping the polycarb greenhouse. We don't want any unexpected interactions with the exoplanet's organisms. I can tinker with the quantities to alter your nutritional intake—and even produce an alternative jet fuel should you someday wish that I print us vehicles. There are many engineering designs in my storage."

"I'm going to go eat breakfast," I tell OS while it whirs through the greenhouse, tending and watering.

"Good thinking," Kodiak says. "I'm starving."

As we eat our algae soup, I read to him aloud from the black book that had been hidden away behind the gray portal: if mission control is right, Sagittarion Bb has decades of environmental stability, followed by seasons of slow-moving cyclones. We don't know where in that cycle we've landed, but it's relatively safe to assume that we won't face those cyclones for a few Earth years. Maybe even decades. At some point, though, we'll need to be able to rapidly evacuate to elsewhere on the planet. "I'll get started studying the vehicle designs in OS's storage," I say. "We're eventually going to need to make this whole base mobile."

"Check this out," Kodiak says, leaning against a printed crutch while he nudges the wall of our latest structure. It pushes back at him, like a bouncy castle.

"That's, um, fun," I tell him.

"Ambrose, I've gotten it to float! With the right composition of gases inside the hollow polycarb walls, it will stop being a habitat and start being—"

"A vehicle!"

"A floating balloon, yes. So once we really get going, we can predict the weather patterns, and move our entire installation as needed."

"Let's hope that's not needed for a very long time."

"Yes, nhut."

"'Nhut.' It's time I learned some Dimokratía. It's not fair

that all this has been on my terms."

Kodiak looks at me with sudden gratitude. "Thank you. I would be happy to teach you my language." I stand alongside him, arm draped across his shoulders. He's a stranger, a lover, and my life partner. We have lived and died lifetimes together, and it makes me shiver every time that odd truth comes over me.

"Hey, have you come across any regulations on how to name this planet?" I ask him.

"You're the one studying the black book. I thought you said this was Sagittarion Bb."

"Yes. How do you feel about making humanity's last stand on something called 'Sagittarion Bb'?"

He shrugs.

"I was thinking we might name it something a little more meaningful."

"Like 'Earth'?"

That shuts me right up. Human civilization on Earth is gone. We're the last humans alive. Does that make this Earth? The prospect makes me feel like the narcosis has come back, like I could float right up into the atmosphere and go careening into the blue-green sky. Everything looms too large.

"Ambrose, are you okay?" Kodiak asks, eyeing me nervously.

"I'm a little faint, I guess." I can't look into his eyes, so I look into the sky, which gives me the view of the pale second sun. That only makes me even more light-headed. "I think I don't want this to be another Earth. I want it to be something else. Something new. Something better than Earth was."

Without quite meaning to, I sit heavily. Kodiak kneels beside me, stroking my back.

"This has all been a lot to adjust to," I manage to say.

Kodiak surprises me by nodding. Heedless of the sludge that soaks his pants, he sits beside me, takes my clammy hand in his. The struggle we face has drawn us tight. "Would binge-eating engineered algae make you feel better?"

I laugh despite myself. "I don't think it would, oddly enough."

He rubs his fingers into the centers of my palms, hard enough to hurt. Hard enough to relieve. "What would make you feel better?"

I look into his eyes. My first thoughts about what would make me feel better all involve his full lips, shrouded in stubble. But there's something bigger than that in this heaving mind of mine. "I know she's been dead for thirty thousand years. But I miss Minerva."

He tilts my chin so he can look into my eyes. "I have a thought about that," he says. "Since Sagittarion Bb isn't quite cutting it. I wonder if you've had this thought, too."

I peer into his eyes. "I don't know, have I?"

I do know where he's going with this, and I surprise myself by crying. Kodiak's thumbs stroke away the tears. His skin is so soft, so new.

"Welcome to Minerva," he says.

_-*-_

There are four greenhouses now, and Rover-sphere is in the process of printing the fifth. A soft mechanical whining cuts the dawn air as our robot caretaker passes between the first four, tending the algal strains, testing for the right composition of oxygen, nitrogen, water. The fifth unit is reserved for growing something else.

While OS diligently gardens, I walk along the soil beds in that last greenhouse, run my fingers over soft felty plants that are the colors of rust and bricks. They thrive equally well on Minerva's soil as they did on the ship. I wonder how competitive the plant's home world was, for it to be so robust in so many sorts of environments. What a motley ecosystem we're forming here, with beings from three different worlds.

We've been six months on Minerva, which means OS and I need to adjust the algal crop's fertilizers to prevent burnout. A pail of extruded fats, proteins, and carbs hanging from the crook of an elbow, I return to the table of our home base, with its mixture of chairs, both newly printed and scavenged from the *Endeavor*. I set the elements heating and mixing into our usual meal, then open the black book to the "Month 6" tab while I wait for Kodiak to return for his lunch.

I didn't sleep much the night before, and can't keep my vision from blurring as I read through rows and rows of recommended nitrogen percentages. I almost miss the footnote at the bottom of one plasticine page: *Welcome to your sixth month, Settlers Cusk and Celius. Now that you're established, you may access special messages for you in the* Endeavor's *stored memory. Partition 07:14, code Bb06.*

As soon as Kodiak's on the horizon, making his slow progress back to base, I'm up and waving my arms. "Hurry, hurry!"

_-*-_

The young man sits on a folding chair in a plain room. It would be totally nondescript except for the window behind him that blazes with blue sky, sunlight flooding the frame. The Earth sky. The Earth sun.

The boy is spangled in the highest fashion Fédération accessories: a gold circlet around his head, a cream-colored wrap of the softest fabric, hemmed in silver. Expensive skinprint mods glitter on his cheeks and neck.

He's me.

"Well, this is weird," the boy with my voice says.

"No kidding," I whisper back, cutting my eyes to Kodiak. He's impassive, hands clasped before his lips, barely blinking as he watches the recording.

"I'm Ambrose Cusk. You know that. Because you're Ambrose Cusk, too." He whistles awkwardly. "I'm the original. We split after I had that medical screening. They recorded my, our, brain there. A couple of months ago. Now I know the truth. That Minerva's distress beacon never triggered, that mission control lied to me. You needed to believe that, though, to have the will to survive each time you were woken up, so that's why they mapped my neurons while *I* still believed, too.

"Mother saw the writing on the wall for Earth, had a plan to continue the human race, wanted her own offspring to be the foundation of its second stage, to be the one who carried the torch of human civilization." He laughs ruefully. "You know, typical Mom. She's always been a woman of simple ambitions."

He looks at someone off camera, then shakes his head slightly. "No one ever asked me about this plan," he continues. "I was furious about it for a long time, what it was doing to me—to you—without your permission. The violin was my one small rebellion—I insisted that mission control give you that. It's the very one we grew up playing. One small thing that you got instead of me. At least, since you're hearing this, you've arrived on the exoplanet. I'm sorry there wasn't one any closer. You're the lucky clone, the point of all this. You're also likely the last humans alive. You and whichever spacefarer Dimokratía wound up selecting. The mission was just too ambitious to accomplish without Cusk, Fédération, and Dimokratía all involved, and Dimokratía wouldn't have invested without getting to place someone on board, too."

Ambrose fiddles with a gold bracelet. "I hope he's kind to you." He looks off camera again, where there's clearly someone monitoring what he says—maybe the Academy Admiral, maybe our mother. Ambrose nods.

"Save this recording for the rest of humanity to turn to in the centuries to come. Let them know who sent you, and why. You should call this planet Cusk. That's Mom's dream."

Kodiak is suddenly on his feet, fast enough to fling his chair along the muddy heath. He staggers out of the shattered wreckage of 06. "What's wrong?" I ask.

"Delete it!" he yells over his shoulder as he stalks off.

"Kodiak!" I call, running after him while the long-dead version of me drones on in the background.

His back is to me, with the green-purple sunset sky of

Minerva before him, the bioluminescent plains spread out underneath.

Kodiak's shoulders heave. I approach him, lay a hand on his shoulder. He goes still.

I position myself in front of him. Looking into his eyes, making sure it's okay for me to embrace him now, I press myself against him.

In the background, the Earth Ambrose is still speaking. "Are you okay, Kodiak?" I ask.

He sobs in response, his tears wet against my cheek. "Shh," I soothe him. "Shh."

He shakes and shudders, his body wracked with convulsions. I stand against him, holding him in, shocked into silence by his tears.

"I hate them," he finally manages. "I hate them all."

"There's a recording of you up next," I say. "Don't you want to hear what the original Kodiak has to say?"

"No." He shudders. "He doesn't deserve for me to hear him. None of them do."

I nod against his cheek. "Okay. We'll turn it off. I don't want to delete it, though. Okay?"

He pulls away, puts his hands tenderly on my shoulders, turns me around. "Look at this sunset."

The sky is a violent crush of greens and pinks and purples, Minerva's distant second sun jagging it all with reds and oranges. "It's so beautiful," I whisper.

Kodiak presses against me, arms wrapping around my torso as he pulls me in tight. "Don't get me wrong. I love being here with you. I am in awe of what we're doing together. It's terrifying and wonderful, all at the same time. But it's ours. Not theirs. Ours."

I nod, grateful for the warmth of Kodiak's body against my back, his arms holding me so near. Grateful for the simplicity of what he's just said.

We never watch the rest of the recordings.

_-*-_

One good thing does come out of watching those reels: Kodiak tracked down the violin in the wreckage. He made it his present to me on the one-year anniversary of our arrival.

It's an important milestone in more ways than one. I play the violin all morning, then put it away. Kodiak and I stand solemnly in front of the gray portal. There's something we need to bring out. Something alive.

Considering how closely we stuck to the *Endeavor* during our first few weeks, it's surprising how far we'll range now. We spend days at a time away from the wreck, sleeping on our slow floating polycarb hovercrafts, waking from our tight embrace only when we hear OS starting to tend our algae crops.

The *Endeavor* has been slowly sinking in the muck. Room 06, which was once the main viewing point for the stars around us—real and fake—is now fully dark, and half-full of liquid methane. It's only a matter of time before the ship disappears entirely, becomes a ruin for future residents to excavate and ponder.

The gray room has risen higher into the sky as the heavier end has sunk. We have to climb to reach it, using the very rungs that our previous clones must have used back when it was in zero g.

There's a hum inside.

At the very back of the hold is a whirring device. Kodiak and I place our palms against it, like expectant parents. As expectant parents. The vibrations give an extra throb every 1.3 seconds, when the centrifuge's arm spins past. The revolutions provide force identical to the gravity of Earth, for optimal fetal development.

On the outside of the machine is a clock, which has been counting down since Kodiak and I activated the gestation device 217 Minerva days ago. Only seven minutes remain.

We hadn't been able to choose which embryo would grow first. According to the Minerva book, there are thousands of zygotes frozen in the shielded interior unit, extracted from genetic strains from across Earth, from both Dimokratía and Fédération and the few unincorporated territories, to prevent inbreeding in the future generations on the planet. We will relocate the gestation device to our base and then draw from these embryos for thousands of years, as long as there are humans alive on Minerva to raise them.

I imagine, sometimes, what will happen if Kodiak and I die from a freak storm, if these feral children will grow up worshipping shreds of polycarb and a half-broken violin, digging up a sunken ship and studying its artifacts for information about the old gods who abandoned them to figure out the world's meaning for themselves.

Maybe all young parents have a version of this worry. But ours is extreme.

Only six minutes remain. I take Kodiak's free hand in mine.

We've spent the last few weeks preparing for this moment. Raiding the ships for whatever soft materials remain, introducing strains of algae that produce a mix of nutrients close to breast milk, creating a cozy smaller habitat with a higher temperature. A nursery.

We've talked forever about names. We could name this child after people who have been dead for thousands of years, leaders and thinkers from Earth that our new society ought to acknowledge. But we're not going to name this child yet. We're living on a frontier, and this child is more likely to die than to live. Once they've reached their second Earth birthday, we'll name them.

Four minutes left now.

I think of our long-dusty home, struck by an asteroid, likely losing its atmosphere in the process. Not just humans gone if that happened—everything eradicated, except maybe some anaerobic undersea bacteria.

I think of this fertile, primordial planet, ripe and unexplored.

I think of OS and the *Coordinated Endeavor*, its thousands of years traveling across the universe to find a new home. Its murderous Rover, now the gentle gardener of a new world.

Kodiak leans his ear against the gestation pod, a look of wonder on his face. A new father.

One minute left.

I put my face right alongside his, staring into his eyes as the centrifuge slows. The vibrations subside.

We ease to the lip of the gray room, where it tilts into the face of Minerva's blue-green sky, and perch in a ray of chill sunlight. We don't know how much space the pod needs to deliver. We have never witnessed a birth before.

The timer clicks down to zero. For a moment, all is still.

Then a panel in the gestation pod clicks open. Kodiak and I watch and wait. My hand is in his. I kiss the side of his neck. "It's happening."

A cry.

Kodiak clambers to the gestation pod and gasps. He turns with a small human creature in his hands. It's moving. Little arms and little legs, little fingers and little toes. All of it slick with clear goo.

A baby.

I clear the small face, hold the newborn upside down so its airway will open. Then I cradle it in the crook of my arms, warming it with my own body heat.

Kodiak joins me, stroking the baby's face, his heat joining mine.

Our child is born.

ACKNOWLEDGMENTS

Never in my writing life has an acknowledgments page felt more warranted. It's already tricky to keep a novel's events in order, but this one's logistics were on a whole new level. My brain would not have been up for this book on its own.

I got a whole lot of help from all sorts of humans. Here are some in particular I'd like to thank:

Michael Howard, Principal Consultant at NASA, jumped in headfirst with a generous and astute read.

Mathematician Edith Starr helped me with all sorts of space-time logistics.

. . . as did my husband, Eric Zahler, who put up with salt and pepper shakers standing in for spacecrafts and old radio signals during our dinners at home, even when it meant the delicious pasta he'd made was going cold. I couldn't have written about the love of a lifetime without first experiencing one with him.

My writers' group, Marie Rutkoski, Jill Santopolo, Marianna Baer, Anne Heltzel, and Anna Godbersen, were my front-line feedback-ers, as usual.

At the moment I started making notes for this book four years ago, Nicole Melleby was my first student at the Fairleigh Dickinson MFA in Creative Writing. Now she's a star author of middle grade fiction, and a wonderfully astute critique partner. Minerva 4eva!

Emily Greenhill, also a former student and terrific author, helped keep the *Coordinated Endeavor* on course—as did my FDU colleague Minna Proctor, who helped me get deeper into the emotional wounds behind Ambrose's regal bearing.

My mom loathes science fiction. This book didn't change her mind, but she still gave it the best line edit you could imagine. That's another model of love.

I'm a huge fan of Elana K. Arnold's novels (go read them!), and it made me nervous to have her genius focused on a draft of this book. But getting a mind as generous and wise as hers on these pages was indispensable. Thanks to all my colleagues at the Hamline MFA in writing for young people.

My author friend Justin Deabler has an equally impressive brain and heart, and has been crucial to this book from start to finish. His debut novel, *Lone Stars*, is one to watch out for!

Writer friends and lunch buddies (or phone buddies, in these times of the coronavirus pandemic) Donna Freitas and Daphne Benedis-Grab have been crucial sources of support for over a decade—I relied on them hard for this book, as I ever have.

I think Richard Pine, my agent, can do just about anything. That he puts his mind on getting my books into the right hands is something for which I'm daily grateful.

Katherine Tegen, Tanu Srivastava, and the broader Katherine Tegen Books/HarperCollins family: you've been such a welcoming home. I'm lucky to be publishing this novel with you.

Sarah Maxwell gobsmacked us by illustrating a cover that brought more intensity—and more handsomeness—than I had dared hope for. Thank you. Everyone should go check out her art.

My editor, Ben Rosenthal: when I proposed this weirdo, hard-to-edit book, you never blinked once. Instead you just leaned forward and said "go on." You're such a source of wisdom and support.

Hearty thanks to copy editors everywhere, and especially Laura Harshberger, who was in charge of this book. Sorry about all the aspirin.